MW01265152

The Kingdom of Arke

Fading Light

Book I

Michael Bergman

This is a work of fiction. All of the characters, names, incidents, organizations, and dialogue in this novel are either the products of the author's imagination or are used fictitiously.

WestBow Press books may be ordered through booksellers or by contacting:

WestBow Press
A Division of Thomas Nelson & Zondervan
1663 Liberty Drive
Bloomington, IN 47403
www.westbowpress.com
1 (866) 928-1240

ISBN: 978-1-5127-2712-8 (sc)
ISBN: 978-1-5127-2713-5 (hc)
ISBN: 978-1-5127-2711-1 (e)

Library of Congress Control Number: 2016900671

Print information available on the last page.

WestBow Press rev. date: 01/15/2016

To my King: thank you for pulling me out of the pit.
To my wife: thank you for sharing in this great adventure.

See, darkness covers the earth and thick darkness is over the peoples,
but the Lord rises upon you and his glory appears over you.
Nations will come to your light, and kings to the brightness of your dawn.

—Isaiah 60:2–3 (NIV)

CONTENTS

Part I

Part II

The Kingdom of Arke

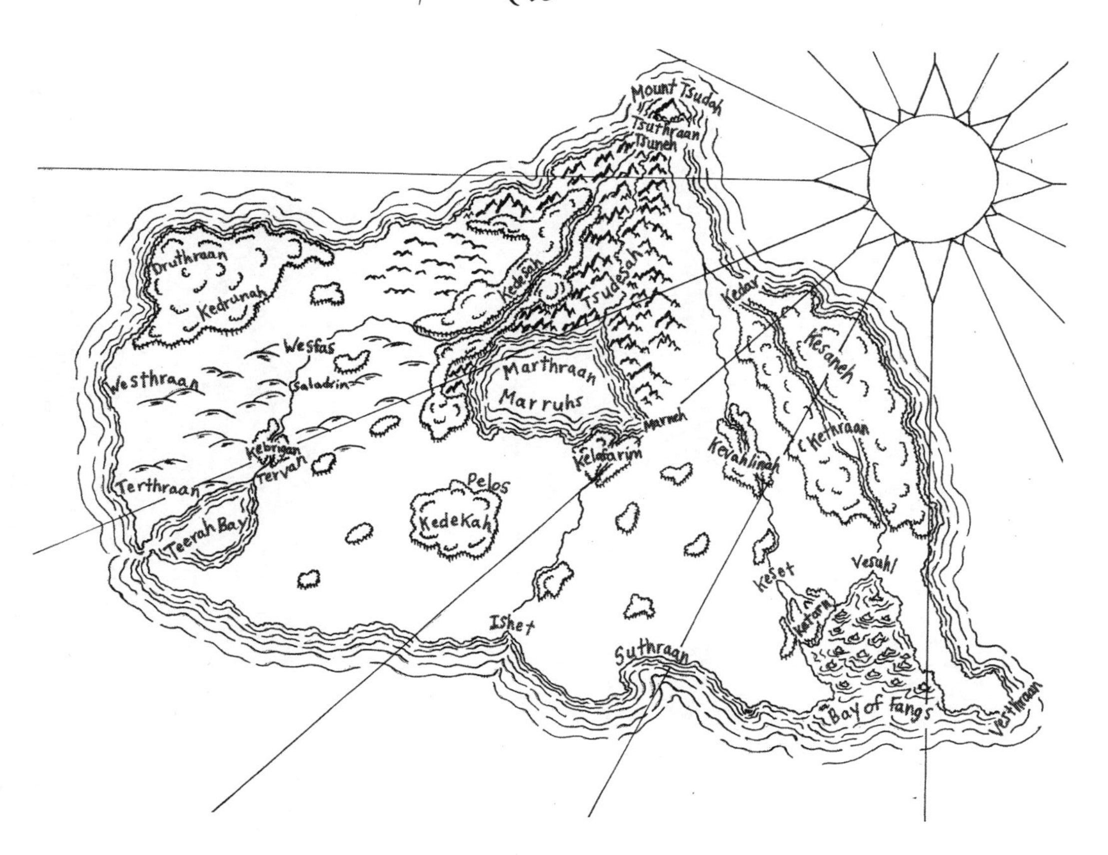

Part 1

1

Flight

Straining, Ryker pulled himself onto the flat rooftop of the house he had just climbed. He now stood high above the streets of Tervan. Ryker cautiously peered over the edge of the roof to search the empty roofs nearby. When he had first seen it staring at him, he had been startled. When it had followed him as he ran, he had begun to grow afraid. Now, after two hours of fleeing over the rooftops, he was terrified.

Wiping the sweat out of his eyes, he smoothed back his hair and took in a deep breath of the night air. Whatever was chasing him was fast and knew how to maneuver up here with speed and skill. Whatever the thing that chased him, it was much faster than any of the Gaur he had run from in the past.

He hadn't gotten a good look at whatever was following him. The first and only thing he'd seen were red eyes. They had looked down at him from another rooftop high above. They'd almost looked like they were glowing, like lanterns in the night. Then, as if a shadow had passed by, the eyes had been gone. Chills ran across the back of his neck as fear of whatever that thing was came over him.

So he ran, not knowing or caring what it was he ran from, and he didn't look back. Leaving the tall rooftop, he continued to run over roofs and leap across gaps between houses. He wasn't completely convinced that this shadowy pursuer really was tailing him.

And suddenly he saw them again, the red eyes—ahead of him and higher up on another roof. The creature was swift to already be ahead and so high up. He quickly changed direction away from the figure watching him. Increasing his speed, he leaped from one rooftop to another, desperate to flee from his frightening pursuer.

A summer breeze blew through the night sky. A storm was coming up the river from Teerah Bay; he could vaguely smell the salt in the wind, bringing up memories of his past that he quickly pushed aside. It was exceptionally warm for early summer. The storm could get bad. Ryker needed to get back to his hideout before the storm began. He didn't want to lead whoever was following him to his hideout. Many other boys lived with him, and he didn't want to put them in danger as well. He had to lose his pursuer somehow.

Using the great tower that loomed over the entire Shuul as a guide, he started for the river. The tower had been built at the center of the Shuul to watch over and protect it. Ryker often used it as a mark to know where he was as he traveled the rooftops. If he could make it to the river, he could dive into the water and maybe hide on the banks under the brush that grew there, until his pursuer gave up.

He had made the jump many times. The first few occasions had been just for fun. The last time he'd jumped, a Shafel Gaur had caught him stealing a bag of coins off a merchant's belt. Ryker had jumped, and the Shafel Gaur, who wore armor, hadn't. He would have sunk like a rock if he had. Ryker had gotten away with enough gold to feed him and the boys he lived with for months. That day, he had run for gold; tonight he ran for his life.

As he ran on the roofs, he looked for the edge of the Shuul. He knew he was close, but how close could mean the difference between escape and … whatever would happen if he was caught. He didn't know what would happen if this thing with red eyes caught up to him. He had heard of people seeing shadowy figures in the night recently. He had thought they were just seeing things or had spent too much time in the tavern. They'd said they had seen dark figures moving swiftly on the rooftops in the small hours of the night. One person swore he saw one of these figures chase a young boy down an alley. When he'd gone to investigate, there had been no sign of them. Both had disappeared. Ryker hoped the man had only been seeing things. It was indeed late in the night, and he was in fact an orphan.

"There!" he said aloud, relieved at the sight of the flowing water. In the moonlight he could see the river. The moon shone on its dark waters as it flowed steadily south to fill up Teerah Bay.

He was near the spot where he knew it was deep enough, so he picked up his speed. In a sprint, he saw his mark on the peak of a roof and headed for it. Two flat roofs lay between him and the point where he would jump. If he leaped from the chimney of the second flat roof, it would give him enough height to reach the peak of the house he would use to dive into the river. He needed to time the jump perfectly to give him enough momentum to continue on into the river far below.

The wind picked up and moved thick clouds above to conceal the moon's light. A fell voice was heard in the wind's breath. As he leaped to the next roof, his body moving fast, expecting to dive in a matter of seconds, something suddenly held him in place. Ryker didn't know if it was fear or an unseen force that held him, but to stop so abruptly was impossible. He couldn't move a muscle. He was locked in a running posture but couldn't get away.

A dark ominous cloud appeared out of the night air before him. It was unlike anything he had ever seen. In the cloud rose the figure that had been chasing him. The red eyes were the only things to be seen under a black hood. The dark cloud evaporated, revealing the rest of his features, which were few. He seemed like a darker shadow in the blackness of night.

"You're quite the little rabbit up here, Ryker." A hissing voice beneath the hood paused as if to let sink in the fact that he knew Ryker's name.

His voice sounded almost like a snake the way it hissed. How did this … thing know his name? Why was he after him? And how was he frozen like this? Ryker shuddered. He had no idea and wasn't sure he wanted to find out.

"My master wishes to extend his hospitality to you," the dark figure continued. The way he spoke was disturbing. His presence made Ryker's insides tremble. The figure clothed in black paced slowing around Ryker, circling him.

Ryker struggled to free himself from whatever unseen force held him immobile. The figure must have seen the expression on Ryker's face change from fear to panic as he struggled to break free. No matter how much he fought it, the unseen force seized him.

"You still have fight in you? Good, good," the stranger said with a wicked laugh. "You will serve the master of darkness well. You should realize now that you have no hope of escaping. Your future has already been sealed." His voice grew louder and more threatening as he spoke. His wicked tongue twisted every word into a cruel, hissing version.

The clouds above exposed the moon to shine down on them, and Ryker got a better look at the shadowy figure. He was tall and lean. The hilt of a sword could be seen behind his shoulder. He wore a long black coat down to his shins. His armor beneath the coat was detailed with many markings and symbols. From his hood to his boots, the only color to be seen was black. Even under the moonlight, shadow still clung to him—save only for his red eyes, which indeed shone with an unearthly light. A dark mist seemed to linger around his eyes, concealing his face further. He turned his back to Ryker, looked up at the moon, and spoke to it, almost like he was speaking to Ryker.

"My master will cover Arke with a darkness that will swallow all light. Even the moon will no longer curse the night sky. No one can escape the fate that will come. He turned around to face Ryker and said directly to him,

"Lucky for you, you will be among us as we drive the light away that blinds this land." He stretched out his long arms. "Come, you must meet your new master!" he finished abruptly, his voice hissing long after the last word.

Another dark cloud appeared and surrounded the dark figure. For a moment Ryker felt himself freed from the unseen force that had held him motionless. He quickly unwrapped his ever-present sling from around his waist and grabbed a stone from his pocket. In one fluid motion, he spun the stone and slung it toward the figure.

Whether it hit its mark or not, Ryker didn't wait to find out. The moment the stone left the sling, he was already on the sloped roof, running along its peak. He planted both of his feet at its edge and leaped. He sailed through the air toward the river. He managed to turn, midair, to see if the figure was still on the roof. He was nowhere to be seen. His black clothes and red eyes were gone. Not having time to straighten his body, Ryker hit the water on the flat of his back, smacking it hard. It stung, but it was well worth it. He had escaped from his dark pursuer.

Ryker held his breath and let the river carry him slowly south. He swam beneath the water for as long as he could. When his lungs felt like they would burst, he broke the surface of the river for a long-desired breath. Scanning the waters, he saw that he was already a long distance away from the roof where he'd jumped. He couldn't see any dark figure on any of the roofs nearby. But that didn't mean that he wasn't being watched. He swam to the east bank and ducked under the tall grasses that grew along the banks of both sides of the river. There he hid and waited.

It was now far into the night, and still there were no signs of his dark pursuer. He waited there in the reeds for over an hour before he moved. Finally he climbed up the bank, dripping wet with mud covering his tattered boots, and left the river behind. His first thought was to head straight to the hideout to warn the other boys. A second thought stopped him from going straight there. First he needed to tell someone what the dark figure had said about his master covering Arke in darkness. He needed to warn the Drudin Gaur of this lunatic's plan. Ryker had dealt with them before but never on this end of a problem. Normally Ryker was the one being caught and punished.

There were many buildings very close to the river. The Shuul was a hub for ships coming up and down the river, and many docks spanned its waters. Ryker often sat and watched as they swiftly passed by. Now he moved swiftly among the buildings. He liked coming to this part of Tervan because it reeked of fish. Oddly, it reminded him of his father. It was an easy place to get something to eat, as most of the time the fishermen just left their nets filled with their catch for the evening. It was almost too easy.

The smells of this place also brought up memories from his past, and he did his best to keep them buried inside him. His wet clothes clung to him as he moved quickly through the alleys and streets, heading east to the heart of Tervan. There he hoped to find the Gaur.

The great tower rose in the very center of Tervan. It was the very reason the Shuul had been built here, for it encircled the tower. His father had told him that when he was young The King had built towers all over Arke to watch over the people. In times of war, great fires were built atop them to signal a warning to others. Now the towers were the headquarters for the Drudin Ashard and his Gaur. Ryker hoped to find someone there who would listen to him and help him.

The river had carried him farther south than he liked, so it took him a while before he reached the tower. Weathered gray stones that had once been white made up the tower and the wall around it. Skilled hands had erected the tower and the walls. Every stone had been cut to perfection and put in place by master craftsmen. Now the tower and wall were beginning to wear with age.

A wall twice Ryker's height surrounded the grounds of the tower. The tower's height dwarfed the wall. It was close to two hundred feet high. Many windows and slits were built into it. He could see the glow from fires and torches through some of them. At the top of the tower was a large deck. During the day Gaur could be seen walking back and forth, always watching the people throughout the Shuul. A stack of logs had long been set ready to be lit in case of an invasion or attack. The roof over the deck came to a tall point. At the top a flagpole was fashioned, although it was now left bare with no flag.

Ryker continued up to the gate, large wooden doors that were shut tight. He walked up to it and knocked on the heavy beams, first tapping with his knuckles. When no reply came, he pounded the boards with both hands. Still no one heeded him. He thought of climbing over, but the walls were smooth, and he didn't see a handhold. Neither home nor shop were close enough for him to jump from. Knowing it would be pointless to wait, he kicked the large wooden gate in frustration and turned away, heading north through the Shuul. He knew if he couldn't find the protectors of Arke here, he could find them somewhere else.

He walked the streets of Tervan now. The hour was well into the night, leaving him alone. If running on the rooftops wouldn't get rid of his pursuer, maybe walking through the empty streets would. Not even a dog was to be seen in the streets. The sky above was oddly calm, but the scent of the ocean was thick in the air. He knew a storm was still approaching. He had grown up around the shore of the great sea that surrounded Arke. He had always loved the sea, but not the storms it brought.

At the pace he was going, it would be close to morning before he reached where he was headed. He began to jog now toward his destination, the Red Dragon Tavern. It was on the other side of the Shuul toward its outer edge. He had lived here on the streets for close to four years, so he knew every street and nearly every shop. He had stayed in the attic of this tavern more than once before he had found his hideout.

He knew he was heading in the right direction when the silence of the quiet Shuul was broken. Coming down the streets was the dull noise of laughter. As he continued down the empty streets, the noise grew until it filled the night air and bounced off the surrounding buildings. He had made it to the tavern.

The Red Dragon was a large three-story building with a small stable built into the lower level. The Shafel of the West and their Gaur were great horsemen and wouldn't stay in a place unless their steeds were given care equal to their own housing—or sometimes even better. Ryker knew he wouldn't find these men of honor in the tavern at this hour. Tonight the tavern would be filled with a crowd the complete opposite.

Ryker stepped up onto the porch that wrapped all the way around the first two stories of the tavern. He stepped away from the swinging double doors to look through the window before he entered. It was broken in one corner and covered in dirt, making it hard to see through. The space beyond the window was packed full of men, each with a large drink in his hand. Women paraded around these men, falling over each other and gawking at them. This was the last place Ryker wanted to be, but he knew this was the last place his pursuer would look for a young boy. And this was the one place Ashard or his Gaur would likely be.

He stood in front of the small swinging doors that beckoned travelers to enter. As Ryker pushed one door open, a man shoved both doors outward, pushing Ryker aside along with the doors. The man wobbled off the porch and down the short steps. He sang to himself as he walked down the street. He had definitely had enough for tonight, Ryker thought. He caught the swinging doors, pushed them inward, and stepped into the tavern.

Ryker quickly navigated his way through the crowd to the far corner. He moved swiftly before anyone could make a scene about his entering the tavern. Once he did, he surveyed the place. It was just like he remembered it, although it hadn't been filled with people when he'd been here last. A long table stretched toward the back of the main room. Behind the table were stacks of barrels and cases upon cases of glass bottles. The main room was huge, with many round tables and chairs. Despite the warm weather, two fireplaces burned on either end of the main room, making the entire place almost unbearably hot. The second story had a balcony that surrounded this main room. Above hung a chandelier adorned with many large antlers.

Ryker scanned the crowd of people in the tavern, looking for the Drudin he had hoped to find here. Not even one of the Gaur who always swarmed places like this was to be found. Maybe it was better this way. He didn't have to deal with telling his story and having the Drudin call him a madman and lock him up. Realizing it had been a mistake to come here, he made his way back to the door.

Keeping his head down, he rushed to the swinging doors. Just as Ryker reached out to push outside, the door was thrust inward. Having his head down caused Ryker to run into the one entering. The man walking through the doorway shoved the boy to the floor with a thud. A deafening silence fell over the tavern with the arrival of the newest patron.

Sprawling on the ground, Ryker didn't dare to look up. From the steel-plated boots near his head, he knew whom they belonged to. Ashard, the Drudin of Terthraan, was here in the tavern. He was the only reason Ryker had come here, though this wasn't the way Ryker had wanted to meet him. He would be lucky to get a word out about his pursuer.

The Drudin brushed passed Ryker without even acknowledging that the boy was on the floor or that he had put him there. Ashard headed straight for the long table in the back of the tavern. The only noise in the whole place was the crackling of the fire and the Drudin's armor shifting as he slowly moved across the room. Without exchanging words, the servant behind the table handed him a frothy mug.

Ryker scrambled to his feet, hoping to get out while he could. As Ryker tried to leave, the Drudin's Gaur stopped him, scooping him up off the ground. They held him tight and half dragged and half carried him toward the Drudin, who had already downed the first mug and was working on his second.

Ashard was the very figure of a fighting man, if ever there was one. From head to toe, he was covered in shining armor, polished until his refection could be seen on each and every piece. His large helm, lying on the counter beside him, had two large horns like a bull's coming out of the sides. An enormous great sword hung from his back. Beneath it was a long, flowing blue cape. Here was one of the great judges that The King had left to govern in his absence.

"Take the boy outside and teach him how to properly respect a Drudin," Ashard said over his frothy mug in annoyance. His voice was deep and threatening.

His Gaur would have obeyed immediately, but Ryker broke free of their grasp. He shoved them away as he spoke. "I'm so sorry for running into you like that, sire. I'm in dire need of help." Ryker was stammering, almost as terrified as he had been on the rooftops.

"I am trying to help you." Ashard smirked, pausing to take another drink of ale. "I'm helping to teach you some manners. Take him!" he said again, and this time his command was quicker and angrier.

His Gaur picked Ryker up by his arms. Ryker fought back and wiggled free of them once more. He stepped closer to the Drudin, pushing away the fumbling hands of the Gaurs. Grabbing hold of him, they held him back from drawing any closer to their leader.

Ryker quickly blurted out his message. "A man dressed in black is out in the Shuul. He was chasing me on the rooftops near the river. He was dressed all in black and had red eyes and appeared out of nothing. He said something about his master covering Arke in darkness!"

Ashard hesitated before he replied. "A man in black, you say? With red eyes? That sounds terrifying! I think you might have had a nightmare, boy!" Waving his hand, he added, mocking, "Tell your momma. Maybe she will care." The Drudin pointed at his Gaur. "Don't make me tell you again! Get this gutter rat out of my sight!"

"She's dead," Ryker said quietly to himself. Speaking up suddenly, he added, "I would be too if I hadn't jumped into the river to escape him." He was ready to leave this man to his mug and take whatever the Gaur had in store for him. If the Drudin wouldn't listen to him, he didn't care if this dark figure was out in Tervan. If the very man who was supposed to protect the people of Tervan didn't care, then neither would he.

The Gaur carried him toward the door despite his struggling, and the silence deepened. Suddenly every light in the place was extinguished. Both fires were turned to ash in a moment. Most of the crowd fled the tavern in a crazed panic, stumbling over one another in the darkness. The Drudin simply took another sip from his mug, his armor still shining bright in the moonlight sneaking in through the window.

The moonlight also showed a figure suddenly emerging from the darkness on the balcony above the Drudin. The stranger stepped up to the railing and placed his thin hands onto it. Those who had remained in the tavern fell over each other in the dark to get out. Ryker wished he could be among them, but the Gaur who held him were as frozen as he had been on the rooftops earlier.

Clouds in the night sky shifted to conceal the moon, leaving the tavern in total darkness. The glow of the figure's eyes were the only thing to be seen. A flash lit up the tavern, breaking up the darkness with an instant of light, and seconds later thunder echoed outside.

Ashard dropped his mug, drew his sword, and yelled at his Gaur. "To arms!"

Both of the Gaur fumbled out of fear and loss of sight to pull out their swords, leaving Ryker free to run to the corner of the room to watch what would happen. The Gaur didn't charge right away; instead they held their swords defensively as they trembled in the darkness. The dark figure above drew his curved sword and leaped from the balcony, landing with a thud on the thick floorboards between the Drudin and his Gaur. With speed that would rival the lightning that flashed outside, the dark figure attacked.

Ryker's eyes remained locked on the figure's red eyes. He couldn't seem to pull himself away from them. They remained constant, unblinking orbs of ghostly light. The eyes moved swiftly back and forth, and the noise of the fight told Ryker that the dark stranger was winning. Between the flashes of lightning, it remained pitch-black within the tavern.

Ryker heard swords clash against each other, and then two separate voices cried out in pain, one almost immediately after the other. Then all was silent.

He heard the rain outside falling slowly at first. Then in an instant it sounded like giant buckets of water had been released from the sky. The roof above leaked a little, and droplets of water fell directly on Ryker's head. He shifted to another spot in the corner. Even knowing that he should flee while he still could, he wanted to see the dark figure fall.

A light appeared as Ashard lit a torch, which cast an orange light within the tavern. The Drudin stood over his fallen Gaur, his curved horned helm looked terrifying, as shadows fled from the torch, its light bouncing off his armor as he waved it back and forth in search of the dark figure.

Ryker couldn't see the dark figure despite the torch's light. Then the red eyes appeared suddenly behind the Drudin. The Drudin must have heard the figure, because he turned abruptly and swung his massive sword. The figure blocked it with his own curved sword and held the Drudin's blade there for a moment.

With a laugh, the dark figure spoke, and his hissing voice could be heard throughout the tavern. "I hope you're not afraid of the dark." Then he blew out the torch and darkness once again ruled the tavern.

2

Consumed

Wasting no time, Ryker dashed out of the tavern. Bursting through the swinging doors, he leaped from the porch. Now he ran through the rain-drenched streets straight toward his hideout. He was already soaked to the bone as the storm continued to pound Tervan with torrents of rain. He hoped Ashard had killed the vile figure or had at least kept him occupied long enough so that Ryker could make it back to the hideout and warn the other boys. He knew they had to leave. Could the dark stranger's words be true? Ryker shook off the dreadful thought.

Puddles of water had already formed in the streets. He tried his best to steer around them, but he couldn't help being soaked from the rainfall. A great flash of light lit up the dark sky, and an explosion of thunder shook everything moments later. He didn't dare climb onto the rooftops in this storm, so he flew through the streets toward his hideout.

He saw something out of the corner of his eye. When he stopped to look at the spot where he'd seen it, it was gone. He shook it off and continued to run through the streets. Surely the dark figure couldn't have gotten away so quickly from the Drudin. He was known by all to be the greatest swordsman in the entire kingdom.

The storm grew steadily worse as Ryker slogged through the streets. Lightning flashed and thunder bellowed as the sky above him released torrents of water. The streets became something of a river as the rain continued. Wind swirled angrily around him, but he pressed on. He couldn't stop until he'd made it back to his hideout.

Thankfully, he reached the place where his hideout remained. A handful of shops there were built in a small rectangular cluster. The shops faced outward, and a small alley was set in the center of them. The shopkeepers used this as a storage area. One of the shops had closed down and was boarded up on the front side. Ryker and Broff, another boy who lived there, had sneaked into the alleyway and broken down a small portion of the back wall. Here they had made a little home of their own, always referring to it as their hideout—like it was a den of hardened thieves.

Ryker ran up to one of the shops walls, and using a crate to catch the edge of the roof, he climbed over it. He crossed the small roof and dropped down into the alley below. They had kept the shop boarded up on the outside to keep unwanted eyes away from them. The alleyway was the only way to get into their hideout.

He ducked down as he entered through the hole in the wall. All of the other boys were sleeping in the left corner, but he saw that Shiloh, the youngest, was awake. When Ryker walked in, another flash of lightning lit up the room. The young boy shrieked when he saw Ryker's shadow near the entrance.

Ryker hushed him and tried to calm him down. "It's okay, Shiloh. It's just me," he said gently as he stoked a small fire. He stayed close by it to dry off his soaked clothes.

"I can't sleep," the young boy said as he came over from his corner to sit next to Ryker by the fire.

Their hideout was small, but it made do. They had a pile of blankets in one corner and a small table and chairs in the other. They had built their own makeshift fire ring in the center of the room, letting the smoke drift out through the hole in the back. A stout post held the roof up near the fire ring. The boys had carved their names in it, declaring that this was their space. It was warm and dry, everything they needed.

Ryker put his arm around Shiloh to comfort him. Shiloh was much younger than Ryker, so he did his best to look after the boy. He hadn't known the young boy long, but when he had found him begging for food, he couldn't just leave him to fend for himself.

Broff, however, had been with Ryker longer than he could remember. He was Ryker's best friend, and they had shared in many adventures together already. He was around the same age as Ryker.

The other two boys were brothers, Kale and Nayori. They could almost pass as twins. They were both a little younger than Ryker, but that didn't stop them from getting into much more trouble than all the other boys combined.

"Can you tell me a story, Ryker?" the young boy asked, looking up at him.

How could he resist? He had lost his own family, but he had gained another with these other orphaned boys. They took care of each other and had each others' backs. They acted like brothers, laughing and fighting with one another simultaneously.

As Ryker thought of which story to tell Shiloh, he was surprised to hear Broff's voice ask him, "When did you get back, Ryker?"

Broff was up now, rubbing sleep out of his eyes. He sat next to Ryker near the fire. The rain had brought a chill, and the fire was welcoming to them all.

"You won't believe the night I've had tonight!" Ryker began, not knowing where to start.

Broff laughed as he said, "Get chased by the butchers dogs again? Those things are ferocious!"

"No, much worse than that." Ryker then told him about the crazy night he'd had. By the time he got to the part about the tavern, the other two boys had woken up, so he had to start all over. Kale and Nayori didn't believe him, but Broff did.

Little Shiloh piped up at the end. "Not that kind of story! Like the ones you always tell." Clearly he thought that this was the bedtime story Ryker had chosen for him. Ryker laughed and ignored Shiloh for a moment.

"That's a little hard to believe, Ryker," Nayori said.

"Yeah, you expect us to think a man in black with red eyes has been chasing you all night?" Kale said. "I thought the stories you tell about The King are tall. This one trumps them all."

"Tell us a story about The King," Shiloh cried.

"In a minute," Ryker told him, patting his curly hair.

Broff piped up, "You said the Drudin fought him? Then maybe they locked him up." Broff always seemed to hope for the best.

"Regardless, I think we should pack up and leave here," Ryker said. "The Drudin will send his Gaur out to find me." He hoped the others would agree.

"I'm fine with that," Kale said.

"We need a change of scenery anyway," Nayori agreed.

"Then its settled," Broff said. "We'll pack up at first light. Where should we go?"

"We'll figure that out in the morning," Ryker said. "Let's get a good night's rest—at least for what's left of the night." He hoped Shiloh would forget about his promise to tell him a story.

The other boys got up to head back to bed, but Shiloh wouldn't have it. "I want to hear a story about The King!"

"Okay." Ryker laughed. "Let's head to bed, and I'll tell you there."

Shiloh agreed, and when they were all settled in their spots, Ryker began to tell them a story his father had told him when he was young. He had heard it almost every night, so it had stuck in his mind. He didn't wholeheartedly believe in the stories he told, but the thought of having a King seemed nice.

"A great and mighty King once sailed across the sea with his Paladin," Ryker began. Having heard and told the story many times, the words came naturally to him. "Long ago, Arke was a desolate wasteland and covered in darkness. Its only inhabitants were evil and terrible creatures. When the King arrived, He and His Paladins drove the darkness away and destroyed all of the evil creatures that plagued the island.

"When the fighting was over and the dust had settled, The King climbed to the peak of Mount Tsudah. There, atop the mountain, He dug through it and into the surface of the island. There he discovered a spring of the purest water. Using His power, The King drew the water up and pooled it atop Mount Tsudah. Soon water flowed down the mountain and across all of Arke in wide rivers from the same source.

Soon after, The King and His Paladins sailed back to His own island. They quickly returned to Arke with the next tide. Their ships were heavily laden with white stones. They used these stones to build the Thraans. When they had finished construction, many people came from all over the sea seeking refuge and safety. The King gave them all a home in the Thraans. Then there was peace, and the Kingdom of Arke was established."

A smile was spread wide over Shiloh's face as he lay sleeping, even before the story was finished. The boys bid each other good night as they drifted off to sleep. As much as Ryker didn't want to admit it, he always loved telling stories about The King and all his adventures. Many of the other stories he recalled about The King played in his mind as he drifted off to sleep. The rain continued to fall, pelting the roof above them. He was thankful he had a roof above his head. The rumbling sound of thunder could be heard far off in the distance as he slowly drifted off.

Thunder crashed close by, abruptly bringing Ryker out of his sleep. A sudden flash of light peeled his eyes open and revealed that they were not alone. Thunder bellowed again shortly as the storm raged outside. The chaos outside seemed peaceful compared to the storm that he sensed was close at hand.

The dark figure had caught up to Ryker. He had been joined by more figures like him. Out of dark clouds they came, and the same red eyes were the only things to be seen in their shadowy hoods. The fire gave off its last bit of light, enough to see what was going on.

Silently the brothers, Nayori and Kale, headed for the hole in the wall to escape into the storm. They were chased by two of the dark figures. Hearing screams, Ryker feared the worst and leaped to his feet. He shook Broff and picked Shiloh up out of the covers he was hiding under.

"We didn't realize you had friends, Ryker. How rude of you not to introduce us." Ryker recognized the voice, and he shivered against the fear and cold as it hissed.

Ignoring the voice, he shoved Shiloh into Broff. "Get him out of here! I'll try and hold them off!" He would do his best to protect the boys who had recently become as close as any family to him.

As Ryker turned to face the dark figure, another appeared behind Broff and snatched both him and Shiloh into a dark cloud. Ryker watched as the cloud dissipated and all three of them were simply gone. No trace of them was left. He turned back around and charged, diving toward the one who had spoke to him.

Instead of hitting the figure, he passed right through him, crashing into the table and chairs in the corner of the hideout. He stood, throwing a chair off him. He could hardly see. The fire had died, and all that was left was fading embers.

He ran over to the pile of blankets and looked through them to make sure Shiloh hadn't tried to hide under them again. He wasn't there. Ryker was left alone in the hideout. Looking out of the hole in the wall, he searched the rooftops of the shops overhead. The only thing he could see was rain pouring down from the storm.

A different voice spoke behind him. He could feel its icy breath on his ear. "We can't leave you without your friends. Why don't you join them?"

This time Ryker wasn't frozen by an unseen force; it was fear that held him. A dark cloud formed around him. Starting near his feet, it slowly drew closer until it enveloped his legs and climbed up his chest. The darkness was ice-cold. It seemed to swallow him up and reach even into his mind. As he left the hideout behind, darkness replaced everything. The last thing he remembered was a sense of falling, as if the black cloud had dropped him into a bottomless abyss.

3

Darkness

Wind from the east swept across choppy waters, blowing white spray into the air. Waves crashed against the haul of the boat, splashing water on Ryker's face. He immediately realized that he was now on the deck of a small fishing boat, no more than twenty feet long. It had a single mast with its sail folded up. Connected to it was a long pole that stretched out over the water to one side. It didn't take him long to realize that this was his father's boat. Whenever it was pulled ashore, Ryker's father had always let him play on in while he tended to the nets. Ryker knew every board, every net, and every bit of tackle. How he was aboard it now, he had no idea. It had to be a dream, or something similar.

"Enan, we need to throw the nets out once more. We don't have nearly enough to go in for the day." The voice caught Ryker by surprise.

He turned to the voice that had spoken. It was his uncle Vahl. The man had raised him after his father had passed. His uncle looked just like his father. He was tall, and his features were hidden behind a scruffy beard and long messy hair, which were soaked and clung to his face. He wore a long-sleeved tunic stained with the blood and grime of fish.

"If we don't head in soon, we'll be caught out here by the storm. Then we won't even have a boat to fish with." Another voice answered, Ryker knew it as well.

It was his father. Somehow he hadn't noticed either of them standing in the boat with him. Much like Vahl, his father wore a long-sleeved tunic, though his hair and beard were trimmed and well-kept. His father had gray eyes—like the waters of the bay he fished on, his mother had always said.

Even knowing it to be a dream, Ryker ran toward his father, spreading out his arms to hug the man he longed for. He passed straight through him like a cloud. Luckily, a pile of nets lay behind his father, and they broke his fall. He rose up out of the nets to look at his father. Though Ryker knew he was gone, seeing him brought a yearning to be with him just once more.

"You worry too much about these clouds," Vahl remarked as he looked overhead. "They always look worse than the storm actually is."

Walking over to the pile of nets, Vahl passed right in front of Ryker without even noticing him. He began working out the mess of nets while Ryker was still tangled up in them. It was strange seeing his uncle again. The last time he had seen him was more than three and a half years ago. He had hoped to never see him again. Even this being a dream—or whatever it was—didn't make it better.

"I'm afraid you don't worry enough about them, Vahl. We must head back," Enan urged his brother. "I have a family to support too, but we won't do much good to them at the bottom of the bay."

Getting aggravated at the nets, Vahl threw them back down. Putting his hand on his forehead, he blew out a deep breath. "Maybe you're right."

"Tell you what," Enan began. "I'll get the nets untangled. You prepare the sail, and on the way back we'll drag the nets along with us," he said, trying to convince his brother.

"Dragging toward home has never got us many fish," Vahl said under his breath.

"Better than nothing," Enan exclaimed.

Vahl agreed, and the two brothers got to work. Ryker pushed the nets off of him and stood on the deck. He watched as his father and uncle worked together. This was a completely different side of his family that he had never seen.

His father had almost finished with the nets. He had the weights on the bottom edge over the rail. Now he worked on fastening the top corners of the nets to the long pole that extended over the waves.

The bay was getting worse, and the boat rocked like a bobber. The wind was pushing the storm clouds closer in by the second. His father began singing an old shanty he always sang when he worked, not appearing to be worried about the storm. Ryker had always loved hearing him sing.

Ryker turned and watched his uncle Vahl work on rigging the sail. He pulled on a rope to begin hauling the sail up the mast. As he did so, a huge gust of wind raced across the waters and filled the sail. The boat suddenly was brought into motion.

With no one at the tiller, the boat turned to the left abruptly. Not expecting this, his father was caught up in the nets. Having the weights hanging over the rail, he fell overboard with them. Vahl quickly dropped the rigging of the sail, and the boat drifted to a stop.

Ryker was already holding the rail and peering into the murky waters of the bay. The heavy weights of the nets carried his father down into the void a short distance behind them in the wake of the fishing boat. All that remained on the surface was a cascade of bubbles of his father's last breath.

Within this dream—if that was what it was—a strong childhood memory played back in his mind, a memory of watching his father sail off from their home on the banks of Teerah Bay. Every morning he had loved sitting and watching his father sail off until the fishing boat could no longer be seen over the waters. Every evening he had sat and waited patiently on the shore for him to return. He had done this for as long as he could remember, until one evening when a storm rolled in over the bay. His mother had told him to come inside and watch for his father through the window. He'd obliged, but when the fishing boat had returned, his father had been missing from the deck. Deep down, Ryker had always denied the truth; he'd always thought his father was indestructible.

Ryker knew that the story in this dream ended with his being an fatherless. But in the grip of the current vision, he decided that if he could have one more look at his father, it was worth the risk. Diving in headfirst, he splashed into the water after him.

The moment Ryker was submerged, he swam with all his might, following the bubbles that led to his father. Though he didn't realize it at first, the water was ice-cold. His body ached, but he pressed through and swam. Soon he couldn't see a thing under the waves.

There were no sign of his father anywhere. His lungs longed for air, but his heart urged him to continue. He longed for his father, for nothing could replace his love. Before his breaking point Ryker realized that he too would drown under these waters. So he gave up and swam toward the surface.

He was ashamed for giving up. He knew his father was gone, and there was nothing he could do about it. Even in this dream he couldn't change the fact that his father had been entangled in the very nets he used to support his family. His livelihood had been his demise.

Ryker knew the surface was close, but though he moved toward it, it evaded him. He swam, yet he couldn't reach it. Fear and anxiety sent him into a frenzy as he fought to reach the surface of the water.

His lungs felt like they were about to collapse. Desperate for air, he continued. He wouldn't give up yet. His mind suddenly began to fade. He needed air. His mind slowly drifted, like the current made by the waves just out of his reach.

No sound. No sight. No sense of anything. Nothingness engulfed him, drawing closer until it was suffocating him. This was true darkness: not only the absence of light but the absence of everything.

Somehow Ryker broke the surface of the water, breathing precious air back into his lungs. As he looked around him, he was astonished at his surroundings. The choppy waters, the fishing boat, and the storm clouds blowing through the sky were all gone. What replaced all of them was nothing. An abyss of utter darkness surrounded him.

He treaded the freezing cold water. It was so cold that his body locked up, which made it almost impossible to swim. Without light he couldn't determine where the water ended and the air began. Though he couldn't see it, he sensed a huge expanse above him. The black void seemed far away, yet it felt like it was about to crush him.

Fear sank its teeth deep into Ryker's heart. He frantically searched for any kind of light or marker to guide him in one direction. Seeing nothing, he hoped his eyes would adjust to the dark. He waited a long time between blinks to help his eyes. When his eyes didn't adjust, the fear planted by the darkness grew until total despair filled him.

This was unlike any kind of darkness he had ever experienced. A cloudy night still had some glow from the moon. But this emptiness was completely absent of all light. It was so thick, he could feel it.

Where his eyes lacked, his ears began to pick up. He could scarcely hear voices in the darkness. They were muffled at first, almost as if he had something blocking his ears, but they were all around him. Then they grew louder until they filled his ears with yet more terror. Screams of other boys cried out in desperate pleas, their voices echoing off the tall, cavernous ceiling. All of them cried out in the darkness. Terrified voices rang out and echoed above the waters.

Ryker tried to regain his ability to think. Hoping not to receive an answer, he called out for his friends. "Shiloh? Broff? Nayori, Kale? Can you hear me?" he shouted.

His heart sank when he heard a reply from little Shiloh. "Ryker!" he cried in terror.

Ryker knew the younger boy had a hard time in the water. When the boys had found the rooftop from which they jumped into the river, all of them had jumped except Shiloh. He wouldn't even wade along the river's banks. Ryker had hoped to help him become a good swimmer that summer. With the added fear of this huge, dark expanse, it was only a matter of time before Shiloh went under. Unable to see, Ryker swam in the direction of Shiloh's cry.

"Shiloh, keep talking to me! Don't give up! Where are you?" Ryker paused to listen, treading water again.

"Here!" The reply came through a mouthful of water.

He was headed in the right direction, so he continued. When he thought he had swum too far, he called out to him again. Another reply came from

Ryker's right. It sounded like he was right next to Ryker, as if Ryker could just reach out and grab him. But he couldn't. This scenario repeated itself again and again. Soon Shiloh's voice sounded faint and far away, as if he had drifted away from Ryker. Then no reply came.

Ryker swam frantically, looking for the boy, calling out his name until his own voice became hoarse. Knowing Shiloh had gone under, Ryker started swimming underwater, flailing his arms in hopes of finding the younger boy. Ryker had been looking for him for longer than he cared to think. His limbs were growing weak. He couldn't keep swimming like this for much longer.

"Shiloh!" he screamed.

Ryker had just been viciously reminded of losing his father, and now little Shiloh was drowning in the dark. He couldn't take it. Grief took him, and he wept in the waters, even as he continued to scream Shiloh's name. Other voices called out names in the water. There must have been dozens of them.

Ryker let their terrified voices ring in his ear. He considered just letting this black sea consume him as well. He let that thought linger in his mind. He would rather die than be left with grief over a helpless boy he should have been able to save. Just as he let his arms and legs go numb to lose himself to the black sea, a voice rang out above the dark waters.

"A light!" one of the boys exclaimed just before Ryker's head went under.

The hope of light brought Ryker out of the dark place where he had let his mind wander. If the voice had come a second later, it would have been too late. Hope spurred him to look for the light. The voices all around him cried out now in relief. If only the light had appeared sooner to help him find poor Shiloh. Those dark things that had brought them all here would pay!

A feeble light was shimmering over the dark water off in the distance. It didn't look like the orange flame of a torch or fire. It was far more red and hazy. From this distance it was hard to tell.

Regardless, the light must mean something, so he swam toward it. Being a fairly good swimmer, he passed many boys. As he approached the light, he suddenly stopped. He treaded water a short distance away as he gazed at the light.

Those dark figures with the red eyes were the reason he was here, the reason they were all here. Why would he trust a light like this? It was more than likely coming from them. He searched the place where the red light shone. The light emitted from a jagged metal torch thrust into one of many flat rocks surrounding the red light in shallow water and creating a forbidding look to it all. Beyond the shore was what looked like the mouth of a cave, a passageway deeper into darkness.

Not seeing any of the dark figures didn't put Ryker at ease. He let some of the other boys pass him by in the water. He watched them crawl up and fall onto the dry rocks in exhaustion. He had exerted all of his strength and didn't know how much longer he could tread the thick, dark water.

Not seeing the dark figures led him to believe that they wouldn't come—at least not right away. So he swam toward the shallows. Until he found out what this place was and who these dark figures were, he would keep his eyes and ears open. He hoped to find the other boys he lived with—Broff most of all.

Searching among the boys lying on the shore, he recognized a boy swimming toward him in the low light. Standing up, he had to squint to make sure it was him. "Broff?" he called out.

He ran through the shallow water to help him up. Broff could hardly stand, so Ryker put his arm around him and led him up on solid ground. He helped him sit and fell down next to him.

"Boy, am I glad to see you!" Broff said as he hung his arm around Ryker's neck.

They rested there on the rocks together. They had swum for what seemed like hours until the light had showed up. Though Ryker was glad it had, it still made him feel uneasy. His eyes continued to search the darkness around them for more red lights.

Ryker didn't realize till then how utterly cold it was. He was soaking wet now as he sat up out of the water. The darkness around them felt like the dead of winter. In all the earlier excitement, his blood had been pumping so fast that he hadn't stopped to think about the cold. Now it was the foremost thing on his mind–that and this intense darkness.

He looked out over the dark waters. The faint red light showed little of what they had endured. The calm water now looked like a sheet of dark-red ice. The darkness beyond the glow of the light let them know that they were indeed inside a large cavern—how large was hard to tell, for all that was to be seen was darkness.

Ryker and Broff shivered and clung close to each other. They were lucky to have each other to help keep warm.

"Did you see Shiloh?" Broff asked. "I held him when we were both taken in that … cloud. After that, I don't know how we got here, but we were separated."

A grim look stretched over Ryker's face. He knew even in this low light that Broff could see his expression. Broff didn't press Ryker with questions; he remained quiet. The expression on Ryker's face told the story.

"What about Nayori and Kale? Did they get away?" Broff asked, changing the subject.

"I don't care if they didn't," Ryker said angrily. "I saw them try to slip away without even trying to wake the rest of us. If they had, maybe we all could have gotten away."

Between the bitter cold, the grief he felt for Shiloh, and the memory of his father, he was furious. He hoped Kale and his brother had been taken shortly after them. It wouldn't have been fair if they'd gotten away. It was almost their fault that Shiloh was gone. If Ryker saw them again, he would make them pay for what they'd done.

Ryker slowly scanned the faces huddled on the shore. He couldn't remember seeing any of these boys in Tervan, for it was a big enough Shuul for Ryker not to know everyone. Still, it was small enough for Ryker to recognize most of the other boys who lived on the streets. Most of them were around Ryker's age. Some of them could have been a little older. A few were around Shiloh's age.

Could there be this many orphaned boys living in Arke? Without a family to care for them, they probably lived the same way Ryker did—stealing for a meal each and every day, not knowing if they would go hungry or when their next meal would be.

Ryker overheard the boys around them as they spoke in hushed tones about the state they were all in. All of them wondered how they'd gotten there and what would happen to them next. No one had answers.

Some of the older boys began consoling the others. Ryker stayed silent and listened to them. He knew it was useless. Some of them exchanged names and where they were from. Ryker heard many claim to be from the surrounding Shuuls, including Tervan, Wefas, and Pelos. Some of them were even from the Thraans. They all had the same story. A dark figure with red eyes had chased them down. They'd been enveloped in a cloud of dark smoke and had wound up here. Where "here" was, no one had a clue.

The older boys started talking about a plan for what they should do next. Ryker thought it was stupid. What hope did they have in this place? There was no way to escape. They didn't even know how they'd gotten here. He knew it was only a matter of time before the dark figures showed up. He hoped they didn't make him suffer. He was at the end of himself and didn't care if he escaped. He knew of only one way to escape this darkness and it was looking more appealing by the second.

The red light emitting from the orb suddenly went out. Darkness surrounded them all. Most of the boys cried out in terror. The darkness seemed to press in on him. It was thick and heavy, crushing into his body and making it hard for him to breath. Broff held his hands tight. Ryker whispered encouragement and held on to him. Pairs of red lights broke the black expanse. They weren't like the soft red light like had been. They belonged to the dark figures that had escorted them here. Twenty of them surrounded the boys on the shores of this black sea.

4

Despair

All of the boys, surrounding the now extinguished light, jumped to their feet. With no place to run or hide, they all huddled close together. Ryker and Broff joined them in the center of the island as the dark figures moved in closer. The figures surrounded them, laughing with evil, hissing voices. Many of the boys whimpered and cried.

The figures near the entrance to the passageway moved aside. As one, the dark figures all drew their swords. Most of the boys were shrieking in terror now. The figures nearest the shore advanced. With only one place to go, the boys stayed huddled together and moved toward the passageway. The figures herded them into the deeper darkness.

Ryker took Broff's hand as they pushed through the packed-in boys and ran through the passageway. Faint red lights hanging on the walls revealed the path before them. His soaked, wet clothes stuck to his frame. His boots spit out remaining water as they ran.

Clamoring noises came bouncing off the walls behind them. More of the other boys followed their lead and ran with them. It was obvious that the dark figures wanted them to go down this way, so something bad was probably at the end of it.

The dark hall rose steeply as they ascended from the black sea. A long while later, the hall evened out and opened up on their right. Ryker stopped to gaze at the opening. A few of the boys stumbled into him when he paused. They too were caught up in the sight.

An enormous cavern lay beyond the opening. Many small red lights set in metal holders could be seen shining throughout the cavern. The height of the ceiling and its ominous rock walls was lost as every eye was drawn to a great hole filled with a black void. The level ground that spread throughout the rest of the cavern fell away in the center. Like a round stair, it led down into the depths. The steps fell away, each one sinking deeper than the last, spiraling down into the darkness until they were out of sight.

They could see many boys like them, all dressed in black and mining the rocks in the hole. Hundreds of boys could be seen swinging pickaxes and carrying away rocks. Some of the closer ones saw the boys above them stop. They waved them on, telling them to keep moving. A dark figure with a whip came out of nowhere in front of them. He cracked his whip and signaled for them to keep moving. Ryker pulled himself away, Broff along with him, and continued down the passageway.

They ran down this hall for a long time. Soaking wet and cold, they pressed on. Running was getting his blood pumping again, which helped against the bitterly cold air.

Ryker grew tired as they ran. After swimming and now running, his strength was beginning to wane. Broff was a little heavier than Ryker and not as athletic, so Ryker pulled him along, trying to be strong for them both.

Then the passageway ended, and the walls beside them fell away to reveal a far more massive cavern. A huge domed roof was lost in the darkness above, like a starless night. Many rock columns were spread out all over the floor of the cavern. Atop thin mountains of jagged rocks were fixed some kind of metal torches. There were at least a dozen of them in a circle, all giving off a faint red light to illuminate the cavern.

In the center of the jagged mountains, a single peak rose higher than the rest. A huge pillar held the domed roof aloft. It had to be at least as tall as the tower in Tervan, Ryker thought. Its black walls almost shone from the glow of the light. Its edges looked sharp and dangerous.

Surrounding the base of the pillar were many groups of boys close to his age—training. The clashing of swords could be heard echoing throughout the cavern. On the opposite side from them, other boys hurled knives at planks with targets painted on them.

Running around the circular cavern's walls were numerous platforms and ledges about twenty feet wide. Pathways running within them were cut from smooth rock. All sorts of strange platforms could be seen in the dimly lit cavern.

The sight before the boys was chilling. Many of them stood still, their mouths wide open, gazing at everything going on in the busy cavern. Ryker heard Broff whimper next to him.

"Where are we?" Ryker said aloud. His thought had escaped through his mouth.

Suddenly the dark figures were all around them once more. Their red eyes were nearly the only things to be seen in the darkness. Herding the boys once more, they led them to the edge of a bridge that stretched before the passageway. Shoving the boys to the very edge of the smooth rock, the dark figures now lined the track. Hundreds of them could be seen, each of them with a pair of red eyes glowing in the darkness.

A single voice rang out and bounced on every wall in the cavern. It wasn't anything like the voices of the dark figures. It was deep, and it thundered as it filled the cavern: "Begin."

It was all some of the boys needed as they leaped from the platform onto one of the three ledges running straight. Some of the other boys needed a little more coxing. One of these was Broff. He had never been very good at running on the rooftops like Ryker.

Red lights hanging on the wall gave off little light to see by. The faint glow splashed on the stone pathways. Darkness filled the gaps between the ledges and obstacles of the track. The blackness beneath them waited to consume any victim. If you fell, you fell into the nothingness.

"C'mon, Broff. We have to do this," Ryker told him, looking behind them. The red light revealed many dark figures carrying cruel-looking whips.

"I can't, Ryker!" Broff began, tearing up. "This is all too much! I want to get out of here!"

Ryker took him by both arms and shook him. "We can't go back. We have to keep moving. Whatever this place is, we have to get through it. You and me, we are in this together!"

A whip cracked near them, and a boy yelped in pain. Many of the boys that remained began running on the ledge ahead. Ryker hurried Broff to the edge of the platform.

"Jump!" Ryker said and gave Broff a push.

Broff shouted and leaped. It was a good thing Ryker had shoved him, or he wouldn't have made it over the first jump. Broff looked back as he ran, and Ryker cheered him on. He had to be brave enough for both of them, but all he wanted was to break down and cry, to let whatever kind of sick nightmare this was end.

He shook himself. If he was to survive, he had to conquer the fear that already plagued his heart. Jumping onto the smooth pathway that spanned the thick darkness below, he moved forward.

Ryker followed close behind Broff on the ledge as they both ran. The red lights above them helped a little. They could make out the basic shapes of things, but their eyes weren't accustomed to this kind of dark, so everything was difficult to see. This darkness was unlike anything Ryker had ever witnessed.

Soon the ledge gave way to nothing. Ahead, dozens of ledges ran horizontally before them. Some were farther away than others, separated by gaps of darkness. A long jump would be needed to reach each one.

They ran along these ledges, jumping from one to the next. If they stopped, they would lose momentum and fall. One of the other boys did this. He jumped too far and overshot the jump. He caught himself and pulled himself back up on the ledge. When he tried to jump to the next one, he didn't quite make it. He screamed as he fell, his voice dwindling away until he was lost along with his failing voice. What lay beneath them? Was it just a void of darkness? Or was there something at the end? Ryker hoped he didn't have to find out.

What lay before them made even Ryker stop in his tracks. The tops of pillars rose up out of the void. They were at many different heights and spaced out randomly. They were just big enough to get two feet on. He watched as the boys ahead of them moved from pillar to pillar. One after the other fell. This would be his doom, he thought.

"Take your time," Ryker said to Broff, who nodded and took a deep breath. Ryker needed a moment to collect himself just as much as Broff surely did.

Broff made it to the first pillar fine. Gaining confidence, he jumped to the next pillar. Soon he was nearly halfway to the next set of obstacles. It was Ryker's turn. Taking a different path from Broff's, he began his journey on the pillars. He had only made it across a few pillars when he heard Broff cry out. Taking his eyes off the pillar at his feet, he quickly looked up and saw Broff lying flat on one of the pillars. A dozen pillars stood between them, so Ryker picked up his speed.

"Hang in there, Broff! I'm coming," he shouted.

He kept his eyes on Broff as much as he could while staying focused on the pillars. Broff tried to get to his feet, but he slipped and fell. He shrieked Ryker's name. Looking up, Ryker saw him clinging to the pillar by his fingertips.

Ryker was close. He moved as fast as he could. When he heard another shriek, he watched his friend slip into the darkness below. Ryker's eyes were instantly filled with hot tears. He wanted to dive down into the darkness and save him.

He had already lost Shiloh and now Broff. What was this place? Had they been brought here just to be filled with despair and killed for some kind of sport for these dark beings?

Filled with rage, he looked for the closest pair of red eyes. They would pay for this! They were off ahead of him in the next set of obstacles. He could hear their voices mocking another one of the boys as he struggled to pull himself up onto a ledge.

Locking his teary eyes onto them, Ryker ran toward them. After the pillars, the ledges ran yet again horizontally. This time the ledges were at different heights, some lower and some even higher. Ryker leaped from ledge to ledge until he was on one higher than most.

He was above the dark figures now. He moved to the right side and put his back to the wall as he stood on the tall ledge. He took a deep breath. *This is for Broff,* he said to himself. Then he pushed off the wall and ran along the ledge in a sprint. He pushed off with his legs and flew through the air.

Aiming for one of the dark figures, he dove. The figure saw him coming through the air and caught him by the neck, forcing the air out of his lungs. He slapped Ryker to the ground and then slid him to the edge of the chasm beneath the track.

Shoving its face close to Ryker's, he was almost swallowed by its hood. Shadow lingered within the hood and shrouded his face. "Don't stop now," its voice hissed. "You were doing so well! If you want to become one of us, you have to train harder than that!"

Many of the others laughed. The entire cavern was soon filled with evil laughter. The dark figure stood. Ryker still lay on the ground, stunned and gasping for air.

The dark figure spread out its arms and spoke again, this time loud enough to be heard by all. "We are the Shadow Keepers, the Dwellers of Darkness. We are the mighty Khoshekh. Soon all of Arke will know our name. The kingdom will be covered in thick shadow. Welcome to your new home. You will soon grow accustomed to even more than just this darkness."

Then two of them picked Ryker up and carried him to the edge of the floor. "Good luck finding your friend in the Pit," one said just before they threw him into the air.

Ryker spun over himself as he flew into darkness. Losing sight of his captors, he was soon surrounded by utter blackness. As he fell, the temperature went from cold to terribly bitter—almost too much for his body to handle. It seemed that time stood still as he fell. If he was indeed falling, he couldn't tell. His head hit something hard, taking him away from it all as he lost consciousness.

5

Numb

Pushing himself up off the ground, Ryker was amazed to find himself under the light of a moon and standing in knee-deep snow. His feet were already wet, which made them immediately go numb. A gust of wind blowing over the snow-covered ground brought chills over his entire body.

The place looked and felt familiar to him, even with the snow masking everything. The night sky held the moon and stars above him, their light seeming bright compared to the darkness he had just endured.

His body shook in the cold. He was wearing the same clothes he'd been wearing when he was captured, and they weren't near warm enough for this weather.

The area around him had many trees, all holding white powder within their boughs. The limbs were stripped bear from a harsh winter. Only sticks remained over a white canvas, longing for the warmth of spring.

The land beneath the snow was sloped, and Ryker followed it down. He crossed his arms to conserve heat and began walking in the knee-deep snow. His boots packed the snow down and kicked it up as he walked, leaving a path behind him. In no time, everything from his waist down was soaking wet, which made matters even worse. He really needed to find somewhere to get warm.

He could only remember once in his life when it had snowed like this. When he was a child, a terrible winter storm had swept across Arke. It had concealed the entire island in deep snow for over three months. Many had starved during the snowstorms and blizzards. Some had fallen ill and died of sickness.

For the first few days, Ryker had loved to play in the deep snow, making walled forts and sliding over the frozen bay. But the joy he'd found in the cold snow had soon been replaced with hate. Now cold weather only brought him bitter memories of that snowstorm.

Soon Ryker broke through a cluster of trees to see a large body of water. Teerah Bay lay frozen over before him. Sheets of thick ice covered the waters. Drifts of snow lay on top of the ice and piled high against its banks. The strong winds from the sea created tall mounds of snowdrifts. The moon shone over it all, creating a bluish tint to the white snow.

The wind howled like a hungry wolf in this open area, blowing over the frozen bay and chilling Ryker's face to the bone. Pain tore at his bare skin. He rubbed his face with his hands, blowing on them to try to get warm. It helped a little, but his body was quickly becoming numb from the cold—especially his hands and feet.

Down the embankment to his left was a small house, a cottage built close to the banks of the frozen waters. He made his way toward it through the snow with the guidance of the moon. The front door overlooked the water.

Drawing closer to the cottage, Ryker noticed that no prints had been made around its threshold. His were the first footprints in the snow since it had piled up outside the door. He had hoped no one would be home so he could stay there in peace and get warm.

Luckily for him, the house had been built with care. Strong lumber held back the elements, and a thatched roof kept it dry inside. The roof continued over a porch, sheltering the threshold of the door. It was mostly cleared of snow, and Ryker shook himself off when he stepped onto it.

He walked toward the door to try to peer through the window. He noticed that the door was already open slightly, letting a thin line of snow drift in. Maybe someone was here after all. He pushed the door open and peeked in.

A bed covered by a thick quilt was the first thing he noticed. The bed was made up, and as Ryker looked over the rest of the cabin, he saw that its single room was very clean. A dresser stood next to the bed. A table with three chairs sat near the large fireplace. Seeing no one there, he stepped in quickly and shut the door.

He hurried over to the fireplace. It was built with many large stones held together with mortar. Near the fireplace, a small rack held many split logs. He stacked the logs and found kindling and flint near the fireplace in a small bucket. He made quick work of building the fire, despite his numb and clumsy hands. He hit the flints together to create a spark. He hit them again and blew softly on the spark until the tinder began to burn.

Soon tiny flames from the kindling grew and made their way up to the logs. Not long afterward, the dry logs took up the flames. Once the fire was burning, he felt warmth wash over his body immediately. The flames grew and his spirits rose. He stayed close to the fire, holding his numb hands near the flames. He was so glad to have feeling in them once more.

Then something moved in the cabin behind him. He heard it—or thought he did. It was hard to tell over the popping of the logs on the fire.

He scanned the small, one-room cabin behind him. When he saw nothing, he turned back to the fireplace and put another log onto the roaring fire. He drew closer to the heat and closed his eyes, letting the warmth soothe his cold skin.

Then he heard it again. Finally he got up to see what the noise was. He looked out each of the many windows but saw nothing in the moonlight. Crossing the room to peer through the door, he thought he saw something move in the bed. He thought at first that the light from the fire was playing tricks on him. As he stared at the bed, he saw something move underneath the thick quilt.

He walked slowly to the bed. As he stood over it, he thought he could see the outline of a body lying under the quilt. He reached out to pull the covers back. He paused, hanging his hand over the quilt. He pulled back, thinking it might be best just to slip out without waking the owner of this home. Something about this place seemed very familiar, but for some reason he just couldn't figure out why. He stretched his hand out again. This time he took hold of the hem of the quilt and pulled the covers back to reveal the one resting beneath them.

Ryker saw the beautiful, pale face of a woman. He knew her. He had loved her. He was staring at the face of his mother. He knew now why this was all so familiar. It wasn't a dream but another memory—one he had tried to forget, one he wished he had forgotten. Emotions he thought he'd buried deep inside himself came back to light and took over his body with grief. The pain this memory brought overcame him. Tears filled his eyes, and anguish flooded his heart.

Her eyes were shut, and she lay completely still. Her dark hair was combed and lay alongside her head and tucked under her slender frame. Her arms were folded over her chest. Despite what he knew, she looked peaceful. A slight smile was spread on her pink lips.

Ryker had always loved his mother. She had taken such good care of him, though she had never been the same after his father's death. She had loved his father dearly. His parents' love for each other had been deeper than the sea, and he had seen it. They had showed Ryker what true love was: selfless. He had tried to keep these memories of his past at bay. But this darkness he had been thrown into seemed to search through his mind and bring his worst memories foremost in his mind.

As tears fell down his face, he reached out to touch her. Her gentle touch upon him had always been so warm and loving. The moment his hands met her icy skin, the door swung open, and the glass in the windows shattered. An explosion of wind and snow engulfed the small cabin. The tiny cabin was subjected to the center of a full blizzard. A whirlwind of ice and snow blew through the cabin.

Soon everything was covered in deep snow. The warm fire Ryker had lit was extinguished by the snow. Its flames hissed angrily until only a thin cloud of smoke remained. His mother was suddenly gone.

The wind became stronger and the air colder. It was nearly impossible to see. The wind felt beyond cold. His body hurt from the icy air. He crouched down and held onto his legs, trying to hide from the blizzard's wrath. He felt like he would freeze to death here. When the cold became unbearable, he lost all of his senses and faded into darkness.

Ryker gasped when he realized that he wasn't frozen to death. Though it was still cold, he was lying on his stomach on a rocky floor. He face was pressed hard against the cold stone. He quickly shoved himself up and stood, groaning.

Again, pitch darkness surrounded him. He tried to feel for something in the dark. Not daring to call out to anyone, he stayed as quiet as he could, hoping to avoid detection by any unseen foe lurking in the shadows. He searched the dark with outstretched hands and found a wall. Spinning around, he put his back to it, slid down its smooth edge, and sat, drawing his knees up to his chest. He sat there and wept. He missed the love he had always received from his mother. He missed the joy of his father. He shook his head. He was alone now, and he had to be strong in this place or he might loose himself.

"What did I do to deserve this?" he spit out from his tear-streaked face. Despair was the only thing that made sense in this dark place.

Again he asked himself why he was here. How had he gotten here? Those things—those dark figures—had stolen him away from the miserable life he had. At least he'd been able to see the light of day while living in the streets. Here, there was only darkness, no matter what time of day or night it was.

Here his free will was cut off, and he was subject to—what had they called themselves before throwing him down here? The Khoshekh? He had never heard anyone in Arke refer to them as the Khoshekh. He guessed it was the name they'd given themselves. And now he had a name for these dark things. He felt like they were all around him even now, pressing in closer to him. Although he couldn't see any intense red eyes, fear gnawed at him. His fate now rested in the hands of these Khoshekh.

No! He couldn't allow these things to win. He needed to find his friend Broff. Together they would figure out a way to escape this place.

First he needed to see if he could find Broff—if he was still alive. He had fallen a while before Ryker, but in which direction he did not know. He stood up and looked in every direction, trying to find some kind of light to guide him. When he saw none, he made up his mind to go straight ahead.

He pushed off the wall and walked slowly forward, keeping one hand outstretched in front of him so he wouldn't run into anything. In a very short time, his hand felt another smooth wall. He realized that this place probably ran directly beneath the track.

Letting his hand glide along the rough stone wall, he headed to his left. He thought maybe it would guide him back behind the place where he had fallen. He walked slowly through the darkness. One hand was on the wall, and the other was before him to keep him from running into any unseen sharp corners.

Moving slowly, his heart beat faster, and his mind began to play tricks on his senses. He thought he saw shadows moving in the darkness. The fear of losing his friend was greater than the fear of being stuck in this dark pit.

In the darkness he could pass right by Broff unless he ran into him. So Ryker began to softly call his friend's name. Barely a whisper came over his lips. He called Broff's name every so often as he walked in the darkness, hoping to find him soon, but he began losing hope as time went on. He called out over and over as he moved slowly along the wall.

"Who's there?" a voice whispered.

Ryker froze in place. He hadn't expected to get an answer from anyone but Broff. He didn't recognize the voice, and he didn't want to draw attention to himself, so he kept quiet. He tried to see where the voice had come from. He could hear labored breathing and rustling on the ground ahead of him.

"I'm not one of them, I swear!" said the voice frantically. "My name is Kegan. I am from Pelos. Please help! I think I broke my leg."

Ryker played out different scenarios in his head. He could just pass by without a word, or he could carry this stranger someplace a little safer. Or he could come back to help him when he had Broff to help. He honestly didn't know what to do. He would have hated for someone to pass him by without helping him if he was in need.

But Ryker didn't have time to carry this boy. He needed to find Broff first. He considered leaving the boy and quietly moving on, but he knew that would be wrong. This poor boy was in this darkness just like he was, taken from the streets and thrust into this evil place. Ryker couldn't just walk away from him.

His conscience got the best of him, and he replied, even though he knew time was short. "Kegan?" Ryker called his name softly.

"I'm here!" the boy answered, practically yelling, hope resounding in his voice. "Please help."

"Shh," Ryker hissed. "Not so loud."

"Here!" the boy called again much more quietly.

Kegan's voice led Ryker through the darkness to find him. Ryker walked toward him and stumbled over him in the dark. Bending low, he stretched out his hands to find him. Even at arm's reach, he still couldn't see the boy's facial features.

Already knowing the boy's name and what was wrong with him, Ryker spoke to him in a hurry. "I'm Ryker. I'm looking for my friend. Has anyone passed you since you were here?" He hoped he was going in the right direction.

"No, you're the only person I've heard since I fell," Kegan said, grimacing in distress.

Realizing that Kegan was in a lot of pain, Ryker kept the conversation short. "Where did you fall?" he asked, hoping to get an idea of where he was in this dark place.

"I fell after the square platforms. Something tripped me, and I fell into this pit." He took a sharp breath as if he suddenly experienced a jolt of pain.

Ryker didn't even remember seeing square platforms. He was going the wrong way. How far he had gone, he didn't know. He wanted to help the boy, but he didn't know if he could carry him to someplace where they could escape from this darkness. He thought he could at least help him to the wall.

"Can you stand?" Ryker asked him.

"I can try," Kegan replied. With much effort, he stood, leaning on Ryker for help.

"Let's get you to the wall," Ryker said.

Placing his shoulder under Kegan's arm, he helped him walk over to the wall. Kegan had to hop on one leg to move. Though Ryker couldn't see his leg, he was sure it was broken. He kept his free hand outstretched so they didn't run into the wall. When they reached it, Ryker gently helped him sit down with his back propped up against the wall. Kegan breathed a deep sigh of relief as he sat.

"I know you're going to leave me here," Kegan said. "I would do the same thing. I don't want to slow you down." Ryker could feel the sorrow overwhelm Kegan's voice as he spoke. "I was so scared before you showed up, but I don't want to get you hurt while trying to help me. I'd rather die here than kill the both of us." He paused, and Ryker heard the boy break into weeping. "Just leave me!" he said between tears.

"Once I find my friend, we'll come back for you," Ryker stammered, shocked at the boy's attitude. He didn't want him to die just because of a broken leg. But he had to agree with Kegan: he needed to be light on his feet to endure whatever else these Khoshekh had in store for them. Kegan would only slow him down.

"Great," Kegan spat out. "Then I'll be the reason for both of your deaths. Just leave me here and forget about me. There is no hope for us in this place. I have always been scared of the dark. Now I have good reason to be."

Ryker tried to argue with him, but Kegan cut him short when he yelled, "Leave me!" He pushed Ryker away, his voice bouncing off the walls and echoing down the long hall of this pit.

"Once I find my friend, I am coming back for you!" Ryker exclaimed.

He then stood and followed the wall in the direction he had come from. He felt so sorry for the boy. He had to admit that he was more terrified than he had ever been in his life, but he tried not to think about it. He pushed all fear and despair to the back of his mind, keeping his thoughts only on Broff, who was still alone somewhere.

Quickening his pace, he called Broff's name a little louder. When he thought he had backtracked to the place where he'd started, he slowed his pace. He called Broff's name again, and again there was no reply. He was sure to pass more boys who were hurt.

Somehow Ryker didn't feel any kind of pain from his own fall. If this was because of the dream he'd had of the snowy cabin or the way he'd landed, he wasn't sure. He knew one thing for sure: between all of the swimming and running, he was tired. Weariness came over him, and he had trouble continuing.

If not for Broff, he would have quit long ago, sat down in the dark, and let this fear and despair eat away at him until the cold took him. He knew if he stopped he wouldn't be able to keep going. He couldn't stop now. He needed to find his friend.

He briefly thought about the day he had met Broff. Ryker remembered watching him from a rooftop as Broff had tried to steal a loaf of bread from a bakery window. An older woman had seen him and begun calling for the Drudin Gaur. Broff had frantically tried to eat the entire loaf of hot bread, burning his tongue and hands in the process. Ryker had rolled with laughter as he'd watched.

When Ryker had seen the Gaur coming up the street, he had leaped down, grabbed Broff and the bread, and helped him escape. Later, Broff had told him that he'd just lost his mother. He had never even met his father. He was newly orphaned and had no idea how to survive in the streets. From then on, they had been inseparable.

What if Broff had gotten seriously hurt and was groaning in pain on this cold, hard floor? "Broff!" he called again. He could almost picture his friend rolling on the ground in pain. His heart ached to find him. He had lost Shiloh to the dark waters, and he wasn't about to lose Broff. He never gave

Kale or Nayori a second thought. They had abandoned him to whatever fate the Khoshekh would bring.

Time wore on, and still Ryker moved in the darkness, calling Broff's name. He was sure he had passed the place where he had been thrown into the pit. Soon he figured he would pass the place where Broff had fallen.

Suddenly Ryker had a thought. What if Broff was unconscious and couldn't respond? There was no way he could scan this entire area to look for him. He needed a light. He knew there was no material in these depths with which to make a torch. The red lights that burned in this place look like something other than flame.

Broff had to be awake. It was the only way for Ryker to find him. "Broff!" Ryker now yelled his name in panic.

6

SURVIVAL

"RYKER? I'M HERE!" CAME AN answer in the dark.

The voice belonged to his friend! He could hardly believe it. Broff was conscious after all. A few tears came to Ryker's eyes as he heard Broff's voice.

Ryker eagerly responded, "Keep talking to me so I can find you!"

The boys found each other's outstretched hands searching in the dark. They fumbled in the darkness and embraced one another in a hug.

"Are you all right? Are you hurt?" Ryker asked, unable to see his friend, even right in front of him, to see if he was injured or not.

"Yeah, I'm fine. Are you? I didn't think you would fall like I did. You've always been so swift on the rooftops." Broff was almost laughing. Only he could find humor in a place like this.

"I tried to fight the dark figures," Ryker replied solemnly.

"You did what?" Amazed, Broff hit Ryker jokingly. "Are you crazy?"

"I didn't know what would happen to you down here!" Ryker said. With the grief of Shiloh still heavy on his heart, he stopped and shrugged his shoulders, the movement going unseen in the darkness. "I figured I would go out fighting. They threw me down here, and I was knocked out." Ryker recalled the dream of his mother, but he couldn't talk about it just yet, so he pushed the thought aside.

"Let's find a way out of this place," Broff said suddenly, almost in a panic. "This place is so cold and dark." He shivered.

"When I was looking for you, I found a boy who broke his leg," Ryker said. "I told him we would come back for him after I found you."

"You've always been the hero," Broff joked. "Lead the way."

Ryker certainly didn't feel like a hero. He was just as scared as anyone else would be in this vile place. Broff depended on him, and he wouldn't let him down. Broff put one of his hands on Ryker's shoulder as he led them both back the way he had come.

Ryker thought about telling Broff about both of his dreams, but he figured it would be better if he kept them to himself. They didn't exactly make for a happy story. The two boys kept quiet as they went, not exchanging any words as they walked through the darkness. With no markers and nothing to let them know where Kegan was, Ryker called his name every so often.

Using the wall to guide them, Ryker knew they would run into Kegan sooner or later, whether he answered them or not. After a while Ryker knew that they had already traveled much farther than the place where he had left Kegan, so he stopped calling his name. Maybe another boy had picked him up. Or maybe Kegan had heard Ryker calling and had crawled to the opposite wall to keep to his word, wanting to be left so he wouldn't bring Ryker and Broff down with him.

Though Ryker's hand was numb from the cold, it quickly became raw as he used it to guide them along the rough stone wall. Despite the numbness, he felt warm blood drip from his fingers. Broff kept a firm grip on his shoulder while they traveled through the pitch-blackness. The darkness was cold and still. It held neither sight nor sound.

The silent darkness was abruptly torn apart by terrified screams. Hysterical shouts echoed through the walls of the pit. Broff gripped Ryker's shoulder even tighter. Ryker stopped advancing in the dark for a moment. He too was petrified at the howls of fear.

As they listened, the cries in the darkness became clearer. When Ryker realized that the cries came from other boys, the pair continued. The commotion was a group of boys who had fallen beneath the track down into this dark hole. They had wandered in the dark pit until they'd found a faint red light glowing above a barred metal door. The red light illuminated the area around the door. It seemed bright compared to the darkness they had endured. Ryker and Broff stayed in the shadows beyond the red light to watch the other boys. Ryker looked for Kegan among them but didn't see him.

Two of the boys held on to the bars and shook the door, making a loud jarring sound that echoed up the hall on the other side of the door. Most of them huddled together on the floor, shivering in the cold. Some of them paced in front of the door, taking turn shouting pleas up the corridor beyond the door.

Desperation hung in every single heart within this dark place. The darkness they were made to endure provoked total anguish. Ryker felt it as well. The feeling only grew as their stay in this dreadful place lengthened.

Easily seeing that the door was locked with no hope of opening it, Ryker sank down to his seat. He felt defeated, cold, and exhausted. He didn't think he could go on.

Pulling on Broff's hand, he pulled his friend down next to him. Without seeing Broff's face, Ryker knew he was tired too. They needed to rest and wait until someone opened the door. If that time would ever come, it was hard to say.

"What do we do now?" Broff asked in fear.

"Nothing," Ryker replied quickly. "There is nothing that we can do. We're trapped in this hole until we starve or freeze to death."

"I'm scared too, Ryker, but we need to stay strong," Broff replied tenderly. "At least we have each other."

"You're right, Broff. I'm sorry for losing it."

"I know how strong you are. It's okay to admit you're scared. If you weren't scared in a place like this, I would think something was wrong."

"I am scared, I'll admit it. I just wish there was something we could do."

"There is," Broff said as he settled himself. "We can get some sleep."

Broff was right. They needed to rest while they could, despite their situation. Ryker closed his eyes and leaned his head back against the cold wall. The temperature in this hole was almost unbearable. Though his clothes had dried as he ran, the bitter cold and darkness made him shiver.

The boys surrounding the door were humming with activity, so Ryker found no rest. Broff didn't mind; he snored softly with his head resting on Ryker's shoulder. Ryker hoped he was having a dream of somewhere warm and full of light.

Ryker knew, even without all this noise, that there was no way he could fall asleep with the dreams he had been having. Even if they weren't dreams, they still hung foremost in his mind, reminding him that he was alone in this world. He had been through enough in his short life, through more than most people went through in their entire lives. What had he done to deserve so much sorrow?

Ryker watched as the other boys kept shouting through the barred door into the hallway. No answer came, and no one could be seen up the dark hallway. Some of them shook the bars, trying to shake them loose. Others gathered what random things they had in their pockets, trying to find something they could use to pick the large lock holding the door secure. They tried everything from bits of bone to old rusty knives, but nothing budged the lock. Soon the boys saw that there was no hope of breaking through the door by force or otherwise. One by one, they all gave up. Gathering in small groups, they fell asleep.

Still, Ryker stayed awake. Resting here while he watched the others was enough for him. There was no way he could get any kind of sleep while thoughts of his parents plagued his mind. If he were to let his mind become still, the grief of losing them would catch up to him.

He looked around at all the sleeping boys. The light above gave everything it touched an unnatural red hue. He looked up at the red light and studied it. Before, he hadn't had a chance to look at it, but now he was captivated by it. There was no flame producing it. The red glow seemed to come from an orb. What it was made from, he had no idea. The orb sat in a metal bracket connected to the wall. It appeared to pulsate with a faint red light.

It was far different from normal light. Instead of pushing back the darkness and replacing it with wonderful white light, it mingled with the darkness, marrying it in deep shadows. The red light didn't hinder the darkness around them; it only seemed to make the shadows lengthen, letting the darkness flourish in a terrible way.

Here, beneath the dark light, they stayed. The Khoshekh were the only ones who could let them out. How long they would have to suffer in the pit, Ryker couldn't guess. All he knew was that he was bitterly cold. He had suffered through many things in his life and he had survived. He was sure he would survive through this. After some time, the sleeping boys woke, one after another. Some of them tried shaking the barred door again and shouting up the passageway. This woke Broff momentarily, but he fell back to sleep again.

Ryker was exhausted, but the moment his eyes shut, he saw the faces of his father, mother, and Shiloh. So he fought against sleep. The other boys soon realized that there was truly no hope, so they all sat and waited. Some fell back asleep, while others spoke about trying to explore the pit to see if there was another way out.

Time was hard to tell without the light of the sun or moon. Ryker guessed that they had remained in that hole for days—until a sudden gust of wind came up through the pit. It blew Ryker's hair back, chilling his already freezing face. Shivering, he clutched his knees tighter to his chest.

The red light above seemed to diminish. Now dimmer, it gave off less of its eerie light. Ryker could hear footsteps coming down the hallway toward the door. Ryker shook Broff, who rolled off his shoulder and into his lap. Ryker pushed him up and dragged him toward the door. He hoped they would be the first ones out of this dark hole. They were both eager to trade this dark pit for anywhere else.

A few of the other boys woke to the sound of echoing footsteps. They roused the others, and by the time the Khoshekh were opening the gate, all of the boys were awake. Everyone was exhausted, freezing, and ready to be free.

Ryker was anxious about what the creatures holding the key would do. He and Broff were the closest ones to the door, so he watched as the Khoshekh unlocked and swung open the heavy barred door. The Khoshekh turned without saying a word, was enveloped by a black cloud, and was gone. Ryker remained on the outside of the open door, wondering what had just happened. The door was open, but he didn't feel free.

"C'mon, Ryker. Let's get out of here!" Broff begged.

"This doesn't feel right," Ryker said loudly enough for all to hear. Most of the other boys were quiet, feeling the same way Ryker did. They had an unlocked door, but they were hesitant to escape.

"Nothing about this place feels right," Broff replied.

Ryker looked up at the red light. It grew brighter and splashed its strange light on the others as he looked around at them. Boys just like him and Broff surrounded him. Scared and alone, none of them deserved being thrown into a place like this.

Knowing that Broff was right, Ryker said, "Good point. Let's go. Just keep an eye out for anything." Looking through the door, he searched the darkness in the hallway. It was no more than four feet wide and just tall enough to walk through. The light above them threw little illumination into the hallway. Ryker's eyes slowly grew more accustomed to this low light. He didn't know where this hallway might lead, but he was sure it would be better than this pit.

He led Broff up the passageway, and the other boys followed quickly behind them. Not knowing where it led, Ryker kept an even pace and scanned as far ahead as he could, not wanting to find any surprises. The red light at the door gave little light into the hall, but when it was spent, another light shone in the hallway from the wall, making the walls, ceiling, and floor look blood-red with cruel shadows lingering nearby.

The hallway rose upward steeply and curved slightly to the left as they climbed out of the pit. Another red light could be seen farther along in the hall, and this one looked fainter than the rest.

Without realizing what was ahead of him, Ryker stepped through another barred door and out into a wide hallway. It was exactly like the hall they had gone through after swimming in the dark waters. He hadn't remembered seeing a door on the side.

Ahead of him at the end of the hallway stood five Khoshekh with their backs to them, looking out into the cavernous room as they guarded the entrance to this hallway. Their black armor and swords looked frightening in the glow of the red light. Their silhouettes were outlined in shadow by the red light. None of them turned to the boys behind them. They stayed still as statues, looking at all the other captive boys who were training in the large cavern. The sounds of steel echoed throughout.

Another hall led to their right, and Ryker decided it would be their best option, so he headed in the opposite direction from the Khoshekh. More red lights hung in this hallway, two on each side every few hundred feet, which was more than enough to see clearly.

Ryker heard some of the other boys behind him beg the Khoshekh to let them leave this place. He knew better than to ask. It all seemed clear to him now; they were here for a reason. They had all been taken because no one would miss them, and this master of darkness that led the Khoshekh was creating an army.

They continued through the hall, and soon the smell of food enveloped his senses. It didn't smell like freshly made pie or cake from the baker's shop, but it smelled like something edible. Either way, his stomach growled at the thought of food. He, and probably the rest of the boys following him, hadn't eaten in a day or longer before they'd entered this darkness. After enduring that black hole, he was almost faint with hunger. He hadn't been this hungry in a long time.

A doorway was cut into the hall on the left, and the smell of food poured out of it. Ryker stepped into a large room with a low ceiling, unlike the large caverns this place seemed to be filled with. Four large red lights were set in each corner to illuminate the room. Long tables lined each side of the room, with benches set on either side of the tables.

At the other end of the room, a fire burned in a shallow hole in the floor. Hanging above it was a large pot by a chain attached to the ceiling. A table behind the fire held bowls and pitchers of water. The red orbs in the corners of the room seemed to consume any natural light that escaped from the fire.

From the excitement that followed, one would have thought it was a grand feast set before them. Ryker and Broff led the pack as all of the boys dashed over to the steaming pot. Bowls went flying as each one tried to take two or three for themselves. On the outer rim of the pot hung a ladle. They tossed it to one another as they filled their bowls to overflowing with the soupy contents.

Ryker sat with his bowl at a table close by. Broff sat across from him, looking into the bowl. Ryker didn't stop to think what was in it and had already eaten half of it. Broff still looked into the bowl, fingering the contents. Most of the other boys did the same, but then the room fell silent as all of them stuffed their mouths with the food.

"What's in this?" Broff asked in disgust.

Ryker, who had all but finished his food, looked into the bowl at its contents. It was a milky kind of soup. It had no taste, but it was filling. Whatever it was, it was meant for them, and he was going to get another bowl.

"Just eat it, Broff," Ryker said. "You don't know when your next meal will be." He rose from his seat and headed over to the pot of food.

A Khoshekh was now guarding the pot. He must have showed up while Ryker was eating. Ryker reached out for the ladle, but the Khoshekh grabbed his arm and said, "Don't be greedy. Save some for the others."

Ryker turned toward the glasses and pitchers but looked back at the Khoshekh before reaching for them. The Khoshekh was preoccupied with another boy who also wanted seconds. Ryker poured out something for him and Broff to drink.

He hurried back to where Broff was sitting, hoping the Khoshekh didn't see the two glasses. He slid one to Broff, who was now eating out of his bowl. Ryker took a long drink and set the empty glass down on the table. He looked over the room and saw that many of the other boys were done eating. Now there were two more Khoshekh standing by the door.

"I hope you have all eaten your fill," said the hissing Khoshekh near the entrance to the room. "Follow me and you will find rest."

All of the boys obeyed and stood. Passing by the Khoshekh, they entered the hall once more. Another Khoshekh was waiting for them outside under the red lights. Having his stomach full, Ryker felt much better. However, the fear these Khoshekh brought whenever they were around made him feel uneasy. He never knew what was going to happen, and he always expected the worst.

"Follow me," another one hissed. Turning and walking slowly, it led the boys down the hall. A large ring of keys dangled from its belt, resulting in a chorus of jingles that bounced off the walls with every step.

They continued down the hall until they came to a series of wooden doors with small metal grates in their centers. All of them were tightly shut. From the muffled voices escaping through the metal grates, Ryker could tell that they were filled with boys like them. How many orphaned boys were these dark things keeping down here? he wondered.

The Khoshekh approached a door on the right. He found the right key on his ring and unlocked it. Swinging it opened, he motioned for the boys to enter, and they obeyed. All of them ran past him into the room.

Once they had all entered, he slammed the door shut. Ryker stuck his face by the metal grate and watched the Khoshekh lock the bolt. When it did, it suddenly looked up at Ryker. Its face was hidden in the darkness that shrouded it beneath the hood. Its red eyes glowed in the dim light and seemed to brighten as the creature laughed.

Its voice hissed as it spoke. "Rest your weary head. You'll need your strength for tomorrow!" Its high-pitched, hissing laughter echoed in the long hall.

Ryker found out quickly that everything about the Khoshekh was vile. They were cruel beings shrouded in darkness. He would do everything he could to defy them, to fight the fear they had sown in him. He shuddered to think about what would happen if he gave in to their plan for him.

He turned from the door to look over the room. It too had a low roof and was smaller than the room they had shared their meal in. It was lined with a few dozen cots and many of the other boys had already sprawled out on them.

A single red light shone above him. Ryker was still not used to the red hue it gave to everything. It made the darkness even more frightening, and it even made the other boys' eyes look lifeless.

Ryker found Broff, who had picked out two cots for the two of them, and walked through the crowd of boys toward him. The boys had fought over what they'd thought were the best beds. Ryker sat down on the cot opposite Broff. A chill ran up his back and made him shiver. If nothing else, he hoped he would get used to this cold air.

"So, why do you think we're here?" Broff asked, looking up at Ryker.

Ryker snapped back impatiently, "Isn't it clear to you?"

He was cold and exhausted and had already gone through enough for one day. He had been taken from the place he had only recently called home. He'd had dreams reminding him of his parents' tragic deaths. He had lost Shiloh, a friend he looked at like a little brother. Ryker didn't care about their fate in this dark place. He only hoped it would cloud his memories and cover up the pain they brought with them.

"I'm sorry, Broff," Ryker said after his mind had settled down. "I didn't mean it like that." He didn't want to lash out at the only friend he had ever had. This darkness seemed to be pressing in on him, stifling his thoughts.

"It's okay," Broff said, shrinking away from him.

"Broff, I apologize. This is just so much to take in. We really do need to stick together down here. We have already been through a lot back in Tervan. Now it looks like we'll be going through even more." Reaching out across the gap between the beds, he put his hand on Broff's shoulder, trying to comfort him.

"It's okay, Ryker. I can feel it too. It's not just the fear of what's going to happen. There's something else in this place in the darkness. Like it's hiding something." Broff shuddered as he finished.

"You're right. I can feel it too. Whatever it is, we need some rest up for whatever tomorrow has in store for us. If we stick together, we can survive long enough to figure out how to escape." Though he tried to sound hopeful, Ryker knew their chances of escape from a place like this were very slim if not impossible. He didn't know if they would ever see the light of day again.

"Escape is the furthest thing from my mind," Broff said as he lay back in his cot. "I just want to survive." He shuffled around on the mattress to get comfortable. He clasped his hands behind his head and shut his eyes.

Ryker did the same and lay back on his cot. "Good night, Broff," he said. Broff mumbled a reply but was already fast asleep.

Ryker smiled at his friend. He knew this place would destroy any kind of light they held inside of them. He would try with all his power to hang on to the hope he had for freedom for both himself and for Broff. He would use the fear as fuel to help him strive to see the light once again.

The cot he lay on wasn't terribly uncomfortable, though it was a little scratchy and it stank. It was far more comfortable than he would have expected it to be. With no blanket, he had to cross his arms tight to try to keep as warm as possible. He shivered as he lay there on his back. He felt tired enough not to care about how cold he was.

Before he shut his eyes, the red light above the door went out, leaving the room in darkness. He had never liked to sleep unless he had a small fire going or a little candle burning. The unknown things that his imagination always placed in the darkness hindered him from sleep. Now, living in a place filled with things that actually resided in the darkness, he felt even more fearful of what lay beyond where his eyes could see. He rolled over onto his stomach, hoping it would keep him a little warmer. Soon he too drifted off to sleep.

7

Separated

Ryker should have known better than to get a good night's rest in this dark place. That night his sleep was plagued with terrible dreams. He was standing in utter darkness with no light to guide him. The only sound he could hear was his own heavy breathing. His body shivered in the bitter cold. The temperature felt far worse than what he had endured before. He squatted down and pulled his legs in close to his chest, hoping to keep warm that way.

Then in the distant darkness a light appeared. It was not a light he was hoping to see. In fact, it was a pair of lights. It looked like the faint red glow of eyes he had seen before, which reminded him of the fear he had felt the first time he had seen them. The glowing red eyes didn't stay still. They seemed to bob up and down quickly. As they bobbed, they seemed to grow, but in actuality they were getting closer to him. Then he could hear running footfalls to match the movement of the red eyes. A Khoshekh was charging toward him.

Fear seized Ryker. He rose and ran in the opposite direction of the red eyes, and the Khoshekh they belonged to came toward him. Running for a moment, he turned his head to see if the Khoshekh was still in pursuit. It wasn't. The red eyes were nowhere to be seen. Once again he could see nothing, and darkness surrounded him, pressing in from every side.

How could he escape from the unseen in a place where he was blind? he asked himself. He stopped to catch his breath and scanned the darkness to see if another set of eyes would appear. He quickly looked in every direction, not even knowing when he had made a complete circle in scanning the darkness.

He kept searching until he saw yet another pair of eyes. They seemed much closer than the first. Ryker quickly turned on his heels and ran. Then, ahead of him, another set of eyes appeared. The red glow of the eyes illuminated the darkness around them, barely revealing the hem of the hood that shrouded the rest of the Khoshekh's features. Ryker turned his direction slightly to avoid the new set of eyes. He looked behind him and saw that the first set of eyes was still in pursuit. Now two of them were after him.

These two chased him for a long time until they suddenly disappeared. How many times would these things appear? he wondered. How long would he have to endure this nightmare?

He knew he was sleeping, but he didn't know how or when he would wake. The fear and panic he felt every time he saw the red eyes felt so real. He stopped again to take in deep breaths and prepare for the next chase. He looked into the darkness again, expecting to see eyes appear somewhere in the darkness.

And they did—everywhere! A dozen Khoshekh appeared in a semicircle around him. All of them stood still, only fifty feet away from him. Ryker's eyes grew wide, and his jaw dropped. What hope did he have now? Fear and despair were a constant feeling in this darkness, and they only grew at the sight of so many Khoshekh after him.

He reminded himself that he had escaped the pursuer on the rooftops for a short time, and he could do it again. They didn't stand there long. Soon all of the Khoshekh ran toward him. Ryker ran away from them with all the strength he had left, hoping he could find somewhere to hide, somewhere to get away. He ran through the darkness to escape from the things that resided within it. The darkness almost seemed to be part of the Khoshekh, like the air they breathed.

He looked back at his pursuers and saw them failing to keep up with him. He was losing them. He felt hope spring up in him. Then his feet no longer ran on solid ground. They fled on open air. The ground beneath him had stopped at an edge unseen in the darkness. Without any way of stopping himself, he fell, plummeting headfirst into the darkness. A scream of terror broke away from his lips. Falling in the darkness, he had only one thought: his hope of seeing the light of day again was fading, and this darkness was going to be his end.

Ryker shot up in his bed, gasping for air. The last thing he remembered was falling in the darkness and thinking he was about to hit bottom. He was covered in sweat, and his body almost welcomed the coolness of the room. He wasn't the only one up. The red eyes of the Khoshekh could be seen throughout the small room. A single red light was burning by the door. It was dimmer than before, but it still revealed their guards' dark armor and menacing swords.

"Time to rise. I hope you are all well rested!" one of their captors hissed as he tossed a sleeping boy out of bed. "Today you will find out who is worthy to serve our master, which I'm sure many of you are eager to do." Many of the others laughed along with the Khoshekh who had spoken.

Then chaos resonated off the walls in the bunkroom. Khoshekh were appearing wherever a boy was still sleeping in a cot. They threw these boys out of bed, creating panic within them first thing in the morning. The boys scattered out of their beds and hit the floor running.

A Khoshekh yanked Ryker out of his bed. Shoving him along, he asked, "Didn't you hear him? Don't you want to serve our master?" The Khoshekh did the same to Broff, and soon the friends were beside each other in the line heading out of the room.

"Did you get any sleep?" Ryker asked, whispering quietly for only his friend to hear.

"Yeah, well, kinda. I know I fell asleep, but all night I had dark dreams. As if being awake in this place isn't a nightmare already." Broff spoke quickly in a voice so low that Ryker could barely hear him in the hectic room.

"Me too" was all Ryker could get out before they were shoved through the door and into the hall.

The Khoshekh surrounded them and ushered them down the dark hall at a run. The only light to help guide them was the one from the room they'd left behind. Shadows lengthened out of the doorway and shed a red glow over a small expanse of floor.

They headed down the hall toward the main cavern. Ryker was afraid they would again be made to run the track that had almost claimed their lives. He didn't know if Broff—or even himself—could endure that cold darkness again.

Many of the boys rubbed sleep out of their eyes. Ryker could see the looks on their faces by the red light. They looked as if they wanted this to be a dream they would soon wake from. He knew better. This was their reality now: bitter cold and intense darkness. Fear changed to numbness as time wore on.

Despite the dark dreams he'd had during the night, Ryker's body felt rested. Even lying on the smelly cot in the cold darkness hadn't bothered him. However, it seemed that the moment he'd closed his eyes, he was opening them again to the shouts of the Khoshekh.

He was also very surprised about the dream he'd had. He would have thought he'd continue to dream of his past as before. But this dream was different. It was a nightmare of the reality that waited for him when he woke.

The times when he had relived his past, he hadn't been sleeping. He was sure he had lost consciousness, but he knew he hadn't been sleeping. Those visions had felt so real, so vivid. This darkness must have something to do with it.

"Where do you think they're leading us this time?" Broff panted as he ran alongside Ryker.

Broff's voice startled Ryker. He hadn't known that his friend was next to him. The question brought him out of his thoughts. He was barely able to see a few feet in front of him, let alone his friend next to him.

"How are you feeling today, Broff?" Ryker ignored Broff's question, wanting to know how his friend was. Their short conversation earlier had ended quickly. He knew they would spend many nights inside this dark place, and the first few would be the hardest.

"Fine," Broff replied.

Ryker could tell by Broff's voice that this friend knew what he was doing. "Good. I wish they had at least let us sleep in on our first day," he joked, trying to make light of the situation.

"Ryker, come on," Broff said, getting back to the point. "Where do you think we're going? What do you think those things meant about serving their master?"

"I don't know," Ryker said, trying to get out of answering him outright. "Just keep up with the rest. I'm sure we'll find out soon enough." He could guess where they were going, because they were headed toward the domed room. They were probably going to run the track again. Hopefully, Broff would do better today, and Ryker could keep himself out of trouble. He would try to help Broff more this time.

More shouts echoed throughout the hall as they continued running. The Khoshekh ran alongside, their eyes the only things to be seen in the dark hall. Ryker hoped for Broff's sake that they wouldn't run the course first thing, though he did have confidence in him to do better this time. He could only hope that Broff wouldn't fall into the pit again. If he did, Ryker would have to make a choice to follow or continue.

The hall gave way to the wide-open space of the main cavern. The darkness that dwelled within made it seem larger than it really was, though it seemed that all of Tervan could fit inside. Only half of the red lights circling the pillar were burning this morning—or whatever time it actually was. Their glow fell on the large pillar holding up the cavern's ceiling, and the other pillars that held up the lights made everything seem sharp and dangerous.

The Khoshekh led the boys toward the center pillar. It was almost the size of a small mountain but very thin. Near the pillar, a ring was drawn on the rock. By the lights surrounding it, the circle looked as if it was painted with blood. Ryker shuddered at the dreadful sight.

One of the Khoshekh spoke. "Surround the circle, but do not enter it. You will each get your turn." All of the boys complied and stood around the circle. Only a handful of the Khoshekh remained, one of which walked to the center of the circle.

A booming voice of unknown origin spoke. "You have been brought to this beautiful darkness to become my mighty Khoshekh. You shall be forged into deadly weapons. Soon Arke will see us in our full strength, and you will have the honor of fighting for me as your master." The voice continued to echo in the great cavern long after it had stopped speaking. Ryker thought he saw a shadow move on top of the pillar as the voice spoke.

Ryker shuddered at the voice. Obviously, this was the master the Khoshekh kept talking about. However, he didn't have a hissing, high-pitched voice like the Khoshekh. Who was he?

"Welcome to the Hollow, where you will be tested and trained in order to serve our master well," said the Khoshekh in the middle of the circle. "This is your first test. Yesterday was nothing compared to what you will endure today. It was no more than a welcoming party." He laughed at this. "Two of you will enter this circle. The first one to leave it will be sent to the mines. The one who remains will be declared the victor. He will have the glorious opportunity to train as one of us, the Khoshekh. Now, let us begin." After the Khoshekh had spoken, he disappeared into a black cloud. Wisps of it remained for a moment and then faded into the dark air.

Two Khoshekh shoved the first pair of boys into the circle. They were facing each other from opposite ends. All of the boys took a step back from the circle and watched as they began. Neither of the boys looked like they had ever been in a fight before. The red lights above distorted their features, making it hard for Ryker to guess their ages. Maybe they were a little younger than he and Broff, he thought. They charged and grabbed each another. They groaned and panted, straining to push and pull at one another, hoping to get the other off balance. They held on to one another for a few minutes before they grew tired.

The smaller of the two boys was weaker, and he lost his balance and rolled onto the hard floor. However, he was still in the circle. The boy on the ground did his best to rise off of it quickly. Seeing his opponent get up, the boy still standing charged at him and shoved him hard. The smaller boy hadn't stood up completely, so his feet gave way under him as he was pushed out of the circle.

A Khoshekh immediately scooped the boy up and swiftly carried him toward the second hall across from them. The boy didn't put up a fight. He seemed fine with mining instead of training to become one of the Khoshekh. Neither of the choices appealed to Ryker, however. The boy who had won was sent to begin training on the track. Ryker could faintly see him start on the platform near the hall leading to the bunkroom. While he began the series of obstacles, another pair of combatants was chosen for the ring.

Many of the boys fighting in the ring only tried to push each other out. The Khoshekh didn't seem to care about picking fair opponents. They picked boys randomly, not paying any mind to the size or age of the two boys. Usually the older or stronger boys won, leaving the younger ones to mine. A few of the younger, smaller boys were faster, so they could outmaneuver the bigger, slower boys. Using their weight against them, they could get them off balance and push them out of the ring.

Some of the older boys threw punches, demonstrating their strength. A few of them really put a beating on the boys they were paired against. Ryker was surprised at the ferocity of some of the boys, it seemed they took their anger out on their opponent. Soon only a few remained. The victors ran the track, and the losers were carried off to work in the mine.

Broff was shoved past Ryker into the circle, and Ryker's heart sank as Broff entered the ring to spar with another boy. He tried to grab Broff's hand to pull him back, but it was already too late. Ryker lost all hope for his friend when he saw the boy Broff would face off against. He was almost twice Broff's size and much older. He held up his fists, declaring that he was ready for a real fight.

"You can do it, Broff! Use his size against—" Ryker felt the back of a Khoshekh's hand strike his head to stop him from encouraging his trembling friend.

"Quiet! You will get your turn," it hissed. The Khoshekh stayed close behind Ryker in case he tried to interfere again.

Ryker watched as Broff and the other boy prepared themselves. One would stay and train, and the other would be sent to the mines. For a moment Ryker didn't know if he wanted Broff to win or lose. Either way, he didn't want him to get hurt.

"Begin!" said a Khoshekh close to the ring who was growing impatient with the combatants.

Without letting a moment pass, the older boy closed the gap between them and struck Broff in the face with a swift left jab. Broff held his nose and cried in pain. Beneath the red light, Ryker saw the other boy smile at the pain he'd caused and back away from Broff. Broff's nose was bleeding, so he wiped the dripping blood away from his mouth and put his hands up in defense.

Ryker and Broff had often wrestled with one another, but they'd never made such violent contact with each other. Suddenly the other boy attacked Broff. Again and again he struck him, and all Ryker could do was watch.

Broff tried to block the blows, but the other boy found most of his hits landing. With each successful hit, Broff backed away, inching closer to the edge of the ring. When he finally came very close to the line, the older boy hit him in the gut and pushed him hard. Broff fell onto his back outside of the circle. He had lost.

Ryker saw relief come over his friend's face. He seemed to welcome his loss as two Khoshekh picked him up. He was on the far side of the ring from Ryker, so he didn't have a chance to say anything to him. If Ryker ran over to him, he was sure to get a beating for it.

All he could do was watch as the Khoshekh carried him off. They headed for the hall across the cavern under the glow of one of the lights and were lost to darkness. Then he saw them again as they entered the glow of another red light.

When they entered the hall that led to the mine, Ryker lost sight of them. Ryker had been the unspoken protector of all the boys that had lived with him in Tervan. Now he could only protect himself. He couldn't even keep his eye on his only friend in this dark place. Hope continued to slip through Ryker's hands, only to be replaced by the despair of this pressing darkness.

If Ryker lost his match on purpose, maybe he could once again be reunited with Broff in this darkness. He would have to make it look like he was just a bad fighter. For all Ryker knew, he might actually lose to a better fighter. *Don't worry, Broff. I'll see you soon*, he thought as he looked across the cavern at the hall leading to his friend.

8

Welcomed

Having his focus away from the circle got Ryker pushed into it. A Khoshekh shoved another boy in to fight with him. The boy was no older than Shiloh. Ryker couldn't believe it. Why couldn't Broff have faced off with a boy like this and Ryker have faced the older, larger boy?

"Begin!" a Khoshekh shouted.

Although Ryker wanted to lose to this young boy and mine with Broff, he couldn't allow himself to force this boy into training with these evil beings. Simply being in this place had plagued his mind with something unseen. Who knew what would lie in store for him once he began training?

But could he abandon Broff to whatever the mine had in store for him? Surely it would be just as bad as the training, if not worse. He didn't know what to do.

The younger boy put his hands up in two fists and began walking slowly to Ryker. Ryker looked at him in dismay. When the boy got close enough to hit Ryker, he stopped and looked up at him with terrified eyes. He whispered suddenly, "Please beat me. Throw me out."

Ryker wanted to help this boy, but he also wanted to lose so he could help Broff. He knew this younger, smaller boy wouldn't last long in the Khoshekh training. But could he himself last?

Looking at the boy again, he pitied him. This young boy was asking for help in a hopeless place. He saw Shiloh when he looked at him and couldn't deny him what he asked. He would help this boy, no matter the outcome for himself.

Ryker nodded and put his hands up as well. He began pushing the boy to the edge of the ring. The boy began putting up a little fight so the Khoshekh wouldn't become suspicious. He shoved Ryker's hands away and pushed back. Ryker caught on and did the same, shoving the boy toward the edge again.

"Hit me!" the boy whispered desperately.

Ryker didn't know if he could do that. He could really hurt this kid if he hit him. To make it look real, the younger boy struck Ryker in the gut. The blow surprised Ryker and made him gasp.

Ryker then hit the boy, holding back his full force. He unintentionally knocked the wind out of the boy. Then, to complete the act, Ryker shoved him out of the ring.

He had done what the boy had asked, but Ryker still felt like he had sent the boy to his doom. Ryker knelt down to make sure the boy was all right. Along with the groaning, Ryker caught a wink from the boy's eye. He would be all right. Two Khoshekh shoved Ryker out of the way and picked the boy up to carry him off to the mines.

Another Khoshekh led Ryker to start his training. They headed for the large platform near the bunkroom hall. Following the Khoshekh, he was close to the sword strapped to the creature's back. If only he reached out, he could slide the sword out of the scabbard and kill his captor.

Just as he was thinking about this, the Khoshekh slid the blade out, only to slide it back in. The metal on the hilt and the edge of the scabbard hitting each other made a clanking noise.

There was no way he could follow through with his plan now. He wondered if the Khoshekh knew that he was thinking about taking the sword. Even if he had managed to get the sword, he would have had to answer to countless other Khoshekh before escaping.

They were on the large platform that bridged the gap over the pit from the main cavern to the hall leading to the bunkrooms. A few Khoshekh blocked the hall. The Khoshekh led Ryker to the left-hand side of the platform and signaled for him to start.

"Begin when you're ready," it said. "May I be the first to welcome you, for soon you will be on your way to becoming one of us."

The Khoshekh spoke as if it was a good thing to become one of them. These things were twisted. It laughed as it left Ryker and returned to the ring of boys, where only a few remained.

Darkness stretched before Ryker. It was the same darkness that led down into the cold pit he had endured yesterday. Pillars similar to the one Broff had fallen from came up out of the void, dotting the darkness with stone. These were slightly different though; they were not the same height, making it far more difficult to cross.

Ryker didn't have any other option, so he leaped to the first one. His landing was a little shaky, and he steadied himself before continuing. He leaped to the next pillar, steadied himself, and then jumped to the next. He continued this process until he made it to the next obstacle.

Like the very first obstacle where he had followed Broff on the previous day, long, thin platforms ran before him. Moving across the pillars had led him to the platform on the far right, so he was close to the wall. He ran atop these with no problem, although a few times he grew overly confident and nearly lost his balance.

The next area held narrow platforms that spanned the track diagonally. The first began high on his right, connected to the wall, and then ran steadily down, meeting low on the cavern floor to his left. He had to jump toward the platform to his left to accommodate the height difference on the diagonal platform. Many of them lay before him. The next started high on his left and low on his right. These platforms went back and forth like this. He stayed near the center of these platforms and found he could jump them easily, because each one met at the same height near the center. He jumped off a little higher on his right or left, depending on the platform he was on.

After those, he was on another wide platform that spanned the gap of the pit below. Another large hall led to his right and was shut off by a large metal gate. The red lights above showed that it had many hooks and barbs all over it. At the top of the gate, every bar came to a sharp point like a spearhead. Five Khoshekh guarded the gate with long, curved spears. Ryker's curiosity got the best of him, and he wondered what lay behind those gates.

One of the guards hissed as it came quickly toward Ryker with its spear pointing at him. "Move along," it said. "The master will let you through here when you finish your training."

Ryker realized that he had better move. He jumped to the next obstacle. These were like the ones he had done the day before, and they spanned the track horizontally. He leaped from platform to platform in succession. Running on rooftops for so long had made him agile and brave when it came to heights.

However, this track was far different from the rooftops. Here the height over the darkness was unknown. The void beneath the platforms was terrifying. He had to keep himself focused and look ahead in order to keep his balance.

Ryker leaped off the last horizontal platform onto a square one about four feet wide. Many of these spanned the darkness. Like the pillars, they were at many different heights, making it harder to cross. Looking for the best route with the closest platforms, he began.

The one he started on was higher up than most so the next one he jumped to was much lower. He jumped to another about the same height, if not a little lower. The next was a platform much higher. He reached up as he jumped, getting hold of the edge with his fingertips. His body slammed on the side of the platform. He held on tight as the impact nearly knocked him into the pit below. Straining, he used his feet to help push off as he pulled himself up.

He rolled onto the square platform and rested. He was being watched, and not long after he stopped, a Khoshekh from the cavern floor began cracking a whip for him to continue. Knowing the Khoshekh could easily appear on the platform with him at any moment, he didn't delay in jumping to the next platform and finishing quickly.

He stood on the last of the square platforms, looking at the obstacle before him. These would be the hardest yet. Large rectangular platforms were balanced on beams at their centers. These large platforms slowly tilted left and right under the orb's red light.

If Ryker were to jump on one side, his weight would push the platform down. Three of these lay in succession in front of him. He had to cross them one way or another, so he decided to go for it. Leaping from the platform he was on, he landed toward the left side of the teetering platform. It quickly sank down with his weight.

While trying to keep his balance, he ran as fast as he could along the platform toward the other side. His weight pushed the rising side back down, leveling it out. The moment it was relatively level, he jumped to the next platform. Landing near the middle of this platform, his weight didn't affect it much. He did have to balance himself to find the center of the platform.

The next platform was much farther away than the other two had been. He would have to gain altitude in order to make the distance. He slowly moved toward the right side, shifting his weight to slowing raise the left side. He waited until he thought it was high enough before he moved. The platform was close to sending him down into the pit, but he knew he needed all the height he could get. Without losing any of the height he desperately needed, he bolted to the left side and jumped from the very edge. He sailed through the air and landed on the next platform. He rolled across it, nearly sliding off.

The platform descended quickly, giving him no time to rest. He ran to the right side, jumped off it and onto the main platform, and landed with his feet dangling off and his stomach flat on the main platform. This one held firm and didn't move, so he took his time rolling up and onto it completely. Lying on his back, he slowly caught his breath.

He rose, looking back on his accomplishment. He hoped he wouldn't have to do that again, but he was pretty sure he would. He thought for a moment. How long he would be forced to train?

The sound of metal hitting rock stole his attention. It came up from the hall and filled his ears. He looked down toward the sound. Only one red light illuminated the hall where his friend was being held. Against his will, Broff was being forced to mine the rock that held them all captive in this dark and evil place.

He wondered what they could be mining for down there—or if they were really mining for anything at all. Maybe they were chipping away needlessly at rocks in order to break their backs along with their spirits. Ryker would train hard to escape with his friend one day.

"Hang in there, Broff," he said aloud to himself.

On the next three obstacles, Ryker knew what to expect. Platforms ran straight ahead of him, and then more ran horizontally. Next were the pillars that Broff had fallen from.

In a short amount of time, Ryker had finished them all and was on the next large platform. The hall leading to his right stood unguarded. No red lights shone against the cavern's dark entrance. Unnatural darkness spewed from the hall, giving Ryker a new sense of fear for it.

Yesterday, in the heat of the moment, he hadn't seen that dark hall when he'd tried to fight the Khoshekh after Broff fell. Was he allowed to enter there? Was it part of their training? He wasn't sure, so he backed away from the dark hall and went to the next obstacle.

Before him, horizontal platforms at many different heights were stretched over the black void. He had used these to try to jump onto a Khoshekh. It hadn't worked so well, and he had been reunited with his friend in the darkness below. He wasn't going to fall into the darkness this time. He would show these dark things he was a fighter, despite his fear.

The moment he had been brought to this terrible place, his fear had begun eating away at him. He had tried to push it back, but it had been persistent. Now he was fighting for more than his own survival. Fear or no, it was up to Ryker to escape for the sake of both Broff and himself.

Ryker jumped to the platform, landing without second-guessing himself, and immediately jumped to the next. It was lower than the next one, so he had to stretch to move forward. He moved through these challenges with renewed strength.

Looking at the next obstacle, he saw that it was familiar. Small, square platforms stretched before him, sitting within the darkness. All of these, unlike the ones before, were at the same height. Ryker leaped from one square platform to the next with ease. Not all of these obstacles were so bad, he thought. He jumped to the final platform and stood there. Fear had waited for him there and was renewed in his heart.

Nothingness lay before him. No obstacle spanned the final distance between him and the large platform where he had started only two hundred feet away. What was he supposed to do? Were there unseen platforms he was to jump on? Was this a final test to see if he was brave enough to join them?

Maybe the final obstacle was to see if he could survive the fall into the pit far below, only to be rewarded with bitter cold and utter darkness.

Ryker stood there, frozen in dismay for a long while. He knew if he stayed on this platform any longer, he would be punished. He could see red eyes watching him from below.

He backed up as far as he could on the square platform to get as much speed as he could. Taking two short steps, he leaped into the darkness. He didn't hit any unseen platforms in the darkness, and now he was falling through the void.

Crying in terror, he once again fell into the pit. Suddenly darkness enveloped him—not the darkness from the pit but the darkness of a black cloud. It constricted his skin, grasping him tight with its black, misty hands.

The next thing Ryker knew, he was splashing into the frigid water of the dark sea. He was shocked, not only by the cold but by the fact that he hadn't fallen into the pit. He immediately began treading water as he searched for the red light.

The shock of the cold water reminded him of Shiloh. Suddenly he could see Shiloh's desperate, terrified face in the darkness around him. Everywhere he looked, Shiloh's face was there. Even when he closed his eyes, he could still see him.

Ryker tried to shake the terror away, but he couldn't seem to rid himself of it. Seeing Shiloh ahead of him, he began swimming toward the phantom. It stayed just out of Ryker's reach, no matter how hard he swam.

Shaking his head, Ryker wept in the water. His body quickly started tightening up from the temperature. He needed to flee from these waters before they claimed his life too.

He searched once more for the red light in the darkness. Shiloh's face was now replaced with the glowing red light. Ryker swam as fast as he could, pushing the cold water away with his hands and feet, drawing closer to the light.

His body soon locked up after all the running and swimming, for he was exhausted. He pressed on through the pain and the cold, knowing he would drown if he stopped.

Reaching the rocks near the light, he flopped onto one to rest and closed his eyes. He sat near the red light, not knowing if he could go on, the sounds of the mine echoing down the passageway. The thought of Broff suffering there gave him strength to press on. A moment later he climbed completely out of the water to dry off as much as he could.

The red light seemed bright to him. He had lingered too long in this darkness. Shivering, Ryker longed for the warmth of the sun and the glorious light it brought with it every day. He had taken it for granted. Every day it had risen out of the dawn to shine on Arke. Every evening it had fallen on the opposite horizon, bringing the coolness of night. No matter what happened, it always returned the following day. Even if storm clouds covered it, it still shone behind the clouds. He promised himself that if he ever saw the sun again, he would never again take it for granted.

Rising up from the cold, wet rocks, he and a few others lingered close to the red light. There were a handful of boys he didn't recognize. One boy he did recognize: the one who had beat Broff in the match inside the circle. He knew now that if Broff had won, he couldn't have handled this training. Ryker was still furious at the boy for hitting Broff over and over when he could have just pushed him out of the circle.

Ryker thought of ways he could get back at the boy for what he had done to his friend, but now wasn't the time. Eventually the boy would get what was coming to him, whether it was from Ryker or the Khoshekh.

Ryker didn't wait around for the other boys to get up. He was the first of them to leave the shores of the black sea. Before he left, more of the boys who had completed the track began swimming up to the rocks under the glow of the red light. He could hear some of them whispering to one another as he headed up the dark hall. With no Khoshekh herding him, he walked slowly in the darkness. Without any light to guide him, he ran his hand along the wall, letting his fingers slide on the cold stone.

The steep climb beyond the shore gave way to a more level passage. A red light appeared ahead of him in the hall. From the sounds echoing off the walls, he knew he had reached the mine. With two Khoshekh standing in front of the passageway, he wasn't able to enter. He did walk very slowly though, peering around them, trying to get a glimpse of Broff.

All he could see past the shadowy figures was the large, black room beyond them and the massive hole in the center of it. He hoped Broff would be all right in there. Ryker could only imagine what agony awaited any who were forced to work even deeper in the dark.

Ryker felt great agony himself. He had been separated from his closest friend. He had been separated from the light of day. Broff was the last thing he had held on to from his old life, and now he had been separated from everything he had ever known. Darkness and fear were now the only things in his life. Ryker was alone and afraid.

The Khoshekh standing nearby noticed him lingering. One said, "Did you change your mind about training?" The other added, "We can get you a pick, and you can join the others." They both hissed in laughter.

Ryker quickly left them—and his friend suffering in the mine—and continued up the hall. Reaching the end of the hall, he stopped and looked at the huge cavern. If not for the fact that he was surrounded by evil captors and a consuming darkness, he would almost say it was an amazing sight. He wondered if the Khoshekh had taken it over or had stumbled upon it. Maybe if they hadn't infected it with their darkness, the place could have been beautiful. The idea stayed with him as he looked at the cavern from this distance.

A hideous voice spoke from behind him. "Darkness is a beautiful thing, isn't it?" Ryker wondered if someone had just read his mind. "It hides everything in its black cloth. Nothing can escape from it, oncc it is enveloped by it." The Khoshekh was so close that Ryker could feel its vile breath on the back of his neck. "Our master has aptly named this place the Hollow. It is a marvelous name, isn't it?" It didn't wait for Ryker to respond. "You have done well to last this long," the Khoshekh continued. "You show promise in becoming a weapon worthy for our master to use."

Ryker was filled with fear and overcome with horror as it spoke. Evil flowed out of its twisted mouth. The Khoshekh placed its hand on Ryker's shoulder. He would have shrugged it off if not for the Khoshekh gripping him so tightly that he couldn't.

"The next stage of your training is to scale the Pillar, which holds our marvelous dome aloft. Reach the top, and you will be rewarded with food and rest. Fail, and you will have to try again until you reach the top. Be careful. Either way, it's a long way down." Then a cloud of darkness enveloped the Khoshekh, and he was gone. His hissing laughter remained, echoing in the cavern and down the hall.

Shaking off the encounter, Ryker ran toward the Pillar. He could see from a distance that it was tall. As he neared its base, he realized just how tall and ominous it was. Many of the red lights were suspended around the Pillar giving the boys already scaling it the light they desperately needed to climb.

Ryker stepped up to the base of the Pillar and searched for the perfect trail to climb. Climbing on buildings and running on rooftops came naturally to Ryker, but he had never once climbed a rock like this. He would need to learn to survive this rigorous training if he was going to escape with Broff.

He must have circled the Pillar twice before he found the spot he thought was the best starting point. Extending his arms, he reached for a good handhold. He pulled his feet off the cavern floor, placed them on the rock, and began his ascent.

Hand over hand, he pulled himself up the face of the Pillar, keeping its height as far out of his mind as he could. Its jagged edges made it somewhat easy for him to get a firm grip. One small slip, however, would easily cut his hand. He was very careful not to do this.

The red light nearby gave him plenty of light to see where the best handholds were. It made the rock glow red as if it was ablaze in hot flames.

Shadows covered the face of the rock, indicating where deep holds were located. Though the light was sinister, he was thankful for it.

He made his way slowly up the Pillar, keeping a steady pace. His arms and legs were growing weary, but he knew he had to either press on or fall to the cavern floor far below. Falling from this point would cause serious injury or worse. He tried not to think about how high up he was, so he thought instead about how much farther he had to go. Getting a sure grip, he pushed himself away from the face of the Pillar to see if he was getting close to its peak.

He began again, hoping his arms wouldn't give way from the abuse of this long, jagged climb. Standing on the tips of his toes, he reached as far as he could to grab ahold of a large chunk of rock. His fingertips were just about to make contact with it when his feet slipped out from under him.

In an instant, his arm seemed to have grown another foot. As he fell, he grabbed ahold of the rock and held it tight. His body swung under his arm as he held on for his life. His arm burned and grew numb under the stress of his entire weight. Throwing his other arm above him as well, he gripped the rock with both hands, pulled himself up, and scrambled to find a place for his feet to rest.

He let out a long, deep breath and continued. He needed to be on flat ground soon, but he would prefer that it come by climbing safely to the top rather than falling to the ground below. Reaching up, he pulled himself to the next handhold. Making sure his feet were as firm as they could be, he pulled himself higher. He climbed on, hoping the top was near.

Reaching for the next hold, his feet slipped again. This time he wasn't fast enough, and he groped at the open air as he fell. He fell from nearly half the height of the Pillar and plummeted toward the cavern floor. This fall would certainly be his end.

The dark embrace of a Khoshekh cloud enveloped him as he fell through the air. Then it hurled him back into the chilly water of the black sea. Ryker was alive. The Khoshekh had saved him.

Swimming through the dark, chilling waters once more, he pressed on, passed the red light on the shore, and swiftly made his way through the hall. He was determined to scale the face of the Pillar.

He was glad the Khoshekh had saved him, but would they do so every time? Finding a new place to begin, he set one hand over the other and began his ascent once more, hoping he would complete the climb this time.

How long would he be made to train? He knew it had already been a full day of training. His body ached, and his mind felt cloudy. He pressed past the aches and pains of his body and continued climbing. The Khoshekh had told him that once he reached the peak he would be given food and rest.

The higher he climbed, the less the red lights shone up from below. Darkness reigned high above the cavern floor. Below him the red lights were no more than a flicker.

He was reaching now, feeling almost blindly for a good hold. He could only see a few feet in front of him, which wasn't ideal, being so high off the ground. Reaching up into the darkness, his hand held on to something he didn't expect, but he was relieved to find a hold. He was gripping the beginning of the ledge he had been climbing toward.

He pulled his feet up close to his body, planting them on a small cleft in the rock. He reached up with his other hand to grasp the ledge. Now that both hands were holding on to the ledge, he pulled himself up and rolled onto its flat surface, careful not to slip off.

He gasped for air as his exhausted body lay limp on the cold surface of the ledge. He laughed to himself. He had done it. He had climbed the Pillar.

The Pillar rose past the ledge another ten or fifteen feet to meet the domed ceiling. At its peak, the Pillar was not much wider than the length of Ryker's arm. He could only see a shadowed image of it in the dim light around him.

Ryker pushed himself up to stand. The dim red lights below only showed what was near them. Ryker was higher up than he'd thought, and his knees grew weak. He watched the cavern floor, busy with activity far below him.

There must have been hundreds of boys training in many diverse ways. Some of them stood on a thin platform above the ground. They held what looked like swords and fought one another. Dozens of these platforms were spread out near the left hand side of the Pillar. To his right, there were many boys throwing things at the ends of logs placed in stone. He couldn't see what they were throwing, although the projectiles glimmered in the red light, so he guessed they were knives. Around the other side, fresh boys were being placed into the circle to see who would train and who would mine. Surrounding the Hollow were many boys running around the perimeter on the track. Their agile forms moved stealthily in the shadows far away from the red lights.

"Well done!" a Khoshekh said from behind him.

Ryker quickly turned to face the Khoshekh as it stepped out of the shadows. Its eyes lit up the blackness surrounding them. Ryker backed away from him, almost to the very edge of the ledge he had just climbed over.

"You continue to show promise. My master was right to send for you. Soon you will enjoy your training—and in time, the darkness as well." The Khoshekh extended his arms into the darkness around them.

Ryker could barely see him. The red lights below appeared very faint from this high above them. The only thing he saw clearly were the Khoshekh's glowing red eyes. The Khoshekh stepped closer as a cloud of darkness formed around him. Its darkness enveloped the little light reaching them from the lights below. It then extended, reaching out toward Ryker. Soon it consumed them both.

Ryker seemed to be thrown out of the cloud and was suddenly at the entrance to the hall that led to the bunkrooms. He was on the other side of the Khoshekh that were guarding its entrance. He didn't see the Khoshekh that had sent him through the dark cloud, so he journeyed into the hall.

His echoing footsteps broke the silence of the dark hall. Very few of the red lights showed above him. He walked slowly down it until he came to the room where he hoped to find food. He would gladly take a bowlful of whatever they had fed him the day before.

Entering the room, he found himself alone. He eagerly crossed the room and picked up a bowl from the table in the back. He used the ladle to fill his bowl to the brim. He would get as much as he could, if the Khoshekh weren't watching.

He ate that bowlful along with another before he was full. He found a metal pitcher on the table, full of clear water. He poured the contents into a small metal cup that rested beside it. When he had drunk his fill, he left the room and continued down the hall to rest.

After getting his stomach full, he was ready to rest. He quickly came to the part of the hall with the series of doors on either side. The red lights spread throughout the hall lit everything up enough for him to see that all of the doors were closed.

If he didn't find a bed soon, he wouldn't mind sleeping on the cold, hard ground. Up ahead he saw a door swung wide open. He headed for it and entered the room. He saw that half of the cots lining the room were already filled with snoring boys. He was sure they deserved rest as much as he did.

He found a cot to lie in, one that had a blanket lying on it. Ryker slipped under it to find that it was indeed warm, but it stank. He didn't mind the smell, for the warmth was worth it.

This isn't so bad, he thought to himself. He had trained hard today—or for days. He wasn't sure. He deserved some rest and comfort. He could only hope that Broff was faring as well. He had forgotten how warmth felt. Within minutes of lying under the blanket, Ryker fell asleep. Snoring in his own cot, he joined in the choir of other boys as they all slept in the darkness.

9

Alone

Ryker's head bobbed along with the rhythm of his uncle Vahl's cart. He sat in the back of its long bed with his feet dangling off the boards. His head rested on the side plank, knocking against it as the cart rolled.

He had dozed off again but was awakened by a large rut in the road. The cart jerked as it passed through the rut, wrenching his limp neck along with it. His head hit the side plank, waking him roughly. He squinted beneath the sun's warm rays. It was late in the summer, and the air was hot in the midst of the dust the cart's wheels had stirred up.

Ryker's eyes were greeted with the sight of the long road they had left behind. He could see dust rising in the distance as they passed over the weathered ground. He swung his legs lazily and looked at the countryside they traveled through.

He turned forward to see his four younger cousins sound asleep between pillows and blankets piled throughout the cart. It was usually filled with fish being hauled off to the market. The boards had been marinated with many years of fish entrails. Ryker had been stuck with the task of washing the cart out, though he could never remove the smell completely. His aunt and uncle sat on the driver's seat, talking quietly as his uncle steered.

They were heading north to Tervan for a few things they couldn't normally get in Hidah. They all made the trip once or twice a year, gathering in the cart and traveling to the Shuul. When his parents had still been alive, they had all traveled in one cart. Now Ryker felt like he was imposing on the tradition. They all loaded up in the same cart and traveled all morning to reach their destination. Ryker's parents had been gone for close to a year, and their memory still stung his heart.

"Gretel, wake the children," he heard his uncle say roughly to his aunt. "We are getting close to the edge of Tervan."

"Wake those sleepy eyes, my little loves," Gretel said lovingly to her children. "We're close to the Shuul."

Ryker turned to look up at Gretel, but she was busy waking her children. She averted her eyes when she noticed Ryker watching her wake the children. He turned back around and watched the road behind them.

Neither of his relatives showed Ryker the least bit of kindness. They made it clear to him that he was an unwanted burden to them. After his parents died, they had been charged with his care. They didn't let Ryker stay with them without his fair share of chores. Despite still being so young, he worked longer than Vahl most nights, and he had to sleep in a shed near the smelly boats.

This was another dream. He hadn't realized it until now because it all seemed so real, so vivid. This was another memory he was reliving. The darkness was playing more cruel tricks on his mind. It felt so familiar because it was a memory. He recalled the last trip they had all made to Tervan. He went along with the vision like it was a rehearsed play, for he knew how it ended.

Soon the sounds of the busy town drowned out the creaking cart. The four children ran around in the storage bed of the cart enthusiastically, excited for their first stop of the day. His uncle steered the cart through the busy streets of the Shuul, and soon they had made it to the place where the children were so excited to go: the sweet shop.

They had already jumped out of the cart and gone inside before anyone could tell them to do so. Their mother, Gretel, was after them, pulling up her dress as she ran. Vahl's usual hard demeanor never showed any emotion, but a smile actually broke on his face. With a twist of his wrist, he brought the horses into motion, and they were headed to their next stop.

Ryker stayed in the back of the cart but turned to watch where they were going. In a short time they stopped again, and Vahl pulled something out of his pocket. They had stopped in front of what looked like a blacksmith shop. It had a low, wide roof and was completely open inside. Shadows from the sun made it hard to see anything beyond the eaves of the roof. Ryker jumped out from the back of the cart and walked around it to where his uncle was seated.

"I need you to pick up some fishing hooks from the blacksmith here," Vahl told him, tossing him two gold coins. "I'll be back to pick you up after I'm done getting tackle for the boat." Without waiting for Ryker's reply, Vahl left him outside the shop.

Why was he buying hooks here? Ryker wondered. They always got them in Hidah. It was a strange request, but he turned and entered the shop. The embers of a fire burned in the back of the shop, but the smith was nowhere to be seen. Many benches were burdened with an assortment of different kinds of hammers and tongs. Almost all of the posts that held up the thatched roof held even more tools. Ryker walked through the crowded shop, gazing at all the tools.

"You Vahl's boy?" a gruff voice asked him.

It startled Ryker, for he hadn't realized that anyone was around. He spun to meet the blacksmith. He was a short, burly man dressed in a sleeveless tunic and a thick leather apron. In his hand he held a large leather bag tied with a string.

"Yes, sir," Ryker stammered. "Are those the hooks for my uncle?" He pointed to the bag the smith held.

Without answering, the man threw the bag to Ryker, who fumbled to catch it while holding the small bag of coins already in his hands. Ryker completed the transaction and handed the smith the coins. Without another word, the blacksmith turned and headed through a small door past the furnace.

Ryker, glad to be finished, quickly left the shop. He stood outside under the hot sun. He looked left and right down the street, hoping to see his uncle soon.

Ryker had been waiting quite a while. The sun had begun to dip down behind the shops and homes around him. When his uncle had dropped him off for the hooks, the sun had just crested at its highest point in the sky. His uncle was still nowhere in sight.

Ryker knew where the other shop was, so he headed down the street toward it. When he reached it, he was distraught that he didn't see Vahl's cart or horse anywhere. Knowing that going into the shop wouldn't solve anything, he ran back in the direction he had come.

He passed the blacksmith shop where he had ben dropped off and continued down the streets of the Shuul to the sweet shop. Still he didn't see his uncle or the cart. He looked in through the window, seeing many mothers and fathers with their little ones, getting them prized treats. His relatives, however, were nowhere to be seen.

Panicking now, he bolted to where they had entered the Shuul. Fighting his way on foot through the crowd near the main square was hard, but he made his way through. When he made it to the outskirts of the Shuul where they had entered just before noon, he didn't see the cart waiting for him.

He peered down the road, using his hand to shield his eyes from the setting sun's glare. He couldn't see anyone down the long road from the Shuul. He didn't even see a dust cloud left by the wheels of the cart. They had long since gone. He knew even then as he stared at the empty road that he had been abandoned.

He had been left here by the people who were suppose to love and care for him. A gut-wrenching sorrow tore tears out of his eyes. He dropped the bag of hooks, and it fell to the dirt road. He sank to his knees as hot tears streamed from his face, and he wept bitterly.

His parents had left him with his aunt and uncle, hoping they would raise him like one of their own. They had promised Ryker they would love him in his parent's absence. He realized that this had been a lie. They didn't care what happened to him. They had forsaken everything they'd claimed by leaving him here all alone.

They had left him to fend for himself here in Tervan. How could he hope to do so? He was still a boy and nowhere near manhood. He stood wiping the tears from his face. Despair quickly formed into hate for them. They had left him here, unwanted, and he realized that this was fine with him. They had never shown him any kindness. He was better off without them, he thought. He was better off all alone so that no one else could hurt him like they had. With no one in this world to look out for him, he had to look after himself.

He slowly made his way back to the busy square, only it wasn't busy anymore. It was empty. Not long ago he had passed through the square by fighting his way through the crowd of shoppers, carts, and horses near the main entrance of Shuul. But now the only thing that remained was a fountain. Its waters flowed in streams through each pool until they reached a larger pool at the bottom.

Ryker stepped over to it and peered into the clear water. What he saw was something he did not expect. He saw a reflection of himself. Only it wasn't the face he remembered.

Instead of his youthfulness and simple clothes, he wore dark clothes. His face was almost totally hidden under a dark hood. His youthful face and features had been replaced by a thin and pale face. His eyes were bright red as if filled with blood.

The image of himself as a Khoshekh disgusted him. This would be his fate. He would become like them because he had nowhere else to go. He couldn't escape this fate that was set before him. He desperately splashed the waters, ruining the reflection that stared back at him. The touch of the water sent a jolt through his body, and the vision was gone.

Ryker sat up abruptly in his cot. He was soaked with sweat and was terrified in the darkness that surrounded him. He shivered against the cold.

He quickly scanned the room. The red light illuminated the room slightly, showing him that he was indeed all alone. He had been completely abandoned, and that was exactly why the Khoshekh wanted him.

It was his uncle's fault that he was here. If he had cared for Ryker like he'd promised he would, Ryker would still be on the shores of Teerah Bay where he belonged. Instead he had been swept off the streets and forced into training in this dark place.

He had to fight back. He completely blamed his uncle for where he had ended up, but his uncle was far from this place. He needed to be free before he could get revenge on him. Still, he would never abandon Broff to this darkness. He would continue to train and do what he was told until he could find a way out. He couldn't let this darkness consume him. He wouldn't let it. He would fight back with all his strength.

Despite the terrible memories the dream brought, he did his best to push them aside. He needed to get to the Hollow before one of his captors came looking for him. He rose from his bed and saw that a new set of clothes rested on the floor beside him. It was a black tunic, gray pants, and dark leather boots.

He hesitated to put them on. Once he put them on, he would surely resemble the Khoshekh. He truly wanted to escape and wanted nothing to do with this utter darkness. But he knew he would have to play along if he was going to survive and find a way to escape.

He quickly put all of these on and went out into the hall. The new set of clothes was much warmer than the tattered clothes he had been wearing on the night of his capture. More of the red lights lit his path as he walked through the hallway toward the Hollow.

The Khoshekh that usually guarded the passageway at the entrance of the main cavern were gone. A single Khoshekh stood on the bridge to the right side. "You're late" was all it said. It nodded its hooded head in the direction of the track. Ryker knew what to do.

He took a running start past the Khoshekh, leaped from the bridge, and began his journey through the track once more. Knowing what to expect, he moved along it with much more speed and a lot more confidence.

He completed it all and came to the place where there were no platforms. Only darkness lay between him and the platform where he had begun. He knew that if he jumped into the darkness it would take him to the black sea. He hesitated. Here, at least, the little light the red lights gave off was much more welcoming that the intense darkness above the black waters. He could see a Khoshekh watching him from the edge of the main cavern floor to his left.

Knowing the consequence of staying there, he leaped into the darkness. Instead of splashing into cold water, he fell to the floor beneath the great pillar that held up the main cavern. Not expecting the hard rock floor, he landed almost flat on his side. From the impact, he guessed that he had fallen far.

He rolled over onto his back and looked up at the Pillar. He could see a few of the other boys already climbing it. Even though he felt all alone, he knew he wasn't¾not in this place. Many other boys had the same story he did. Even though the thought didn't comfort him, it was still a decent thought to know that he didn't suffer alone.

He rose off the floor and stretched his muscles before joining the others in their ascent. Soon he was climbing high above the floor of the cavern. His arms and back were already feeling the abuse of the climb, and they grew weary. At least now he knew how high the pillar rose before he would make it to the ledge.

As he neared the top, he noticed something. He wasn't sure if the lights below were giving off more light than the day before, or if his eyes were growing more accustomed to the little light the entire place was subject to. Whichever was the case, he could see much better, which made the climb somewhat easier.

When he made it to the top, a Khoshekh was waiting for him. As he reached up to get a firm hold on the ledge and pull himself up, the Khoshekh stopped him. It grabbed hold of Ryker's arms and said, "You've climbed so high. You will make a fine Khoshekh. But we can't have you sleep in without a punishment!"

At its last hissing words, the Khoshekh lifted Ryker's arms up and threw them back past his head, sending Ryker falling from the top of the Pillar. Ryker screamed and flailed madly in the air as he fell. Before he struck the ground, he could feel a black cloud consume him. Its misty darkness surrounded him and saved him from his doom below.

The black cloud released him. Ryker's momentum from his fall carried through the cloud, and he struck the dark waters hard, knocking the wind out of his lungs and almost knocking him unconscious. He was barely able to get his head above the water to fight air back into his lungs.

He desperately swam toward the faint red light where he knew the shore would be. As he drew closer to the red light, it went out, leaving Ryker to float among the waves in darkness in hopes that the light would reappear. His body ached from the climb, and his breathing was still labored from the fall.

Then the light reappeared much farther away and in direction different from where he had been headed. So this was his punishment for sleeping in, he thought. He swam toward the light, only to see it go out again.

It reappeared some time later. This time it stayed lit long enough for Ryker to climb ashore and rest his weary body. He was exhausted and breathing heavily as he lay in the shallow, cold waters near the red light. When he'd caught his breath and his body was rested enough to continue, he rose and headed up the passageway.

He hoped he would see Broff while passing the mine. When he heard no noise coming down the passageway, he became worried. He knew that he would soon pass the opening on the right where the mine was. When he didn't, the fear that never left his stomach intensified. He ran now, and the passage became dark and cold. Soon he was in deep darkness and couldn't see the passageway in front of him. He turned to go back but found that he couldn't. He couldn't even see his hand in front of his face. He tried to find a wall or the edge of the floor¾anything that would help him navigate this place.

When he found the wall, he followed it quickly, hoping to leave this darker place as soon as he could. He ran along the wall with his hand brushing its smooth surface for a long while. He continued on for what seemed like hours, running through the darkness.

This place completely reminded him of the pit he had endured while hoping to find Broff. He could only hope he hadn't returned there. The terrible darkness that the Khoshekh wielded made dreams feel like reality and reality feel like a nightmare.

There, up ahead, a dim light shone. It was a red light shining in the distance, pushing back the abounding shadow. The light was like a beacon to him and begged him to draw closer. Ryker doubled his speed and drew close to the light. Letting his hand fall away from the wall, he ran full force toward the glowing orb.

Seeing the closed metal door, he slowed his speed, and his hope sank beneath the despair filling his heart. He knew exactly where he was. He was in the pit underneath the track. He had indeed returned, and this time he was all alone.

He ran to the bars and shook them, pleading for the Khoshekh to come and open it to release him from the darkness. He knew it was pointless, but he tried with all his strength to open the locked door. He lingered at the iron bars for a moment.

Quitting his fight with the locked door, he sank before it, leaning his desperate head against the cold bars. Still wet from his long swim in the black sea, he sat there, shivering. He pulled his legs in tight and huddled behind them for warmth. He hoped he could get a little rest before he was allowed to exit this cold, dark place.

No rest came to his weary limbs, however. The new clothes he had received didn't hold back the cold when they were wet. Hours passed, and still he shivered violently. He thought he was going to die alone down here. He rose again off the floor and paced back and forth in front of the door, trying to get his blood pumping to make him a little warmer. He rubbed his arms and legs, but still his body shook.

Hours later he heard someone coming down the passageway. He could hardly believe it. He ran to the door and awaited his release. The Khoshekh stood behind the barred door. His red eyes pierced not only Ryker but also the darkness surrounding him in the passageway.

The Khoshekh was as still as a statue, not making any move to open the door. Ryker stood on the other side of the door, waiting, unsure of what the Khoshekh would do. They locked eyes, and Ryker found that he couldn't look away. He didn't know if he was supposed to say or do something.

The Khoshekh didn't move, and Ryker found it was impossible to speak. He became terrified of what was about to happen to him. Maybe they had sent him down here alone to be rid of him and to end his training early down here in the darkness. This was the consequence for sleeping in, he thought.

When the Khoshekh finally did move, it made Ryker jump. His heart felt like it was about to jump out of his chest. The Khoshekh quickly withdrew a key from its belt and unlocked the door.

The moment the lock snapped open, a black cloud took the Khoshekh away. Ryker pushed open the door and climbed wearily up the passageway, glad to be out of the pit for the second time. He had been left unharmed, despite his lack of discipline. Soon he was back in the Hollow, running through the track once more.

10

Broken

Ryker trained hard and continued to grow stronger and swifter. Days turned to weeks, and weeks quickly turned to months. Each day was similar. His training followed no real order. He spent his days completing the track, climbing the Pillar, or swimming in the black sea. Most of the time he did all of them and then repeated the cycle.

Every evening he was exhausted and looked forward to the food and rest he received afterward. All day his training was very dark and difficult. Luckily, he spent fewer times in the pit, which they used for punishment.

He memorized the routes up the Pillar. The track became second nature to him. The black sea, however, was always dark, always cold, and always terrible to endure. Every time he was sent there, it felt like he had to swim longer, and the red light seemed farther away.

Anytime he passed by the mine during his training, he lingered in front of the opening in hopes of seeing Broff. As the weeks went by, he still had not seen his friend. He hoped Broff was all right, but he feared the worst. He knew that mining in that hole had to be difficult. He just hoped his friend could take care of himself.

As the weeks wore on, Ryker became stronger and excelled in his training. Soon his eyes grew accustomed to the dark. Slowly, he even began to enjoy the training. It made him stronger and more agile. Of course, he always had it in mind to escape with Broff the moment an opportunity presented itself. For now he was content with the small comforts he found when he ate and slept.

One day his training took a different course. All the boys, including Ryker, were rudely awakened by a small group of Khoshekh. They roused the boys and had them hurry outside, much like the first day he'd arrived there.

The Khoshekh led the boys down the hall into the main cavern. For the first time since Ryker had been brought there, they had led him to the left side of the cavern past the Pillar. Here, many long platforms were raised over the hard floor. They were suspended five feet off the ground and were accessible by two stone stairs on either side of the platform. Ryker had seen boys training with wooden swords on these platforms before. He had watched them a short time after he had scaled the Pillar.

Several platforms were scattered all around them. Some lay vacant, and some already had boys fighting on them. Ryker watched as two boys fought. They moved swiftly on the platform, their swords cracking hard against each other as they swung them. When a Khoshekh shoved Ryker into line, his attention was brought back to the platform where he stood.

The Khoshekh had all of the boys line up at the base of the stairs leading to the platform. On the opposite end, another group of boys did the same, directed by more Khoshekh. A barrel placed by the stairs was full of crudely made wooden swords. Each one of them had been used to train countless boys like them. Ryker was glad they wouldn't start with real ones. He had never held a sword, even a wooden one, and he was intimidated by learning how to use one.

Luckily, Ryker wasn't the first in line, so he watched and learned as much as he could. The Khoshekh did little to teach them. They just threw the boys into the training and told them what they were doing wrong. Many of them stood nearby to watch as the first two boys on the platform closed in with wooden swords drawn and terrified expressions on their faces.

The two boys faltered on top of the thin platform as they drew closer together. When they reached each other, they slowly got their balance. When they had steadied themselves, they both held up the wooden swords in defense. One of the boys lashed out and struck the other with his sword. When the defender was unable to block it, the hit landed on his shoulder and sent him toppling onto the floor. He landed with a thud and lay there a moment before he got up.

The Khoshekh didn't let the victor off the platform. Instead they sent him a new opponent. Another boy in Ryker's line was sent onto the platform to fight the boy who remained. The boy who had won stayed in place and did his best to keep his balance, while the new one made his way to the center of the platform with sword in hand to meet him.

This fight too only lasted a moment before a boy was on the floor. Many more boys fought, and hardly any of them could actually swing the swords properly. Some of them were better than others, but none of them were ready to fight to the death with real blades.

Then it was Ryker's turn. He gripped his wooden sword tight and made his way up the few stairs onto the platform. He understood now why the boys had such a hard time balancing up here on the platform. It was barely wide enough for his feet to stand side by side. He did the best he could to balance as he walked to the middle.

Near the center he looked up and saw that his opponent was a boy close to his age and size. Soon they were close enough to share blows. Both boys held their swords in defense, waiting for the other to strike.

Ryker was first to clumsily swing his sword toward the other boy's head. The motion threw both boys off balance, but they regained their stance and shared a few more swings from their swords. None of them carried any strength.

Ryker was doing his best to block the blows, but he found it hard to maneuver his sword the way he wanted it to go. The other boy stabbed his sword at Ryker, who failed to deflect it. The boy didn't extend enough, so he recoiled and struck again. Ryker didn't have time to try and block it, and the blow sent him sprawling backward.

He landed on his back, hitting the thin platform. The momentum of his fall sent him down onto the ground. He landed on his side with a thud. Ryker grimaced in pain, lying there for a moment.

He gripped the sword tightly as he rose. His entire side burned, but he tried not to show his pain. He stood, still in a lot of pain, and clenched his teeth. Making his way back into line, he did his best to play it off like he was all right. He certainly didn't feel all right. Not only did his gut hurt from the initial blow, but his back and side burned with pain from his fall.

More boys fought with wooden swords on the platform. More boys lost and fell. The Khoshekh still lingered, watching the boys without giving them instruction. The boys knew well enough that they needed to train like this until the Khoshekh told them to stop, no matter how long that would be.

While standing in line, Ryker looked around the rest of the main cavern. He saw newer boys in the first circle, fighting with fists and throwing each other out. More victims for the Khoshekh, he thought. The track ran close to them, and Ryker watched as some of the newer boys struggled to make it through.

He couldn't remember his first time traveling on it. He now knew the track like the back of his hand. He must have run it dozens of times. The Pillar too he knew all too well. He had found the best way up it close to a week ago and had climbed up that same way ever since. He hoped sword-fighting would turn out that way. He needed to learn quickly so he would fall off the platform less often.

Ryker's turn came again. This time he was more confident and waited for the other boy to strike first. The other boy had a hard time balancing, so when he swung, he threw himself off balance. The boy completely missed Ryker. Trying to regain his balance, Ryker saw his opportunity. He quickly swung toward the boy's feet and knocked them out from under him. The boy fell with a thud and a short cry of pain.

Ryker had won! Though he felt bad for causing the boy pain, he was glad it wasn't him. He wouldn't celebrate, because that meant that he would fight again until he fell as well.

The next fight sent Ryker to the ground. This time his opponent swung madly all over the place, but only a few of the blows actually came anywhere near Ryker. Still, Ryker found it hard to block them. He did his best to block as many hits as he could, but couldn't take the onslaught. After a hit to his knuckles and another just under his arm, he fell to the floor. He pushed himself off the ground with the tip of his sword and got back in line.

The next time, Ryker won three fights in a row on the platform. The first boy was terrified, and Ryker didn't even swing his sword. The boy couldn't find his balance, and when Ryker approached, he faltered on the platform and fell. The next time, Ryker traded many blows and thought he was going down. But Ryker prevailed and hit the boy square in the head. He wobbled for a moment before falling unconscious to the floor. A Khoshekh came over, shook him into consciousness, and sent him wobbling back into line. In the last fight, Ryker used a move that sent him to the floor. He stabbed a boy who had no idea how to block it, which threw him flailing backward on the platform and then onto the floor.

In the next fight, Ryker fell after a powerful blow to his leg. He hit his chin on the platform as he fell. Then when he landed on the hard floor, and his ankle twisted under him. Ryker had never felt this much pain in his life. He felt like his entire leg had been wrung out like a washed shirt.

Fighting through the pain, he made his way back into line. He didn't know if he could fight again on the platform, but he knew he had to. There would be no break for him just because his ankle hurt.

Pressing through the pain, Ryker fought many more battles on the platform. He was bruised from head to toe, and his chin, ear, nose, and lip were all bleeding. It was a long time before the Khoshekh had them put away the wooden swords and line up near the Pillar.

Ryker was glad to put the wooden sword back into the barrel near the platform. He was exhausted and could tell that the other boys were as well. He hoped it was enough for the day and that they would be able to rest.

The Khoshekh that had been watching them were standing all around them now. One in the center stepped toward the boys. It drew its sword and pointed it at them. In a slow, sweeping motion, the Khoshekh pointed to each of them.

Then it hissed, its voice echoing in the now silent cavern. "Many of you showed skill today. Some of you did not. Our master only wants the fastest and strongest of you, so you would be smart to train hard and make the master happy."

The Khoshekh sheathed his sword and stepped closer to the boys until he was in their midst. "Now, I know all of you are tired and long for rest. But there is still so much to do. Follow me."

Ryker hung his head. They weren't finished. It was true that he longed for rest, but he knew better than to hope for anything in this place. Falling in line with the other boys, they reluctantly followed behind the Khoshekh.

The Khoshekh led them around the Pillar toward three small walls no more than the height of the Khoshekh. Squares were cut into the walls close to the top. Thrust into the open squares were the round faces of logs the size of Ryker's head. There were twenty of them built into the wall.

The Khoshekh led them to a small ledge only a foot tall. Here each boy stood across from his own log. Ryker guessed that he was probably thirty or forty feet away from his. The distance was hard to judge under the shadow of the Hollow.

The Khoshekh distributed a handful of knives to all the boys. Ryker gazed at the knives when he received them. They were a little longer than his hand and had a blade on each end. They seemed dull, but Ryker still took care in handling them.

When all of the boys were armed with these throwing knives, a Khoshekh spoke. It was close to the center of the boys, near the ledge where they were lined up. "Every time you miss, you must run to the Pillar, circle it, and return here. So do your best not to miss." As the Khoshekh ended, it unleashed several knives in a matter of seconds. They flew out of his hands with blinding speed. They whined as they cut through the air and landed with a thud into many different logs before them.

Ryker's eyes grew wide at the display of skill. He knew better now than to run from these things. They could stick several blades into his back before he hit the ground. He hadn't ever noticed these throwing knives on the Khoshekh until now. They had them stuck in their belts as well as in the straps over their chests that held their swords.

Many of the Khoshekh laughed as they left in a wisp of shadow. Their hissing voices echoed throughout the Hollow. Ryker still couldn't believe how massive it was and how many of these dark beings their were.

Many of the other boys were already throwing knives at the logs before Ryker started. No one had stuck a knife yet, so many were already running to the Pillar behind him. Turning, he saw that it was a good distance away. He hoped he wouldn't miss too many times.

He held one knife in his right hand and the others in his left. He probably held six altogether. He reared back and threw the knife with all his might. It whizzed through the air and, much like the other boys' knives, struck the wall holding the logs. In fact, he was closer to a log he wasn't even throwing at.

Ryker shook his head in disappointment. He clutched the remaining knives and turned, making his way toward the Pillar. He ran along with most of the other boys who had missed. They made a line toward the Pillar, all running at an even pace, not wanting to get back to the knives quickly.

Ryker rounded the Pillar, his ankle burning with pain from every step. Through the pain he was soon making his way back to the ledge where he lined up with the others. By the time he returned, he was out of breath. He tried to catch his breath and waited for his heart to slow down as it raced in his chest.

When he was calmed down, he took aim. This time he didn't throw it as hard as he could. Instead he took careful aim and threw. He did it! It landed near the rim of the log with the blade stuck in. It only stayed there a moment, however, before it fell to the floor. He didn't have enough force behind it to make it stick firmly into the log.

Defeated by the knives again, he limped back to the Pillar. Returning even more winded than before, he took extra care to wait until he thought he was ready to throw. He missed. Throw after throw, he missed. He didn't know how much more abuse his ankle could take.

He was down to his last knife before he finally got it to stick into the log. He could hardly believe it. Between all the sword-fighting, his injuries, and the running back and forth from the Pillar, his energy was spent. It was pure luck that he had stuck a knife into the log. He wanted to celebrate, but he knew he would be punished for it.

When they were out of knives, he figured they were done. He couldn't have been more wrong. The Khoshekh made them gather the knives and throw them again. After every miss, Ryker had to run back to the Pillar. Becoming weary after running back and forth so much, his aim became nonexistent. He felt like he might as well just run and forget about throwing the knives at all.

After throwing several handfuls of knives, the boys were finally allowed to take a break. The Khoshekh had a cruel way of giving them a break, because they made the boys run the track. Ryker couldn't believe how hard the Khoshekh were pushing them today.

Many of the boys even lost their balance and fell into the Pit. Exhausted by the strenuous day, Ryker thought he was going to fall as well, but somehow he managed to complete the track. In the end, he leaped into the long gap and was hurled through a black cloud into the freezing waters.

He lingered in the dark waters and scrubbed his filthy body. The cold water was strangely welcome to his weary muscles and multiple bruises. He slowly swam back to the red light. His body had become accustomed to the frigid temperatures.

Passing the mine, he searched as much as he could for Broff, but he still couldn't see his friend. After not seeing him for so long, Ryker finally made up his mind. He needed to believe that Broff could take care of himself. And Ryker needed to do the same. He couldn't worry about his friend constantly. He needed to focus on his training. He still didn't want to become one of the Khoshekh, but he knew that escape was far out of reach. He pressed those thoughts out of his mind and continued through the passageway to the Hollow.

The memory of the dream he'd had the night before crept back into his mind. He had been abandoned and made to live off the streets. He still felt the same way now that he'd felt back then. Here, he was alone in the dark. Hope was no more than a memory, much like his parents' love. Fear and dismay were the only emotions he felt now. The darkness was finding its way into his head. It poisoned his thoughts and filled his heart with absolute despair.

His fight against the dark felt pointless. He was in a constant battle, with no hope of winning. He longed for a day that would never come. He could never win against this darkness that seemed to consume everything in its path. What hope did he have against the power these Khoshekh wielded? His resolve was broken by the Khoshekh's wish for him to become one of them, to serve the master.

He didn't care. No one cared for him. No one would ever know what had happened to him. The Khoshekh knew this, and Ryker finally realized it. No matter what happened to him down here, he would be nothing more than a distant memory, a memory only to the people who should have cared for him but had instead abandoned him.

He continued to think about this while he ate. His reality now was to train in the darkness and become like those he despised. That was his future. That was the dark fate he was destined for.

Ryker lay in his bunk with his face buried in the blanket he used to keep himself warm. He wept bitterly, knowing he could do nothing to divert his fate. This darkness was winning, and he could do nothing to fight back. He would either become one of them, or he would die down here in the dark.

That was his only hope of escape. The moment he had been brought to this place, he had thought about ending his life. But thoughts of Broff being alone down here had stopped him. Still, he couldn't do anything for Broff now. Tomorrow he would let the cold, dark waters claim his life. Broff would have to be fine on his own. No red light could save him. He would let himself sink beneath the dark waters. He could only hope to see his friend one last time. He couldn't help but think that maybe he would see his father and mother again after his death.

That night, no dreams plagued his sleep. No visions reminded him of his past. His thoughts were dark enough without them.

In the morning, his thoughts stayed the same. They were headed in a dark direction, and Ryker did nothing to hinder them. He had made up his mind. His vision became blurred. His thoughts created a fog he could hardly see through.

What he did see was distorted. Just like every morning, the boys had to run the track. His mind was focused, and he finished every obstacle and platform with ease. When he reached the end, he lingered on the last platform. Before him lay the empty void, his last darkness.

He knew when he jumped he would be sent to the black sea. There he would end everything and finally escape this place forever. Tears welled in his eyes, and despair weighed like an anchor in his heart.

He delayed jumping into the void. His thoughts cleared for a moment, and he began to have second thoughts. No, he had nothing to hope for. The moment his mind cleared, it fogged up again. This would be his only escape. This was his last resort.

Instead of jumping into the darkness, he simple stepped out into it. His limp body fell into shadow. Falling off the platform, he was enveloped by a black cloud.

Awaiting the splash of cold water, he was surprised when it didn't happen. It was like the darkness had heard the language of his thoughts and understood his mind. Instead, the black cloud placed him standing on the shore looking out over the black sea. His feet were standing just before the water.

The darkness taunted him to continue with his plan. He would have to wade out into the water until he wasn't able to reach the bottom. It didn't matter. He had made up his mind. He would end his stay here in a few moments. He was glad to leave. He wished he had just let the water take him when he'd first arrived. He was overcome with grief from losing Shiloh. He hadn't deserved a death like that.

He only hoped that Broff would be okay. This was the first time he had thought about his friend. He would leave him to whatever fate the Khoshekh dealt him. He couldn't do anything for him even if he stayed.

Ryker had been hanging on to a thread of hope as he'd trained. Time had passed beyond gauging. Had it been months? A year? He was unsure. The thread of hope he'd clung to had finally been severed.

His promise to Broff to escape this place with him had been a lie. He was forsaking his friend to whatever dark fate was in store for him. He had no idea what Broff was enduring. He was more than likely being made to mine for countless hours, made to suffer backbreaking labor, driven by a whip swung by a Khoshekh.

Ryker couldn't do anything for his friend. He hadn't seen him in months. Ryker only hoped that Broff would forgive him¾if Broff were still alive.

He slowly stepped into the cold waters, keeping his eyes gazing out into the darkness. The red light shed a frail light around him, casting his shadow over the dark waters. The edges of the shadow were a dark red. The ripples he caused while entering the water made his shadow look even more foreboding. Soon the water was up to his waist. The cold water stung his skin.

The chilling embrace of the black sea beckoned to him. This would be his end. Here Ryker would escape the darkness.

11

Opposed

A piercing cry for help came down the passageway behind him. It filled the cavern and echoed over the dark waters. The cry surrounded Ryker as he waded into the water. It filled his ears with terror. Ryker recognized the cry. He knew that voice. It was Broff! The cry of his friend cleared his mind. What was he thinking?

All of his dark thoughts quickly vanished after hearing his friend in trouble. He turned and ran. He splashed out of the water and tore past the light. He quickly climbed up the steep passageway and continued on. He heard another cry, and soon he could hear the cracking of a whip. It was loud and echoed all around him. He ran harder, pushing himself as he sprinted with all the strength he had.

His vision immediately became clear. The dark thoughts fled from his mind the moment he heard his friend's screams. How could he have been thinking like that? He couldn't believe it. If he ever got the chance, Ryker would tell Broff that he had saved his life. Ryker had saved Broff's life countless times. How could Ryker leave his best friend to this dark fate? He promised himself as he ran that he would never think about leaving Broff alone. They would escape this place together or not at all.

Up ahead he could see the Khoshekh guarding the mine. They stood close to each other, their shoulders almost touching, in front of the entrance to the mine. A red light shone above them. Their shadows stretched across the smooth stone floor. He had to think fast. He needed a way to get past them. Hearing the whip crack again urged him to think even faster.

He slowed himself to a jog as he neared the entry to the mine. The Khoshekh stood in the doorway, blocking him from entering. Ryker looked around them and saw, near the edge of the mine, another Khoshekh whipping a boy curled up on the floor. There was no mistaking him. It was Broff. Ryker had no idea what he had done to deserve the whipping. Regardless, Ryker would intervene. He would stop the Khoshekh by any means.

Where the Khoshekh guards stood, there was no way to get past them both. Ryker knew he couldn't hope to fight his way through, especially without a weapon. Nothing would distract them from their post. Then he noticed something about their shadows. Beneath them, between their legs, was a space big enough for him to crawl through. He knew he couldn't simply crawl through without the Khoshekh grabbing him, but he thought maybe he could roll through.

The moment he passed the Khoshekh, he dove between them at their feet. There was just enough room for him to get through. He ducked into a roll and then leaped to his feet when he was past them. Somehow he had made it through, but then he heard both of them draw their swords. It didn't matter; he needed to get to Broff.

Ryker sprinted toward the Khoshekh that was whipping his friend. A large rock lay near Broff on the floor. Ryker could only guess that he had dropped it and couldn't pick it back up. Ryker would have had trouble picking it up by himself as well. He saw that the Khoshekh had already torn into Broff's shirt with the whip, and Broff was bleeding in multiple places. It drove Ryker into a rage to protect his closest friend.

The Khoshekh had its back to the entrance of the cavern and to Ryker. It was close to the edge of the hole where countless other boys were mining. Ryker's eyes were locked onto his friend's assailant, so he didn't notice anything except his friend's tormenter.

When the Khoshekh pulled his hand back in preparation to whip Broff again, Ryker was upon him. He threw himself at the unsuspecting Khoshekh like a spear. Ryker slammed his shoulder into the middle of the Khoshekh's back, and it doubled over with a hissing screech. Ryker tore the Khoshekh off the floor, and they both fell headlong into the mine below.

He might have saved his friend, but there was no way Ryker would survive this fall. It was well worth it. As he was falling through the air, Ryker was wrapped up in a black cloud. Maybe he would survive the fall after all, but he had no idea where the cloud would take him. He was sure he would pay dearly for his actions. This cloud was different from the others. It seemed to strangle him. He gagged and fought it but could do nothing against it. Gasping for air, he saw the bottom of the hole drawing near. Ryker couldn't fight it anymore. His mind went blank and his body went limp.

When Ryker came to his senses, his head was pounding. He was lying on a cold, hard floor. He lay facedown with his arms outstretched. He must have been unconscious when he landed like this. Now that his mind was becoming clear, he felt pain all over the front of his body. He felt like he had fallen face-first from atop the Pillar. He groaned and pushed himself up to stand. His entire body was in pain, but at least he was still alive. At least he thought he was.

Looking around him, he thought he was beneath the track, stuck in the Pit once more. Absolutely no light could be seen¾or anything, for that matter. As it was in the Pit, he couldn't even see his hand in front of his face. The cold was almost as intense as the darkness, if not more.

Doing what he had always done when he'd found himself in the Pit, he searched for a wall. Keeping both hands outstretched, he walked slowly, hoping to gently bump into the wall to give him a direction to wander in. He started slowly at first. Then, as his steps lengthened, he quickened his pace. Still he didn't feel the wall. He knew he had gone much farther than the width of the track. He might be going parallel to it without even realizing it.

He changed his direction slightly and walked toward the place where he thought the wall should be. Instead of touching the wall, he grasped a pillar¾not something he wanted to find. The feet of the pillars in the track resided in the Pit. However, this pillar was different. It wasn't nearly as large as the pillars in the track were. He wasn't in the Pit.

Letting go of the pillar, Ryker backed away. He was somewhere just as dark as the Pit, but this place was completely unknown to him. He felt somewhat comfortable in the Pit. He had endured it many times and could almost guide himself through it with ease. He knew right where the door was. Now he was somewhere he had never been. He had no idea what to expect, but he knew it wasn't going to be good.

Despair clung to him like a leach sucking out his drive to press on, to continue until he found something or someone. The unknown things this darkness held were beginning to take their toll on him. Where was he now? They must have thrown him into the deepest, darkest hole for what he had done. He knew that saving his friend would come at a price. He hadn't thought about it in the moment. He almost regretted doing it now.

The darkness fed on his fear and seemed to grow and intensify around him. The cold air only became bitter. His skin stung, and his breathing was labored. He sank low in the darkness and clutched his legs to his chest. This would be his end, he thought. Whatever was down here¾or, more likely, whatever wasn't¾would be his undoing.

He would never see the light again, never feel the warmth of the sun on his face. He wouldn't even mind having one of the unearthly red lights to guide him now.

No. No light would ever find him in such a dark place. Light didn't shine here where the Khoshekh dwelled. Only darkness resided here with the dark figures that had done this to him, that had stolen him from the streets and forced him to train and become one of them. Now that they were done with him, they were going let him suffer in this darkness, alone and afraid.

He couldn't help but think about Broff's fate. He hoped Broff wouldn't be punished for what he had done, but he probably would be. Broff couldn't have handled Ryker's punishment. He would have been crying out already. Ryker wanted to cry out, but he knew it wouldn't do any good. He would have to sit and take this suffering. He doubted that he would get a second chance. Maybe in days to come he would be set free and brought back to training. That was a distant hope. He didn't care either way. He was going to end his life today, regardless. At least he had gotten to help his friend in the process, if only for a moment.

Ryker stuck his head between his legs in an attempt to keep warm. He did his best to endure what he was being made to suffer. He had no idea how long he suffered in the dark and the cold. Minutes seemed like hours. Hours seemed like days. He shivered violently on the cold floor. Every so often he looked around him to see if any light that had been hiding would show itself. Every time he looked, the thread of hope he clung to began to fade away slowly until it was all but spent.

Ryker couldn't take this temperature for much longer. The darkness that surrounded him felt like it was slowly consuming him, tightening its invisible grip not only around his heart but his mind as well.

He would do anything for some warmth. He would give anything for a little light. He would gladly endure more of the Khoshekh's intense training if only at the end of it all he could sleep in his warm cot.

Then he heard a soft sound in the darkness. His head shot up, and he looked to see where it had come from. Far off in the distance he thought he saw a spark, a faint glow of orange that seemed to give off the frailest of light. Even from this distance, Ryker could tell that it was a fire. He rose slowly to his feet. He didn't know who or what had started it, but he knew that fire meant light and warmth. He threw caution to the darkness and ran for the fire.

He made it to the fire, which was burning in a small metal brazier. There were many dry logs stacked within it, and the flames licked at them. Soon the fire was burning red hot. Ryker brought his frozen body as close to the fire as he could. He held his hands close to the flames as they rose. Once his limbs were warming up, he then rubbed his chest to revive his cold body. The warmth felt like a distant memory. He could hardly remember the night he'd been taken. He had been soaking wet from the rain and had gotten a fire going to dry himself.

He missed the hideout he and Broff had made. He knew he would never see it again¾or Tervan, for that matter. He wondered if another group of boys would find it and use it as they had. He wished there was somewhere safe for orphans to go, somewhere the Khoshekh couldn't get them.

With his body quickly becoming warm, Ryker wondered who had made the fire. When he'd first seen it, he had run to it without a second thought. Now he wondered if that had been a mistake. He looked around him. The fire gave off plenty of light to see the area around it.

The orange light of the flames splashed on many thin pillars behind him. Ryker had found one of them in the darkness. Now, seeing so many of them, he knew for a fact that he was in a place he had never been before. The pillars were set in two rows that ran straight in front of the brazier. The fire exposed a dozen or so of them before they became lost in shadow past the light. Ryker wondered where the line of pillars led.

He looked in every other direction but saw nothing. Only darkness lingered outside the fire's glow. He knew it wasn't the best idea to just sit and wait around. Without any more fuel for the fire, it would die out eventually. He carefully picked up a small log from the fire. It was burning hot on one end, but the other had yet to be consumed by the flames. He used it as a torch and slowly walked among the pillars. He would find out where they were leading.

The torch in Ryker's hand only showed him a few feet around him. Standing between the pillars, he could see them on either side, so he knew he was going in the right direction.

He slowly made his way down the path where the pillars led him. He passed dozens of pillars, but nothing else was in sight. His torch was slowly going out, and he knew he only had a few more moments before he would be stumbling around in the dark.

He turned around to see the fire he had left far behind him. He could barely make out the speck of orange that the fire had been reduced to. He turned around and resumed his journey through the pillars. He had only made it a few more steps before the flame on the log finally went out. The last flame licked the air until it was sucked back into the embers at the tip of the log.

Ryker quickly reached for the nearest pillar and held on to it for a marker in the black abyss that now surrounded him. He threw aside the log that was nothing more than a smoldering stick. He would have to continue through the blackness.

There was nothing else for him to do. He should have never have tackled the Khoshekh. He should have just fought the creature and taken whatever punishment he'd earned. Maybe it would have been a few hours in the Pit.

He would gladly take that over this. At least in the Pit there was a small red light. He would take the faintest of any color of lights right now.

Then a voice, nothing more than a distant whisper, spoke. A large gust of wind blew past Ryker. In response to the wind, torches sprang to life from sconces on the pillars. A torch burst to life on the pillar Ryker clung to, which made him jump back. In a moment the torches lit the space between the pillars. A path of orange light broke the darkness.

Hundreds of pillars holding these torches stretched before Ryker. He turned to look behind him, and as far as he could see, it was the same: torches suspended on the pillars. He realized for the first time how high up the pillars reached. They climbed until they were lost to the shadow where the light of the torches couldn't reach. Ryker stepped between the pillars. He somehow felt safe between them. It felt like the wall of orange light held the darkness beyond them.

Looking down both ways, he couldn't remember which way to go. If he went one way, he would go all the way back to the brazier where he was sure the fire had been reduced to ash. The opposite way was unknown. He hoped it would hold his exit. He started one way and hoped it was the right direction. His mind was clear. He was alert and cautious now. Someone must have done something to light these torches, something dark and powerful.

Making his way among the pillars, Ryker could see something far ahead of him. The pillars were leading him to someplace he was hoping to escape. Then the pillars stopped abruptly and stood before further shadow.

Thick darkness lay before them. Ryker thought he saw something in the darkness, but it was hard to tell. As he drew near, he saw it more clearly. Set away from the pillars sat a large stone throne. Its edges were all squared and perfectly cut. The stone the throne was cut from looked perfectly black and shining. The light that managed to touch it bounced off of it like a mirror.

Someone sat upon the jet black throne. The light from the torches stopped before they touched the figure's boots. Ryker could vaguely tell that a huge man sat on the throne, hidden in shadow.

12

Surrender

Ryker stopped near the end of the pillars in horror. He knew this man could be none other than the master that the Khoshekh always referred to. The man on the dark throne leaned forward. The light from the torches gleamed in his eyes, which petrified Ryker. He spoke with a voice as deep and threatening as Ryker remembered.

"Welcome." The man paused, letting his voice echo in the darkness. "I have been expecting you!" The man then stood and walked up to Ryker.

His body was now visible in the torchlight. He was the tallest man Ryker had ever seen. He stood almost twice Ryker's height. His large frame made him look even more imposing. Bulging muscles rippled over his whole body. They tensed, as he rose up out of the throne. He wore only a tunic with its sleeves cut at the shoulder to display his large muscles. Dark veins ran everywhere his skin was showing. Ryker wondered who or what this man was. His tunic was slit below his neckline, and many dark veins gathered here and rose up his neck. His eyes looked more like a beast's than a man's. Dark skin surrounded his eyes, although the rest of his skin was a paler color. His head was shaved and his face held a short beard. If this indeed was the master of the Khoshekh, Ryker would rather take the cold and dark he'd suffered earlier.

"I have been waiting here for you to join me. When I saw your light fail, I thought to make it easier for you," said the master of the darkness, gesturing to the torches burning on the pillars. How was that possible?

Ryker found it strange that this man spoke so kindly. The Khoshekh spoke in the same manner, but their words were twisted in a cruel way. His words, however, seemed genuine, like he truly meant what he said. Ryker figured it would be best to play along and be polite. If he was indeed the master of darkness, there was no telling what he was capable of, even if he spoke with kind words.

"Thank you, sir," Ryker answered, hoping to quickly get on whatever good side this huge man had.

"So, you appreciated the light I created for you?" the man said as he walked back to his throne. "Did you also appreciate the fire I made for you? I know it can become rather cold." He stood behind the throne and put his hand on the stone backrest, standing again in the shadow past where the light reached.

"I did, thank you very much. I thought I was going to freeze to death!" Ryker said, stepping back a little into the light beneath the torches.

"We can't have that. You mean too much to me for anything to happen to you!" The large man in the shadows stepped around his throne and drew closer to Ryker. His words were strange, and yet they sounded sincere. "Come! I know you must be hungry," he said, stepping to the left toward a table. Resting beside it were two chairs. He waved for Ryker to follow him.

Ryker hadn't noticed the table before and wondered where it had come from. Upon the table sat all sorts of food that Ryker had never dreamed he would ever eat again: roasted chicken, bread, cheese, grapes, and apples. All of them were on beautiful metal plates. Set in the center of the table were a pitcher and two glasses.

Ryker rushed to the table and began eating quickly. The master of darkness followed him to the table. Sitting back, he watched as Ryker ate. Ryker hardly sat; instead he stood hovering over the food he inhaled.

"So, you were hungry," the master said with a slight laugh. "I figured you would be. I didn't think you would need more food than I had prepared, though." He laughed again.

Ryker hadn't heard anyone laugh since he'd been here¾except for the dark, hissing laughter of the Khoshekh. Their laughter would send shivers down anyone's spine. This man's laugh was far from that. His was almost warm. If not for his situation, Ryker would have said it was a friendly laugh.

"Yes, sir, thank you again!" Ryker said past mouth full of food.

"Please, stop calling me sir. I am Varic. Now, finish your food. There is much we need to discuss." Varic pushed the plate of bread closer to Ryker's side of the table.

The mere mention of his name made Ryker rethink his friendly laugh. He wondered how many of the Khoshekh even knew their master's name. He was anxious to know what they would discuss. The only thing he wanted to talk about was what he needed to do to get more of this food. He thought he had known hunger living off the streets and stealing food, but he'd had no idea what hunger was. Even after being pushed so hard every day, he had only been fed a single, small bowl of odd soup on most days. More than once he had endured days in the Pit with nothing to eat.

When Ryker was done, Varic poured him a glass of water from the pitcher. Ryker sat back in his chair and drank from the glass. He looked over the table at Varic, who stared back with a slight smile on his face. The light from the torches hardly reached where they sat. Ryker gave back a small smile, hoping that whatever Varic had in mind wasn't too terrible.

"I hope you're enjoying your stay here," Varic said, sounding as if this was a marvelous place.

"Yes, I am," Ryker said halfheartedly. "This food and light has made it much better." The food did help, but he knew this was a one-time thing. He couldn't get used to this treatment.

"The darkness is not as terrible as some might think," he said as he turned to gaze into the darkness behind him. "It may conceal unseen things, but you will discover to hide within its shadows." Then he added, "Eventually your eyes will grow accustomed to it. The longer you dwell within it, the more hidden things will be revealed to you."

Ryker looked around the darkness that surrounded them. "The darkness I've gotten used to," Ryker said. Then he shivered as he added, "It's the chill of it I can't seem to grow accustomed to."

"With more training, you will begin to endure anything!" Varic exclaimed, raising his voice.

"When I ended up here, I thought my training was over," Ryker said. "I thought I had been left to die in the cold for what I did." Sorrow hung from his every word.

"As I said before, I don't want anything to happen to you. You are worth more than you'll ever know. I have many Khoshekh at my command, one less doesn't hinder the progress I'm making. Ryker, I need more fighters like you. There is something special about you! I knew it when you ran from your pursuer on the rooftops in Tervan." Varic rose out of his chair. "You will help me bring order back to Arke." He swept his hand through the air.

Ryker could hardly believe what he was hearing. He knew he was training to become a servant of this man. But he had never thought about being the kind of help Varic spoke of. Could he really bring order back to Arke? Was his dark fate, which the Khoshekh had spoken of on the rooftops, the same for everyone, or was it what Varic envisioned? The two sounded opposite from one another.

"I want to show you something, Ryker," Varic said. He signaled to Ryker to rise out of the chair and follow him. Ryker did, and Varic led him behind the throne, away from the torchlight and into the darkening shadows. Ryker could hardly see Varic in front of him.

Varic spoke up and reached back for Ryker's arm. "I have been in this darkness so long I forget that you can't see as well as I can." His touch felt like fire to Ryker's skin. Varic held a firm grip as he continued to lead Ryker away from the light.

Varic stopped and pulled Ryker so that he stood next to him. He let go of Ryker's arm, and Ryker immediately felt relief from the hot grip. The torchlight was far off behind them, and Ryker found it impossible to see Varic.

"Watch carefully," Varic said suddenly, his deep voice rumbling around them.

A thick cloud appeared on the floor, much like the ones that the Khoshekh used for travel. It covered the floor before them and seemed to have a light hidden within it. The light was a pale yellow, and the cloud did all that it could to contain it. Then the cloud melted into the floor.

The cloud revealed a scene on the smooth surface of stone. By a power unknown to Ryker, he was looking at waves crashing upon a small fishing boat¾his father's boat. Ryker could see his father on the boat along with his uncle. It was the same scene as the one in his dream. Ryker looked at Varic, who didn't look away from the scene. He seemed to know that Ryker was staring at him, and he nodded toward the scene. Ryker turned back to the waves and the boat. The moment he did, he watched in horror as his father was thrown off the side, entangled in nets. Ryker cried out as the pain of that horrible memory stung his heart.

The memory of his father's tragic death brought back terrible emotions. He wished he could run away and weep in a dark corner. As he thought about leaving, another cloud appeared.

It swooped in and took away the scene with the water and the boat. The cloud didn't stay idle. It quickly fell away again and revealed another scene. Ryker was gazing down at his mother. Her face was ghostly pale. She looked frail and feeble. She lay wrapped in a thick quilt, and the glow of a fire was dancing in shadows on the quilt. Tears welled up in Ryker's eyes. Why did he have to relive these memories yet again? They tore his emotions to shreds. He closed his eyes. He could stand no more of this torture.

Answering his silent plea, the cloud took the scene away. Although the cloud had removed the scenes of his mother and father, it brought another. Ryker was looking down at himself in a busy market square. He was on one side of the square, calling out for his aunt and uncle. He pushed and shoved his way through the square, trying to reach the other side. On the opposite end, almost where Ryker was trying to get to, his aunt, uncle, and cousins sat in the cart. His uncle drove the cart, paying no attention to Ryker's pleas. He drove on through the busy square and left with Ryker still searching for them among the crowd. Ryker looked on in disbelief. They had left him while he'd searched for them. They had abandoned him despite his pleas.

This scene's emotions were nothing like they had been before. He hated his relatives for leaving him in this way. How could they do that to a young boy? He was their own flesh and blood! Now Ryker was glad they had abandoned him.

The next scene showed Ryker again in the streets of Tervan. This time he looked frail, and his clothes were tattered. It was raining, and he sat in an alleyway. He fought a few rats for a piece of stale bread. Seamlessly the scene changed to Ryker running from a Khoshekh on the rooftops. Ryker watched himself jump, run, and climb to get away from his dark pursuer.

In all this time, Varic didn't say a word. He only watched alongside Ryker. Ryker didn't know how to take all of this. His heart was heavy with all the despair he had ever felt. Then the cloud displayed another scene. He would have to endure more of this. He didn't know what else this dark cloud could reveal. All his dark memories filled with grief and despair had already played before him.

He was wrong. The next scene was the black sea. He watched in terror as Shiloh fought to stay afloat. He saw himself call out Shiloh's name, searching in the dark that he now saw clearly in. He swam and he called. He watched in horror as he swam right past Shiloh, who was just about to go under. Shiloh's face was so desperate for help. He called again and yet again. Then, all that was left of Shiloh was nothing but bubbles. Ryker had failed to save him. He had swum right past him! It was Ryker's fault that Shiloh was gone. He sank to the floor. Hot tears ran down his cheeks.

"Please, make it stop," Ryker finally begged Varic amid his tears.

"I only showed you the past so I can present you with your future," Varic said elegantly, despite the horrific scenes he had made Ryker watch. Ryker knew them all too well. They were his memories, after all.

Varic kneeled down to Ryker's level and lifted the boy's face. "Ryker," he said softly, "I will be your new father, and the Khoshekh will be your new family. With my help, you will never have to hurt again. If you join us, you will never feel this way again." He raised Ryker to his feet.

Ryker liked the way that sounded: he would never hurt this way again. He would gladly accept anything for that promise. He thought about all the memories of his past. Most of them were terrible. Then he remembered meeting Broff. They had gone through a lot together, and he needed to know that Broff would be all right.

"What about Broff?" Ryker asked. "What will happen to him?" It was Ryker's fault that Shiloh was gone. He couldn't take the added guilt of Broff as well. If he could help it, he would make sure Broff would be fine.

"The boy you saved at the mine?" Varic asked, not sounding concerned about him.

"Yes," Ryker replied simply, wiping tears from his face.

"He has worked hard enough," Varic said, sounding indifferent. "I don't find a problem with releasing himif that is what you want."

"You would do that?" Ryker asked, almost in disbelief. At this point, he would believe anything Varic said. He seemed sincere about becoming a father to Ryker, and Ryker desperately wanted a father. He would do anything to have a father again, even if it wasn't his actual father.

"For you? Of course I would," Varic said. "Don't worry anymore about your friend. I will take care of him." He motioned for Ryker to follow. "Now, come with me. There is something else I want to show you."

"As long as it's not more of my memories," Ryker said before moving. He needed to know that was over.

"No, no more memories, I promise," Varic said, laughing. "When we are done, you will be able to forget all about your past. Your future will be the only thing you need to know." He gazed deep into Ryker's eyes, despite the darkness between them.

Once again Varic led Ryker in the darkness. Up ahead, Ryker suddenly saw two red lights come to life. They illuminated the space from above, replacing the shadow with their menacing light. Beneath the red lights, a small pedestal rested. It was made of black stone carved with many markings, all with great detail. Sitting atop the pedestal was something covered by a thick cloth. Varic circle the pedestal, while Ryker walked forward and stopped just before he reached it.

"I'm sure you have wondered how I came to be in such a dark place?" Varic asked, locking his eyes onto Ryker's. "Once I was sworn to the service of The King," he began. "I was one of His Paladin. I was among the first to set foot in Arke. Long ago, only evil creatures and dark monsters inhabited the desolate island. The King and his vast army wiped out all of the evil that dwelled here. I was sent into these caves to search for any other creatures that may have hidden deep within them. I did find creatures, but they were far from evil. They were terrified and looked harmless. I couldn't slay them needlessly, so I left them and exited the caves.

"When I returned to the surface, the wars above had been won. The King then sent half of the ships back to his island to return with many more ships and tools to begin building. Soon we had built the Thraans, and The King established the Kingdom of Arke.

"Those who were with me thought that we were finished and that we too could live in Arke. But The King had other plans. We were to leave Arke and continue on to another island to wage yet more wars and fight more battles. I had seen enough battles for a dozen lifetimes. I told The King that I wouldn't fight any longer. Without a second thought, The King banished me. I was led by my brothers, The King's mighty Paladins, back to these caves. They threw me in and sealed off every exit.

"I quickly found the creatures I had been sent to slay, and they helped me. They lived in this darkness and taught me how to live here as well. These creatures were looking for something, and with their guidance, I helped them search for it. I never would have imagined that we would find it. When we did, I didn't know what to expect. With the creatures' help, we unlocked its power."

Then Varic pulled back the cloth on the pedestal to reveal a black orb. It was hauntingly beautiful. The orb was half the size of Ryker's head. It was flawless, and no mark could be seen on it. The orb's substance looked much like that of the throne Varic sat upon. It was black and reflected the red light shining above it. Ryker felt drawn to the orb. He stepped closer to it and almost immediately reached out for it.

"This is what I found in the darkness," said Varic. "This is how you will become so strong that no one will be able to touch you. This is the Xahlbris. You will never hurt like you did before. Its power is unmatched. Nothing can stand against it. If you reach out and touch it, you will become like me, like the Khoshekh I command." Varic's voice grew louder as he spoke. It continued to grow in volume until it echoed all around them.

Then he paused for a moment. His echo trailed off, leaving them in the silent glow of red light. His voice grew deeper, like the hoarse rumble of a beast, as he asked slowly, "Will you serve me, Ryker? Will you embrace the darkness?"

In a flash, all of Ryker's worst memories raced before him: his parents' deaths, his abandonment, and the guilt he felt over Shiloh. He wanted to forget it all. He never wanted to hurt that way again. He wanted the power. He had been running from this fate since the day he'd been brought here. His running was over. He was done fighting it. He would finally embrace it. He would accept this dark fate before him.

"I will!" Ryker said boldly.

"Then reach out to the Xahlbris, my son," Varic growled.

Ryker took another step forward, reached out to the orb, and placed his left hand on it. At first nothing happened. Then the orb felt like it gripped Ryker's hand with intense power.

Looking up at Varic, Ryker watched the master's eyes suddenly change. His appearance looked like it was changing as well. His eyes soon grew red like the Khoshekh's. He raised his bulky arms and threw his head back and laughed.

A black shadow passed out of the orb and crawled up Ryker's hand. He tried to push it away with his free hand, but he couldn't. The shadow was now under his skin. Its touch burned him, but at the same time, it chilled him to the bone.

The shadow crawled up his arm, and all he could do was watch as it made its way up his neck. Unlike a dark cloud, it consumed him from the inside out. He felt burning pain as the shadow pierced his mind. He screamed out in shock and horror. Varic only laughed louder. The shadow suddenly took hold of his mind and pulled him into the black orb.

Ryker had surrendered to the darkness. He regretted ever speaking with Varic, regretted accepting his dreadful offer. Now the darkness he had feared would consume him had finally done so. He had known this day would come. Nothing could escape from the darkness. Even light trembled in the face of shadow. Darkness, fear, and terror wrapped him in a dreadful embrace and completely consumed his very being.

13

Awaken

He had finally given in to the darkness, and now it was all over. The dark room with the pillars and the throne were all gone. Varic too was nowhere to be seen. Ryker didn't know what had happened when he touched the orb. Whatever it was, he regretted it now. Pain like nothing he had ever felt before had been sent through his entire body. Suffering unlike anything he had ever known had flooded much more than just his mind.

The agony and intense pain that the dark orb had inflicted had vanished. As the darkness had consumed him, he had lost all feeling. He had been overwhelmed by the black shadow inflicted by the orb. It felt like it had thrust him into a dark slumber. He had no control over it and felt nothing within it. His mind and body were completely numb. How long it would last, he couldn't tell. He found no rest in it. He didn't know what was happening to him. The only thing he had felt during this whole time was fear, absolute terror.

Time itself seemed nonexistent. He knew time was passing around him, but his body and mind felt as if they were in a constant state of nothingness. He was never hungry or tired. He tried to recall how long he had been wrapped in shadow, but he couldn't. In this dark coma he barely existed. He was now nothing more than a memory easily forgotten.

However, now he felt weightless. All of the darkness and fear were gone. In fact, he didn't even feel scared or nervous, even though he had no idea where he was. All he could see were tall, thick trees. Their bark was dark, and their branches were full of leaves. The forest was many shades of browns and greens. Beautiful and wonderful things surrounded him. He had all but forgotten what life and light looked like.

Ryker was suddenly in motion without even having to move his legs. He was moving through a forest, sweeping weightlessly between the trees. He didn't know where he was going, but he wasn't scared. Anywhere under this canopy would be better than anywhere he had ever been before.

The sun's rays found their way through the branches and leaves. Through these they became beams of lights stretching above the forest floor. Many of these beams of bright sunlight found their way to Ryker's weary skin. The warmth of the sun felt splendid. Ryker had never seen anything more beautiful in all his life. The colors of the trees and flowers were bright and vibrant. Birds were singing as well, filling Ryker's ears with melodies he had never heard. If this was indeed the end, he was glad to be here.

Through the dense trees he saw in the distance tall walls made of thick white stone. Its aged rock was loosely held together with brittle mortar. Only a few of the once tall watchtowers still stood. The others lay in rubble on the forest floor. Many holes had been cleaved into the walls from long lost battles. Long cracks in the stone stretched along its walls, which appeared ready to crumble at any moment. Some of these places had fallen as time and weather constantly ate away at them. Thick vines grew, covering the walls that still stood. Many large trees grew close to the walls, their limbs stretched over them.

The canopy of leaves almost covered the bright-blue sky above. Still, some white clouds could be seen through the foliage. They hovered above, moving lazily in the wind.

In this dreamlike state, everything felt so real and vivid. He continued his effortless journey toward the walls. A great wooden gate lay in disorder. One of the doors stood firm, while the other had been broken off its hinges and was lying in a heap on the ground before the entry. He passed through the gateway and entered the courtyard.

Much like the walls that had once protected it, the courtyard was in disorder. Many trees grew within the walls. These were much smaller than the ones dwelling in the forest that surrounded this place. Many smaller stone buildings were scattered throughout the courtyard. Most of their roofs were falling in, and many of them lay in piles of rubble. In the center of the courtyard a tall stone structure, once grand and magnificent, now lay in ruin. Even though it was old and unkempt, it was still remarkable. It reached up into the tall trees, surpassing them as they climbed their way skyward. Multiple spires and towers were built in every corner. Stained-glass windows were broken, and the remnants of banners and flags blew in shreds of cloth catching the breeze.

Ryker's mind felt unclear. He couldn't remember if he had ever been here or not. It seemed he knew where he was going, although he had no control as to where he was headed. This place felt so familiar, but he knew he had never been here.

Passing over the tall grasses that grew throughout the courtyard, he made his was to the main door. Many carvings covered the door, which had swung wide open. Making his way through the large doors, he entered the worn-down structure.

It was a dimly lit space, nothing like the bright forest outside. There were many windows, but they were covered up by heavy curtains. What Ryker could see were many carved and handcrafted things of stone and wood. He moved through many hallways and large rooms quickly. Having no idea where he was or where he was going, he continued on this journey of unknown destination.

Making his way farther in, he noticed that the walls became less decorated. The floor, which had once been carpeted, was now bare. Doors on the side of the hallway became few and far between until they stopped altogether. Up ahead in the low light he saw a barred iron door.

He was surprised that this door was still standing. It had held strong while all the other doors he had passed had not. The iron door was locked tight, holding whatever lay beyond it trapped. Ryker could see through the bars, and in the low light he could see that it led to a steep staircase leading down into the depths. He wondered what dark and vile things were locked away down there.

The door then opened on its own. It groaned loudly on its old, rusted hinges. The noise echoed past Ryker down the long empty hall. He moved slowly down the stairs until all light above was lost. To his dismay, he was engulfed in shadow.

Reaching the bottom of the stairs, his movements leveled. Now he was in a dungeon. The walls were lined with torches, but only a few remained lit. The ones that did produced little light. They must have been lit ages ago and had been reduced to no more than flickering flames.

Down through the dimly lit dungeon he went. He still felt no fear being in this place. What would this place have in store for him? he wondered. Ryker still had no power as to where he was headed, but he knew it was somewhere close. How he knew, he had no idea.

He slowed to a halt in front of another iron-barred door, this one leading to a cell on the side of the hall. He turned and looked in through the bars of the door. The torchlight ended at the base of the door, and only darkness was locked away within.

Much like the door to the dungeon, the cell door unlocked with a loud click. The door opened slowly. Ryker wished for the first time that he had the ability to move. If only he could back away from this cell. He wanted to be within the forest once more.

A small candle was lit on a ledge at the far side of the cell. It shed the frailest light in the dark cell. Still, it was just enough to push away the shadow that dwelled within. Under the candlelight Ryker was able to see a frail body clothed in rags lying with its back against the far wall.

It was an old man with long gray hair and a mangy beard. He looked as if he had lived a life of torture and beatings. His body was covered in scars and bruises that his strips of clothes barely covered.

Ryker thought the man was dead. He lay there motionless, and Ryker made no effort to draw closer to him. As Ryker looked on, studying the figure, he saw a few small hairs near his lips move. Wisps of his beard were moving as he took weak breaths. His breathing was slow and fragile. As Ryker looked on, he saw now that the man wasn't dead, although he seemed close to his end.

He looked at the man and pitied him for having to endure so much pain. Who was he to have been beaten this way? Who had done this to him? It looked like every breath he took was a struggle. He wanted to help this man in any way he could.

The old man's eyes shot open as he took a deep breath through his nose. The action shocked Ryker. He drew closer to the frail old man. Wind blew through the corridor of the dungeon, blowing out all of the torches behind him. The small candle remained, despite the wind. It alone lit up this dark place.

Ryker watched as the old man scanned the room. When he found Ryker, his gazed locked onto him. Ryker saw that his eyes were a bright blue, the most beautiful eyes he had ever seen. The light from the candle shimmered off of them. They seemed timeless, as if he had just opened them for the first time. Even though Ryker knew he wasn't actually there in the cell with the man, the prisoner's eyes penetrated deep into Ryker.

Using what little strength he had, the old man spoke a word in a voice with true power and authority: "Awaken!" As he spoke, his voice shook the very foundations of the dungeon.

The moment the word left the old man's lips, Ryker was pulled out of the dungeon and caught up like a leaf in a sudden gust of strong wind. In a moment he had left the forest and was crossing a wide green plain. Then he was on the foot of a mountain, climbing its steep, rocky slopes. He was still moving weightlessly above the ground. A shadow suddenly fell over him as if he had entered a cave. His movements felt like they had ended.

Now Ryker couldn't see anything but darkness. He was once again surrounded by it, remembering now the place he dreaded.

Out of this darkness, scenes appeared before him, much like the scenes he had witnessed in Varic's chamber. A great cloud rose up out of nothing. Many scenes flashed before him. In these scenes he was shown his forgotten memories. He saw now what had happened after he had touched the orb. He was horrified at what he saw. It was like a dark nightmare that he couldn't wake from. He didn't know how he was recalling these things now. He could do nothing against the visions, and he watched in repulsion as he was reminded of the decision he now deeply regretted.

He watched his own body as if he was a spectator high above himself, unable to stop the actions he was taking. He was fighting on the platform with a wooden sword. He fought with speed and skill. Since the day he'd first started training with them, his skill had grown as he defeated opponent after opponent. He swung and struck anyone who was in his way, without mercy.

He wasn't this person! he thought. The darkness he had given in to had taken over. He found the other boys' weak spots and struck them there, drawing blood from his strikes and knocking bodies to the floor. He watched himself strike down every single boy he was put up against.

He threw knives at the logs with skill to match any Khoshekh. He even aimed at targets that weren't his, which were much farther away. The only time he ran back to the pillar was when he was out of knives.

Another scene flashed before him. He was running on the track with strength he had never had before. He had thought he was fast on the rooftops of Tervan. Using them every day, he knew which routes to take high above the Shuul. But here his speed was blinding. He knew exactly which route to take in the darkness, jumping between platforms without hesitation. He completed every obstacle in a matter of minutes.

He climbed the Pillar with ease. The height of the tall climb was nothing to him now. His arms and legs had grown strong. He could reach out in the darkness knowing exactly where every handhold was. When he neared the ledge at the top, he planted his feet on the rocks and jumped. Grabbing the ledge, he swung, and then with a strong pull he rolled up over the top.

The black sea was nothing to him. The icy waters didn't affect him at all. He swam without even the guidance of the red light. How he could see in such darkness was unknown to him. What had the orb done to him? What had Varic not told him?

Still, these flashes of dark memories showed Ryker what had happened while his mind had been succumbing to the darkness. His training had become increasingly intense and grueling. He had never spoken to the other boys, seeing them as nothing more than obstacles like the platforms on the track. He was disgusted with himself. How could he have been so blind? He could clearly see now that Varic was just as twisted and evil as the Khoshekh that served him.

Then the memories he had watched were engulfed in a black cloud. His mind had been numb all this time. His subconscious was in some sort of coma, while his body somehow functioned with the dark powers of the orb controlling him. The dream he'd had of the old man in the dungeon had somehow taken Ryker's mind back from the orb's power.

As the last scene faded into a black cloud, Ryker felt a great force pull him away. The force slung him backward, away from the remaining wisps of cloud. Then the force turned him, and he felt like he was falling through thick shadow. He wanted to cry out but found that he had no voice to speak. He could see nothing, although he felt the ground suddenly rise up out of the shadows to meet him. Instead of hitting the ground, he fell into himself.

Ryker shot up from his cot, gasping for air, instantly overcome with a sense of terror after waking from his long, dark slumber. He felt like he had been cast into the black sea, and cold chills covered his body from his abrupt awakening.

His head throbbed, and his heart beat rapidly, as if it was about to jump out of his chest. The orb had imprisoned him within his own mind. Bars hadn't held him; instead, darkness had surrounded him, holding him captive. Now he was free. His mind had been given back to him.

It felt like only moments ago he had been standing with Varic, surrounded by the pillars and torchlight. Varic had told Ryker everything he'd wanted to hear. Without question, Ryker had reached out for the orb. Now he was alone in a room filled with empty cots. What had he done? His wide eyes darted around the room to see if anything was hiding from him in the shadows.

Ryker put his hand over his chest and did his best to control his breathing. The dreams had seemed so real. They felt vivid, as if he had relived every moment of them. What could all of this mean? Was he reliving memories of his past? Or were they scenes from his future? It was too much for Ryker to take in right now. He needed to rest. His whole body ached as if he had actually endured all of the training he had watched himself go through.

His head swam with all the dark memories lingering foremost of his mind. He tried to lie back down in his cot, but the moment his cold back touched the wet cot, soaked from his sweat, he shot back up as even more chills spread over his skin.

He could find no rest for his dizzy head. He needed to clear his mind and find out what to do next. He swung his legs off to the side of his cot and sat there, letting his head settle. His mind still felt clouded. The darkness that had consumed him was slowly diminishing, though a few remnants still lingered in his mind. Once his mind felt clear, he needed to find out what had happened to him.

"Awaken," the word the old man had spoken, still echoed in his mind. The word seemed to push away the shadow still lurking in his mind. It sounded over and over in his head until the darkness fled. As it fled, the shadows lurking around him in the room seemed to glare at him with unseen eyes. Fear renewed within him as he sat alone in the dark.

The shadow that shrouded this place wasn't just a lack of light; it was something more. The Xahlbris fed this place with unnatural darkness. It had slowly eaten away at Ryker's resolve until, at his lowest point, he had given in to it. The things Varic spoke of were exactly what Ryker had needed to hear. He knew now more than ever that he needed to escape.

Although his body ached, his mind felt clearer than it ever had. He had no idea what time it could be. With all the other cots in the room empty, he figured it was shortly after morning. He expected a Khoshekh to appear at any moment. The thought of one appearing drove him to act quickly. He hoped he would have enough time to devise a plan and get along with it.

Raising himself up out of the cot, he stood, becoming light-headed when he did. He sat back down. When he sat, he noticed that his body felt very awkward to him. He inspected himself closely and saw that he had grown tremendously since he could last remember. How long had it been since he'd touched the black orb? he wondered.

His arms and legs had grown several inches and were covered with lean muscles. From his appearance, he must have been mindlessly training for years. He couldn't be certain, though. He pushed the thought out of his mind. He needed to come up with a plan.

He tried to rise again. This time his head felt fine, so he silently made his way across the room. He crept up to the door and peered through. The red light illuminated the passageway for him. The glow from the red light reminded him of its haunting color. Seeing no one in the hall, he thought of his next move. He knew now that everything Varic had said to him was a lie. He knew he needed to find Broff, wherever he might beif he was still alive.

14

Eclipsed

Thinking that this was the same room he had stayed in for the few months of training before his encounter with Varic and the orb, he turned left. Ryker headed in the opposite direction of where he thought the Hollow was. He would search for his friend before he did anything else.

Very few red lights illuminated the passageway. They helped very little as he looked into every room he passed. Most of the rooms were filled with sleeping boys, weary from training or digging in the mine. He knew their fate would be the same as his was. He wished he could help them all escape, but he knew it would be impossible. He knew that even just two boys trying to escape had little or no hope.

After passing by many rooms, he heard a boy crying inside one of these. Ryker looked through the small bars in the center of the door and saw a boy curled up on his cot. The boy trembled as he wept silently.

Ryker knew at once that it was Broff. He had grown as well, although his body looked malnourished and frail. He had been living a rough life. Ryker pitied his friend and hoped they would be able to escape.

Looking around the rest of the room, Ryker saw only a few other boys sleeping noiselessly. He knew he would be able to slip in without their noticing. He could only hope they both could slip out without waking any of the others.

Ryker tried to open the door quietly, but despite his efforts, it groaned on the old hinges. None of the sleeping boys moved. Luckily, they were in all in a deep sleep from their labors. Broff curled up into an even tighter ball. He must have thought a Khoshekh had entered the room to torment them. Ryker walked over to his friend and called his name softly.

"Broff," he whispered. "Broff, it's me, Ryker."

Broff stopped his crying and pushed himself up with his arm. Wide eyes looked at Ryker in the dark. He was speechless at the sight of his friend. Not waiting for his response, Ryker closed the remaining space between them and wrapped Broff in a huge hug. Broff, who was still speechless, clung to Ryker and wouldn't let go.

They held on to one another for a long time, weeping joyfully with each other. The friends had been reunited.

"I never thought I would see you again," Broff whispered, still holding Ryker close. He shed tears of newfound joy now.

"I didn't think I would ever see you again, either," Ryker replied. He was delighted at finding his friend.

"I am so glad to see you too!" Broff said, still pressed hard against Ryker's neck.

"Are you okay? Can you walk?" Ryker asked.

"Yeah, I'm fine," Broff said, wiping the new tears out of his eyes. "How are you? Where have you been? You look so much taller and bigger since the last time I saw you!"

"Aha." Ryker chuckled shyly. "Broff, as much as I'd like to sit and chat, there's no time to talk! We need to get out of this place as quickly as possible." Ryker pushed Broff away from him so he could stand.

"You know of a way out?" Broff asked hopefully.

"No, but there has to be one. I can't stand to be here for one more second." Ryker was whispering quietly now. He had forgotten about all the sleeping boys surrounding them.

"I'll follow wherever you lead," Broff said, determined. I'd rather die trying to get out of here than serve these dark things any longer." He rose from the cot along with Ryker. Despite his earlier tears, the mine seemed to have forged him into a much harder boy.

Both the boys crept toward the door. Broff was directly behind Ryker as they both peered through the cracked doorway. Ryker looked in both directions down the dark passageway. He didn't see anything, but he knew the Khoshekh could be hiding within every shadow. He cautiously led Broff out into the hall. Ryker wanted to close the door all the way, but he knew it would make another loud noise, so he left it open behind them.

They both slunk down the hallway toward the Hollow. Both of them were as quiet as possible. Ryker led Broff to the right-hand side of the passageway when they neared the room they shared their meals in. Ryker looked in to see if anyone was within. It was empty. They were off to a good start.

Continuing on, they soon came to the end of the passageway. Ryker stayed back until he could see exactly where the Khoshekh were. They had always stood on the bridge at the end of the passageway leading to the Hollow. Now, however, they were gone. They had left their post for the first time.

The boys crept forward and scanned the large cavern, looking for any movement. The dim red lights encircling the Pillar shed little light in the large cavern. Shadows freely filled the Hollow, with no light to hold them back. Somehow Ryker could see exceptionally well, despite the deepening shadows. It actually surprised him how well he could see in this darkness. His eyes had grown accustomed to the darkness after all this time.

"Can you see anything?" Broff asked in a whisper.

"Nothing," Ryker replied.

"This darkness is so thick I can't see anything either," Broff said, sounding defeated.

Ryker had to stop himself from laughing. "No, Broff, I can see, but there isn't anyone to be seen!"

"How can you see anything in this place?" Broff asked, amazed. "It's so dark, I can barely see you standing next to me."

Ryker didn't answer. He took his friend's hand and led him across the Hollow. They ran fast and silently over the smooth stone. The great cavern had been abandoned. The noise of hundreds of boys training constantly filled the air and echoed throughout the entire place. Now the silence was haunting. Ryker wondered where everyone was.

They made it across and continued over the bridge to the next passageway. It would lead them to the mine and the black sea. That was where they had entered this horrible place, so Ryker thought it might be the best place to find some kind of exit. Maybe there was another shore in the deep darkness that he had never seen before. His eyes had grown more accustomed to the darkness, so he hoped that now he would be able to see it if it was there. He hoped for Broff's sake that this was the case. If not … he hadn't thought of any other plan.

A booming voice echoed down the passageway. It stopped both boys dead in their tracks. The words were too muffled to understand, but the deep, threatening voice was unmistakable. It belonged to Varic.

Ryker caught Broff with the back of his arm and threw them both against the wall. His heart felt like it was going to leap out of his chest. He panicked now. Though the voice echoed loudly, it wasn't coming from the passageway. They hadn't been caught yet, but Ryker knew they needed to be more careful.

The boys moved along the wall toward the sound of the voice. Not far ahead was the mine. The booming voice of Varic became louder and clearer as they drew closer to the entrance to the mine. Ryker could see red light above the entrance making its way down the passageway. It filled the space before the entrance with dark-red light. Ryker didn't see any Khoshekh guarding it, so he moved in closer, with Broff following close behind.

Ryker found it strange that they hadn't seen a single Khoshekh. They normally moved through the Hollow and its surrounding passageways endlessly. They guarded every corner. But luck was on their side when they needed it most. The odds of their escaping were in their favor.

Varic's voice was clear enough to understand now. It was silent within the mine except for his booming voice. It filled the mine with a deep, rumbling echo.

"You have all trained well. I am proud of the warriors you have become." Varic's speech was much like the one he had given to Ryker. But Ryker knew better now. Every word out of Varic's mouth was a lie.

Varic continued as the boys edged closer to the entrance. Ryker and Broff stood on the outskirts of the red light. Still in the shadows, they tried to look in through the opening. Even Ryker had a hard time seeing anything.

The red light above them cast a small ray of light that barely reached the drop in the mine. Walking forward, Ryker peered through the entrance. He couldn't see any Khoshekh on their level. He could still hear Varic's booming voice, so he knew Varic had to be deep inside the mine. Ryker felt drawn in to see what was going on. He was about to step into the mine, but Broff grabbed his arm to stop him.

"Wait," he whispered. "Where are you going?"

Ryker wanted to see what was going on. He knew they should continue on to the dark waters to look for an exit, but he was curious to know why, for the first time, Varic had shown himself to everyone else. He knew he could sneak to the edge of the mine and look in to see what was going on.

"I want to see what's going on," he whispered to Broff. He had already shaken off Broff's hand and was crouching to his stomach. He crawled toward the edge of the mine slowly. Broff reluctantly crawled next to him.

The ground fell away, and the mine was now visible below them. Ryker's eyes grew wide, and his jaw dropped when he saw what was beneath him. Thousands of Khoshekh filled every layer of the deep mine. They were scattered all over, some in clusters and some standing alone. Their numbers amazed Ryker. Varic was indeed building an army.

Many creatures Ryker had never seen before were among the Khoshekh. These creatures were dark, and their features were cast in thick shadow. Ryker couldn't see their features, but their eyes were red like the Khoshekh, and horns grew out of their large heads. One thing that Varic had said was true: he had found dark creatures beneath these caverns. At the very bottom of the mine stood Varic. His form towered over all others, even the creatures. Near Varic stood the pedestal that held the Xahlbris.

A line of boys had formed before the orb. The boys who had endured training alongside Ryker stood in single file, ready to take the final step in their training. Ryker had just gone through what they were about to. They would embrace their dark fate and become Khoshekh, serving Varic without question to whatever end he deemed fit.

"When you place your hand on the Xahlbris, you will be gifted with a hint of my power," Varic said to the boys in line.

An awful silence hung among them. They moved forward with blank expressions on their faces. Ryker wished he could cry out and convince them not to do this, but he knew that nothing he could say would deter them.

Varic continued, "I would welcome you with open arms into my ranks and give you the family that you have always deserved. You will become the mighty Khoshekh! With your help, we will submerge Arke into darkness. Out of the shadows, it will rise again—a better kingdom, my kingdom, a kingdom of darkness."

Broff tore away from the edge without thinking to be silent. His movement was not only sudden in the still cavern but also loud. Every head turned to the spot where the boys were hiding. Ryker couldn't believe it. He too pulled himself away from the edge and looked at his friend. Broff's eyes were closed tight, and fear stretched across his face. Ryker hoped Varic and the others below hadn't noticed them.

Varic's voice echoed up out of the mine and reverberated throughout the large cavern. "You cannot hide from my sight in the shadows. I rule all darkness. You think you can escape? There is only one way out, and it does not lead to the light!"

Without wasting a moment, Ryker pushed himself off the floor and pulled Broff up as well. He shoved Broff ahead of him and sprinted toward the exit. Luck had fled from them.

"Where are you running?" Varic growled after them. "There is no place to hide! Nowhere to run! Take them!" he thundered to the Khoshekh.

Ryker knew that Varic's words were true, but he wouldn't let the Khoshekh take them without a fight, or a chase! Before they made it to the passageway, he heard many Khoshekh running after them. Many of them laughed with their evil, hissing voices. The dark creatures in the mine below screeched and growled, making terrible noises. Now they had to worry about beings darker than the Khoshekh. The luck he had thought was on their side had suddenly left them.

They reached the exit of the mine without being caught. Ryker had to push his much slower friend and speed him along as they ran. He knew Broff wouldn't last long in this chase. They tried to turn left where they had intended to going before. Two Khoshekh appeared out of the shadows to block their way.

They fumbled over each other as they attempted to halt and turn to run the opposite direction. Their pursuers inside the mine hadn't made it to them yet, but they were close. They ran hard through the passageway toward the Hollow.

Ryker didn't know how many creatures chased them. It didn't really matter. They couldn't go far without being caught. There was nowhere for them to go. Varic was right: they had nowhere to hide. He was sure the Hollow would be filled with Khoshekh waiting for them. Escape was hopeless, and he knew it.

Looking along the passageway, he saw its end—and theirs—in the dim light. Ahead of him, Broff began to slow down, already growing weary. Ryker sprinted ahead of him and led the way. He quickly thought of where to go next. They could jump into the pit, where they would easily be caught in the deep shadows. They might make it to the bunkrooms and hide among the other boys; most of them were between Varic and the Khoshekh in the mine.

Suddenly he remembered the passageway leading out of the Hollow along the outer wall directly behind the place where they had practiced knife-throwing. He had seen it the first time he'd completed the track. He knew it was unguarded. Why hadn't he thought of that before? Maybe that would lead to the way out. He ran now with new vigor, hoping his friend would keep up.

The passageway opened up to the large domed cavern. It still stood empty. The red light still shed dull light throughout. On the other side of the Hollow to his right was their only hope for escape. Even from this distance, he could see the darkness daring them to enter.

He turned to check that Broff was still behind him. The glimpse he got of his friend's expression told Ryker that he wouldn't last much longer at this speed. But he needed to. Ryker wouldn't leave Broff behind. Ryker turned and headed straight for the dark passageway.

Flying through the cavern, Ryker noticed something glimmer out of the corner of his eye above him. Keeping his focus on the dark tunnel ahead, he continued to run. Fleeing from shadow into a black void didn't seem like the most logical plan, but it was the best one Ryker had.

Suddenly the glimmer he thought he had see blinded him for a moment. Pure light fell upon him briefly. It wasn't the red light he had grown accustomed to. The light that hit him seemed like a distant memory. Although it was very faint, he could tell that it was pure light, like that of the sun.

Gazing at it now in disbelief, he continued running. He had almost forgotten what that kind of light looked like. The faint light was shining within the darkness at the peak of the Pillar. Now captivated by the light, he stopped running and stared at it. Broff ran into him and nearly knocked them both over.

"A light!" Ryker cried out in excitement.

"Where?" Broff asked, out of breath. He stopped next to Ryker and took in deep breaths of air.

"There!" Ryker pointed. "On top of the Pillar!"

"I don't see anything!" Broff said desperately. He placed his hands on his legs and sucked air down into his weary lungs.

"Come on, Broff, we won't get another chance!" Ryker yelled.

As the boys stood near the base of the rock, out from the darkness they came. Their pursuers used the dark clouds and appeared out of them. Varic's horde of Khoshekh surrounded them in the darkness. Their red eyes glowed with intensity. Thousands of them stood around the boys. Ryker knew they had to make it to the pillar. It would either be their doom or their escape.

He had to act fast. For a moment he wondered why the Khoshekh hadn't just appeared in their black clouds right next to them and taken them away. If they had, they would've ended this chase long ago. Ryker knew Varic wanted them to suffer with the thought of hope before he totally crushed them. He was a wicked and cruel man.

Ryker took Broff's arm and headed toward the Pillar. When they reached it, Broff whimpered before it. Ryker took a running start and was already above Broff's head.

"Follow my lead, Broff! We'll get through this together!" Ryker said, looking down at his friend, who reluctantly placed his hands onto the sharp rock.

With Ryker's guidance and the threat of capture by the Khoshekh, Broff climbed. Hesitant at first, he quickly got into the rhythm of it and followed closely behind Ryker. Although Broff looked frail, Ryker could tell that the grueling work in the mine had made his friend strong. He only hoped he would be strong enough for the long climb.

Something flew by Ryker's head and clanged against the rock. He watched it fall and saw the red light glimmer off the metal object. It was a throwing knife of the Khoshekh. More of them flew at the boys. They clanged off the rocks, some even shot sparks as the steel hit the hard stone. Ryker knew the Khoshekh were missing them on purpose. He had seen their skill when he had been handed the throwing knives. If they had wanted to hit the boys, they would have. The Khoshekh were playing with them, cruelly placing fear in the fleeing boys' hearts, crushing their hope until nothing was left.

Ryker looked down after another knife hit the rocks near them. Broff had stopped as well. Now they were nearly halfway to the top. He watched as his friend looked down at the ground far below. He froze and clung desperately to the rocks. His arms and legs were shaking.

"I can't go on," Broff said quietly, almost to himself. But it was loud enough for Ryker to hear.

"Yes, you can!" Ryker encouraged him. "We have to get out of here together!"

Out of the shadows below them, the Khoshekh rose. They also climbed up the Pillar, coming near to the two boys. Ryker cried out to his friend, "Broff, hurry!"

Broff looked below him as well. The sight of the Khoshekh pursuing them goaded him to continue his climb. He hurried upward. Ryker stayed in the same place on the Pillar and let Broff pass him. Switching places would help Ryker defend his friend from the Khoshekh that were now closing in on them.

"Ryker, I can't see enough to grab the rocks in front of me!" Broff yelled, beginning to panic above him.

"Just feel for them!" Ryker yelled back to him. He looked down to see that their pursuers were nearly upon them.

"We're close to the top! Can you see the light?" Ryker asked when they continued on. He hoped they were.

"No, nothing!" Broff said as he grunted to pull himself higher.

"Just keep moving, Broff. You're doing great! We're almost there!" Ryker said, hoping to encourage his friend.

They climbed frantically, scrambling up the Pillar. One wrong move and they would fall, but taking their time would mean imminent capture. Ryker pushed himself away, taking a moment to look above them to see how close they were. It was a moment they didn't have, but he needed to know that they were drawing close. Above Broff he could barely make out the ledge at the Pillar's peak.

"I can see the ledge, Broff! We're nearly there!" Ryker's last words faltered when he saw a pair of red eyes appear out of the shadows on the ledge above them. His heart sank.

"Broff, wait!" Ryker screamed. He raced to climb quickly to reach Broff, but it was too late. Broff reached up for the ledge, and when he grabbed hold of it, the Khoshekh stomped on his hand.

Broff yelled from the pain and pulled his hand away. Unable to balance himself, his momentum sent him falling from the Pillar. Ryker shot out a hand out and grabbed hold of Broff's arm. Ryker clung to Broff with one arm and held onto the Pillar with the other. The act called for all the strength he had within him. The motion from the fall swung Broff directly into the Pillar. He hit it hard with a thud, and Ryker watched as blood trickled down his face.

"Broff, grab onto something!" Ryker yelled through gritted teeth. He knew he couldn't hold his friend for long.

He didn't get a response from Broff. His friend's head was hung low, and his body was limp. Ryker desperately hung on to his friend. The Khoshekh' training had paid off. He needed every muscle he had to keep them both from falling. His arms began to shake from the strain. He knew he couldn't hold on any longer. His gripped loosened not only on his friend but also on the rock that supported them both. Now losing his strength, he could feel his friend shake his head to wake himself. Seeing what had happened, he quickly grabbed onto the rocks to support himself.

Ryker's body was relieved. He didn't know how much longer he could have held them both. He hung his body limp against the Pillar and took deep breaths. He placed the top of his head onto the cold stone. Opening his eyes, he saw that below them, only a few feet away, red eyes approached them.

"Broff, we have to move! Now!" he yelled more to himself than to Broff.

Broff was also taking a break from his near-death experience. Climbing again with renewed strength, they made it to the ledge. Ryker climbed up on it first. Seeing no Khoshekh, he lay flat on his stomach and reached over the ledge to help his friend. He grabbed hold of him and helped him up and over the ledge. They both lay in a heap atop the ledge, glad to be on a flat surface, even if it was a few hundred feet up. They had made it.

Ryker rolled himself upright, reminding himself of the intensity of the situation. Broff followed along as they searched for the light. Hope faded where shadow remained.

"Where was the light?" Broff asked, looking around them.

"It was here," Ryker said, pointing toward the top of the Pillar above them. The domed ceiling was only a few feet above them, so they had to crane their necks to search for it. While Ryker continued searching desperately, Broff walked over to the edge of the platform they were on.

"I don't see any of them, Ryker!" he yelled back to his friend. "I think they've given up!"

Ryker was still looking for the place where the light had come from. He knew there was a reason for it. This could be their way out! Where did it come from? He wondered if there was a crack in the ceiling that somehow let in the light of day. A cloud could be covering the sun at the moment, so maybe they needed to wait for it to pass. It was a feeble hope, but it was all he had. Either this light, wherever it came from, saved them, or they would stay here at the mercy of the cruel Khoshekh.

Broff's scream brought Ryker's attention away from his searching. He turned to see a Khoshekh on either side of his friend, holding on to his arms. The clouds in which they had appear still hung in the shadows around them.

Their red eyes weren't looking at Ryker but at Broff, who did everything he could to break away from them. His attempts were feeble, and the Khoshekh merely laughed at him. Their hissing voices sparked newfound fear inside of Ryker.

Ryker watched in horror as the Khoshekh walked even closer to the edge. They stood on the brink, with Broff still struggling between them. Ryker made a dash toward them. He was halfway to them when the Khoshekh toppled over the ledge. Broff screamed as they fell headfirst to the ground far below.

"Broff, no!" Ryker cried. Tears welled up in his eyes as he watched his friend fall.

Ryker ran to the ledge and tried to get a glimpse of them. They were instantly lost in shadow. He saw nothing in the void beneath him. He knew death would be better than a life of torture at the hands of the Khoshekh. He knew that firsthand. The Khoshekh had now claimed two of his friends that he would have called brothers.

Unexpectedly, the light he had seen from below burned now in brilliance. Not only did Ryker have to close his eyes, but he also had to shield them with his hands. He knew that he had no reason to fear it. It was warm and bright, everything Ryker had been longing for since the day he'd arrived in this black void that the Khoshekh had hurled him into. The light was so bright that it lit the entire cavern with pure white light. No shadow could escape it. It was like the dawn chasing away the night.

The light faded away enough for Ryker to see where it was coming from. Above him at the Pillar's peak, a light like the sun burned through the rock. A mark the size of Ryker's hand was carved into the Pillar. Three curved lines positioned almost in a triangle were cut into the rock, although they didn't appear to have been chipped away by any chisel. They looked like they had been set there ages ago. Ryker climbed until it was level with it, until the light washed over him.

Something drew him to the light. He knew he needed it. It was so beautiful and so warm. Keeping a good hold on the rock with his right hand, he reached out with his left. Before he touched the mark in the rock, the light felt like it sucked his hand down onto it. Immediately he felt a most intense burning sensation. It began in his fingers and then his hand, followed by his arm, until his entire body felt like it was on fire. He couldn't scream out. Although it burned, he was surprised that it didn't exactly hurt him. The sensation he felt wasn't pain. Whatever he felt was good and welcoming.

The carvings from the rock now seemed to be etched into his skin. The intense sensation of pain was the curved lines being spread on the back of his hand. Now the light seemed to be coming from the mark on his hand, which burned brighter and hotter than even the sun.

The light intensified as it eclipsed the darkness within the Hollow. Ryker closed his eyes tightly and tried to look away from it. Even with his eyes shut, the light penetrated his eyelids. As the light intensified, the heat did as well. All the cold and darkness felt like it was being burned out of him. All of the dark memories seemed to vanish from him. He felt the Pillar he clung to evaporate under him. The white light consumed the Hollow as well. He felt himself float safely to a flat space below him. Then, in a single burst like a flash of lightning, everything faded away. A sound like a huge thunderbolt echoed throughout the Hollow.

The dark abyss he had been thrust into was melted away by the intense light. The chill air was replaced by soothing warmth. Ryker was bathed in the light as it slowly burned every last shadow.

Part II

15

Branded

The darkness was over. Ryker drank in a frightened breath and his heartbeat quickened as he took in his new surroundings. He was no longer in the Hollow but in a forest that was cast in deep shadow—though this shadow was nothing compared to the darkness within the Hollow. A moonlit night's veil was cast over the trees.

Ryker stood there, speechless and in shock over what had just happened. His eyes quickly darted all around him, expecting to see red eyes appear at any moment. A bright moon shone somewhere above him, for its bluish light filtered through a leafy canopy. Although he couldn't see it anywhere above him, he was still thankful for the light.

Many tall trees were clustered close to him, and the floor below them was covered in leaves fallen from the previous autumn. Sticks and broken branches lay scattered on the ground, making no clear path for him to follow. His legs were weak, and he found it hard to get a good footing on the ground beneath them. The trees surrounding him were growing on a more or less steep hillside.

His ringing ears made his head throb with pain. He tried his best to shake off the throbbing in his head and the weakness in his limbs. He needed to get away from this place as fast as he could. Not clear on which direction to go, he followed the steep hill downward.

He dashed between trees and over debris littered by the old forest. The slope of the landscape increased his speed dramatically. He was traveling swiftly, narrowly dodging trees as he sped along.

He continued downward hoping to get away from this place before any Khoshekh decided to show up. At any moment they could appear out of their black clouds. Scanning all around him, he kept his eyes and ears open for any movement or sound other than his own breathing and footfalls.

Although he hadn't seen any creatures when he'd arrived, he knew the Khoshekh better than that. They would give him time to run, time to think he could get away. Then, when hope rose within him, they would crush it.

Enduring for so long the darkness the Khoshekh thrived in made Ryker appreciate any kind of light. Even the light of the moon seemed bright and brilliant to him. He looked up every chance he got, in between dodging trees, to see a glimmer of it through the thick foliage above him. He hoped he would make a clearing soon so he could get a better view of it.

After running a short distance, getting his blood and adrenaline pumping, the suffering he had encountered during the bright light slowly faded away. He was still unsure of exactly what it was. Although he started to tire from the sprint, his mind became clear, and his ears stopped ringing.

He began to wonder what the light had been and what it meant. He knew it had nothing to do with the Khoshekh, that was certain. They controlled darkness and instilled fear in the hearts of the boys they stole from the streets. But what power controlled the light that had just saved him from the utter darkness he had endured for so many years? He would try to find out if he could.

From all those nights ago in Tervan, he knew that the Khoshekh could leave their dark dwelling whenever they pleased. He remembered that the moon had been full that night, though it was a little cloudy, but the Khoshekh had persisted in pursuing him. He wondered what kind of light hurt them. He needed to get somewhere that had plenty of it. Still, he needed to stay focused on what was at hand. Not knowing what time of night it was, he could only hope that dawn was close at hand.

Thunder bellowed in the distance. Its sound echoed through the forest, reminding him of the booming sound he'd heard during his contact with the light. This roll of thunder sounded faint and far off.

In the confines of this forest, he couldn't see any clouds, so he wasn't sure if the storm had passed or was drawing near. Peals of thunder and flashes of lighting told him it was drawing closer. The thunder became louder and more frequent, until he heard the gentle sounds of rain begin to fall on the leaves above him. Soon the rain was leaking through the roof of the forest. The ground below Ryker quickly became a muddy mess and made it hard for him to continue downhill at the same speed.

It rained like this for some time, and soon Ryker was soaked. The air around him was warm, so the dampness of his clothes didn't bother him. In fact, the rain was a gift to his weary limbs.

The lightning diminished and left Ryker listening to the quiet sounds of the rain falling on the leafy canopy above him. Despite the situation, he couldn't help but feel something he had not felt in a long time. He wasn't sure if it was happiness, that being the one memory he had almost completely forgotten. Happiness was something unheard of in the Hollow. He had almost completely forgotten how it felt. The cool rain above and this forest reminded him of it. Then he remembered that he needed to run, that he needed to put as much distance as he could between himself and this forest.

The rain above him stopped as quickly as it had started. Still, the trees above dripped down the few raindrops than lingered in their branches. Although the shower had been brief, the ground under his feet was soaked. He was unable to run as fast as he would have liked, and it made him feel uneasy.

He regularly looked behind him to see if anything had appeared out of nothing, but he saw only a dark forest. He almost expected to see the entire Hollow emptied and every Khoshekh hot on his heels, chasing him down this steep forest slope.

Ryker felt like he had run for more than three hours, and still he saw no pursuers behind him. If the Khoshekh were going to catch him, they would have shown themselves already. What if the light that had brought him to this forest had also done something to the Khoshekh to hinder them from following him here? If it was possible for the light to bring him here, he figured it would be just as possible for the light to hold back the Khoshekh.

His sharp eyes caught a feeble twinkle of light up ahead. Although the light would have seemed faint to anyone else, Ryker saw it clearly. Through the trees and beyond, he could see an orange glow far ahead of him. The area he was in now seemed to be sparser with foliage. The trees grew farther apart and had much thinner trunks. Then, as if coming up for air in deep waters, Ryker broke through the last line of trees.

The sight before him forced the breath out of his tired lungs. As far as his eyes would take him, where the rolling landscape met the bleak sky, the sun rose in all its glory. It blended the landscape and skyline in a bright orange glow.

The sun began to rise up out of the horizon to shed its light on the new day, casting thick, bright-orange rays into the dark-blue sky to push away the night. He hadn't thought he would ever see the beauty of the sun again. Now he was feeling the warmth of its rays wash over his cold and weary body. He had finally escaped from the darkness of the Khoshekh.

The feeling that had been lost within the cold darkness overwhelmed him now. He laughed loud and long to himself and began to dance at the edge of the forest. He spread his arms out wide and spun in circles, basking in the sun's warmth.

As the desert drinks from the rain, Ryker's eyes fed hungrily on the light. His eyes had seen only darkness and shadow for what had seemed like an eternity. The sight and warmth that the light brought forth overwhelmed him. He laughed and cried as his emotions overcame him. He fell back upon the wet grass and let his pale skin drink deeply under the rays of the rising sun.

He could hardly believe that he had actually made it out of the darkness, finally escaping from the clutches of his vile captors. Somehow he had held on to the hope of escaping for so long. It had been his only lifeline in the darkness. After suffering for so long, that hope had been reduced to a frayed strand. With the light's help, he had done it. He had been set free.

As he watched the sun climb, a rising-up grew inside him. He felt much like the dawn. Hidden by the shadow of night, he had burst forth from the unknown light within the Hollow and had escaped the clutching darkness. He had risen like the dawn to dwell once more in the glorious light.

The sun was warm and welcoming to Ryker. Reaching up with his hand, he started to wipe the sweat from his face. He stopped his hand midway when he saw a strange mark on it. He had completely forgotten about it.

When he had reached the light atop the Pillar in the Hollow, it had left a large mark covering the back of his hand. His mind had been preoccupied with his escape, and he had forgotten about it. He felt no pain from it, and although it looked like a burn, it was completely healed. It looked more like a scar.

How had the light done this to him? And why? It had helped him escape, and that was all that really mattered. He was free now and had something to remember it by.

The sun rose quickly and was already over the top of the horizon. Its light was very bright to Ryker, but he couldn't bring himself to look away. His eyes were fixed on the beautiful sun. He promised himself he would never again enter any kind of cave or underground dwelling. He never wanted to be separated from the light again. He felt like he could stay here basking in its rays all day long.

The light from the sun showed Ryker long, low-lying hills rolled out in front of him. The forest had led him to a vast plain. A few outcroppings of trees could be seen growing in the rolling landscape. More common were large rocks jutting out of the turf. In the far distance he saw many of these dotting the hills.

He found a tree close by and sat with his back propped up against it. He closed his eyes with a broad smile stretched over his face. Closing his eyes and folding his arms across his chest, he fell fast asleep.

He slept there for some time, the warming his weary body. With it shining brightly on him, he didn't have a care in the world. All his dark memories vanished in the shining sun. His fear that the Khoshekh could appear at any moment was gone. He didn't think even once about the Hollow or the Khoshekh or any other dark thing. The light drove all thoughts of darkness away. Ryker couldn't remember the last time he'd slept so well. And then he dreamed.

In his dream, Ryker witnessed once more the two Khoshekh leaping out of their black clouds to snatch up Broff. Ryker watched in horror as his friend fell with the Khoshekh from atop the Pillar, screaming his name. Ryker ran to the ledge, but Broff had already been lost in the darkness below. He had been swallowed up by shadow, and there was nothing Ryker could do about it.

Ryker gasped as he woke from his sleep, still under the light and warmth of the sun. A sea of emotions rolled in, wave after wave, engulfing Ryker in grief. How could he have forgotten about Broff? He had abandoned him to whatever fate the Khoshekh had for him. Training was torture enough, so he wondered what dark punishment the Khoshekh had in store for his friend. He couldn't believe he had done it again.

The sun's brilliance blinded him for a moment. Living in utter darkness for so long had made his eyes unaccustomed to this amount of light. He shielded his eyes for a while, letting the light flow between his fingers, training his eyes to see in the newfound light.

Soon they adjusted to the sun's light, though he had to squint under its glow. Slowly his eyes adjusted normally. It was a much faster change than when his eyes had had to adjust to the darkness of the Hollow.

Ryker sat up to see that the sun was already making its way to the heights of the blue sky above. He had slept for a few hours, and although he felt rejuvenated, he was sick with the thought that Broff had been captured while they were escaping. There was no way for him to help his friend now. Broff was gone forever. The light had blinded Ryker from everything else, and he had abandoned the friend he'd sworn he would never leave without.

Remembering as well what had happened to Shiloh, hot tears welled up in Ryker's eyes and fell down his cheeks. Both of his friends' deaths were his fault. He should have leaped down and at least have had a chance to save Broff, no matter how slim that chance was. He should have searched harder for Shiloh.

In the scene he had watched in Varic's chamber, Ryker had passed right by the drowning boy. He had been only arm's length away from Ryker, but Ryker had been blind while swimming in the darkness around them both. He had failed his friends when they'd needed him most. Ryker would have to live with the guilt of these memories for the rest of his life. Every memory he had was dark and filled with pain, and these would be no different.

The Khoshekh had done far more to him than just train his body. The darkness had stained him, despite all his efforts against it, despite even the dream that seemed to have driven the darkness out of his mind when it had threatened to completely consume him. His heart felt harder at the loss of his friends. Although he did miss them and felt pain for their loss, he knew he couldn't do anything about it. He knew it wouldn't do any good to wallow in grief. Before, he would have cried until his eyes were out of tears. Now he could easily push the memory away and think about the task at hand. He knew it wasn't right, but maybe he could find a way to help Broff and the other boys who were still held captive. Then one day he could see Broff one more time. He needed a plan, and he needed to keep moving.

He first needed to find out where he was. He looked again over the rolling hills laid out before him. Even with the brightness of the sun, that was all he could see in any given direction. To his left and right, the forest edge stretched as far as he could see, following the steady rise and fall of the ground.

To his right, however, he thought he could see the land fall away quickly. Craning his neck, he studied it, but couldn't determine why the land fell away. Ahead of him rose a hill, so he climbed it to get a better look.

He gradually walked up the hill. When he crested the it, a fast-flowing river came into view. It leaped out of the forest with great speed and cut into the lush green countryside. It followed the low places through the many hills, snaking its way toward the sun until it was lost to his sight.

Remembering the river in Tervan, Ryker was pleased when he looked upon this fast-flowing water. He hoped he had stumbled upon the very same river. He knew if he tried to travel through the green countryside without any road to guide him, he would quickly become lost. If he traveled along this river, it would be his path through the hills. It was something his father had taught him.

Memories sprang up in his mind of the man who had taught him everything he knew. He had always said, "If you're ever lost, just follow the coast or a river until you stumble onto something." It was good advice, and Ryker was glad of it now.

Walking back down the hill, he continued on along the edge of the forest. The wind rushed over the fields and flew past him. Its strong gust blew into the forest, and the leaves of the trees caught the wind like sails.

He couldn't help but watch the many forest creatures scurry to and fro at the sight of him. The forest was alive with all sorts of noises. He couldn't see the source of them all, but he could hear birds and other creatures breaking through the leaves. Many birds sang their beautiful forest songs to each other.

Ryker saw a sudden movement and watched as a deer bounded away from him, its white tail stuck straight up in warning to others. He halfheartedly wished he could simply wander through the forest without any agenda. He wished he could become lost in the woods. He hadn't thought about it until now, but what was he going to do once he found something—or someone?

Varic's dark plan needed to be revealed to Arke. Someone needed to stop him from unleashing whatever dark power the orb contained. He couldn't let Varic's plan go unknown to Arke. The only people Ryker knew to tell would be the Drudins. Everyone in Arke knew they were selfish and arrogant, but they were supposedly their protectors. The Drudin were the only people worth telling. What they would do once Ryker told them was a mystery.

Last time Ryker had talked with a Drudin, it had almost gotten him flogged. He had told the Drudin about a crazy man in black who had been chasing him and had spoken about his master's plan to throw Arke into darkness. Now Ryker had met that master and had heard his evil plan firsthand. What was he to say to the Drudin: that a bigger man in black sought to cover Arke in darkness and that he had a vast army with which to do it? He could hope for the best, but he knew he was likely to be thrown in chains. Someone needed to hear about Varic's plan. Chains or not, Ryker needed to warn someone.

He could tell one of the Shafels who ruled in the Thraans. He knew they rarely ever left their beautiful citadels surrounded by the high walls of the Thraan. Ryker wouldn't even get past the gates before being snatched up. Even if he did, he would have to get through a huge number of Gaur who were solely dedicated to the protection of their Shafel. At least Ryker could find the Drudin again at an inn or tavern. Neither option appealed to him, but they were all he had.

He did have one other option that appealed more to him than the others. If he could find whomever controlled the light, he would surely help. Maybe whoever had saved Ryker from the darkness of the Khoshekh would save the people of Arke from the darkness as well. But Ryker didn't know who that person was. He could be anywhere on the islandor somewhere outside of Arke.

The light could have been nothing more than a random chance, a lucky occurrence. The light could have just been the sun blinding him. He had probably hit his head and fallen out of the cavern into the forest. After all, he was nothing special. He was only an orphan. What would a person with such power want with him?

And if it was indeed someone with great power, what could Ryker offer him in gratitude? His services? Although he could fight, his training was dark. He would rather not fight if he could help it. He didn't know if something buried deep inside him would spring to life if he were put in that kind of situation.

Awaken. The word suddenly sprang back in his memory. The scene of the old man from his dream flashed before him. If it had been a dream, he was glad to have had it because it had roused him from his dark sleep. If it was more than a dream, then maybe the old man in it was real. If he was real, then he must know about the light. Although he seemed to have been close to death in the dream, maybe he had held on and was still alive. It would be a long shot, but Ryker hoped it was true. It was all he had. If he could find the old man, maybe he could find out who controlled the light. First he needed to find out where he was.

Climbing up the hill, he soon crested it and saw the river at the foot of it. The river ran from his right to his left. The area all around was filled with the sounds of the swift current as it crashed against the rocky banks. The sun simmered in reflection off the bright-blue waters. The banks along the river were steep, and many rocks could be seen jutting up within the river, creating white rapids. Very few trees grew along the river. The ones that did were tall and very green from the constant supply of water.

This part of the river was much faster than the portion he remembered in Tervan. He wondered if it was indeed the same river. Regardless, he would follow it wherever it led. If he followed it upriver, he would enter the forests, so he turned left and followed its currents toward the place where the sun had risen that morning. He walked close to the banks of the river toward what he hoped would be Tervan.

He knew that the river that flowed past Tervan continued until it filled Teerah Bay. He wondered if his aunt and uncle still lived near its shores. If only they knew what they had done when they'd abandoned him.

He would never forgive them for what they had put him through. He hoped he saw them again so he could let them know what had happened to him. If they hadn't left him in the streets, he wouldn't have had to endure the Hollow and all of its dread.

Broff and Shiloh might still be alive as well—although if he had never gone to Tervan, they would more than likely have still been orphans there. And without Ryker they probably wouldn't have lasted as long as they had on the streets.

Taking his thoughts away from his friends' deaths, he turned them to the road ahead. The ground near the river rose and fell far less. When it did, it was gradual, and he barely noticed it.

Looking above, he noticed that the sun was beginning to slowly fall toward the opposite horizon. As he mentally traced the line the sun was traveling behind him, he saw something he had only heard his father speak of once before: the Spine of Arke.

A great mountain range rose out of the forest he had just fled through. The rocky slopes sprang out of the trees and reached high into the sun-soaked sky. The Spine stretched from the northern tip of Arke to the lake far in the south. The mountains stretched for miles. Hundreds of mountains were stacked close together in the center of Arke, splitting the island down the middle. No one knew their height for certain, as their peaks were laden with snow year-round.

He wondered what lay on the other side of the mountains. He had heard that a huge forest took up almost the entire east side of the island. He wondered who dwelled in the forest and what kinds of creatures lived there. He had never realized how big the island of Arke was. He had only ever known one small corner of it. Now he had traveled for nearly an entire day without seeing anyone. He hoped one day he would be able to explore all of Arke.

Ryker's eyes followed the range south until the mountains became lost in the trees. When he was a boy, his father had told him that they would make a trip to see the mountains one day. Ryker saw them now and clung to that memory of his father. It was one of the only things that drove him forward. His father had always put others' needs before his own. He'd loved people for who they were, not for what they did. He hoped he could live up to his father's legacy, even if he was only one who remembered it.

He felt a mix of emotions, seeing the mountains. He felt joy at seeing something he had only known because his father had described things so well. His joy oddly mixed with sorrow because his father hadn't been the one to show him. He missed both his parents terribly and wished beyond everything else that he could see them again. They had both been taken away from him when he'd needed them most.

His heart, calloused by the darkness of the Hollow, knew this was the way life went. It was cruel and unfair. He had endured a darkness beyond reckoning, after all. He knew how cruel life could be to a person, even someone as innocent as a child.

Ryker turned away from the sight of the mountains and pressed on alongside the river. However cruel life was to him, he would press on. His mother had often told him that there was a reason for everything. There was a reason for storms to come, and a reason for a bright-blue sky. Ryker would make the best of whatever came to him. He had endured and escaped the worst kind of torment. After that, everything would be easy compared to what he had gone through. He pushed himself with determination and pressed onward.

He traveled along the river, keeping his eyes peeled for any sign of a house or farm or even a road that would lead him to something. He was surprised he didn't see any. Whenever he climbed one of the low hills, he could see for what seemed like miles. He wondered why no one lived around here. Without knowing whether or not to cross the river, he stayed on the near side. It would be dangerous to cross, with the swift current and the many rocks, but he knew he could do so if the need arose.

He hoped he would reach something before the sun went down, before its light gave way to the dark of night. He was sure that the light had helped him escape and had kept the Khoshekh from pursuing him. He didn't know how long the light would hold them back. He might have escaped only last night before the sun had risen. If he was caught in the middle of nowhere tonight, the Khoshekh would surely surround him, excited to bring him back to their master. So he needed to find something, anything, before nightfall.

A short distance ahead of him at the base of two hills, he saw a small outcrop of trees near the river. They grew in a tight cluster on the edge of the banks. When he drew closer to the cluster of trees, he saw that they were growing around a small pool. Their branches stretched out over the pool, shading it from the sun. He noticed that the pool was filled by a small stream near the banks of the river. It flowed through steadily, giving fresh water to the pool.

The water was crystal clear and looked inviting. Ryker thought of nothing better than to bathe in the pool. When he reached the edge he stripped down and walked over to the water. As he knelt down to feel the temperature of the water, he saw something terrible in the water that made him jump back in astonishment.

16

Distorted

The face of a Khoshekh was under the water looking back at him. Realizing that it couldn't be a Khoshekh, he wondered what else it could have been. He had only gotten a glimpse, but the person had looked sickly pale and thin.

Hoping he was wrong, he thought for a moment that it could have been his own reflection, so he looked again. He leaned slowly over the bank until his face was revealed to him in the smooth water. His eyes were wide in disbelief.

His hair was cut close to his head, almost shaved. His skin was ghostly pale, and his eyes were bloodshot. Some stubble grew on his chin, which resembled his father's strong jawline, making him look closer to manhood. He gazed at his face in disbelief. How many years had he spent in those dark depths?

He thought about how old he had been when the Khoshekh had stolen him off the streets of Tervan. He must've been close to fifteen. Now he looked like he was closer to eighteen, or even older. Could he have really spent three years in that place when it had only felt like six months?

He found it hard to believe that the dark orb had truly put him into a dark sleep, even though his training had continued. He wondered if all the Khoshekh had been boys once, though they were now totally controlled by Varic and the dark orb. If they had been boys once, maybe they could be saved as Ryker had been.

Maybe the Khoshekh weren't entirely evil after all. Maybe they were more like puppets used by Varic. They'd often said when Ryker was training that he needed to become a weapon worthy of their master. What if Varic used the Khoshekh as nothing more than a sword in battle?

There had been so many other boys training alongside Ryker. They too had been taken off the streets to train and then be used by Varic. He pitied those boys and wished he could do something about it.

Maybe the person who controlled the light would save them as well. If someone had such power, he could easily shed some light into that dark hole and blind the Khoshekh. Ryker needed to find this person who controlled the light. But he needed to worry about himself before he went on a fool's errand to save all the boys in the Hollow.

Bending down again at the banks of the pool, he felt the water, which was very cool. He walked a few paces back and took a running leap into the water. He splashed water onto the surrounding trees and onto his clothes lying on the bank. The water felt wonderful. It was nice and cool, nothing like the black sea, and very refreshing.

He scrubbed himself well, washing the dirt and grime from his long life of training. As he did, he looked closely at his now unfamiliar body. He was still very thin, but he was covered in muscles—lean but very strong strips of sinew. The Khoshekh training had paid off in the end, he thought.

He couldn't remember the last time he'd had an actual bath. He had swum in the black sea almost every day, but he had never taken the time to wash himself. Reaching down into the water, he pulled up a handful of sandy mud, which he used to scrub himself even further.

When he was finished scrubbing, he let himself float in the water, soaking in its cool embrace and smiling to himself. He had forgotten what happiness felt like. After his hands and feet had become shriveled, he waded over to the banks and pulled himself up. Using one of the tree's roots as a ladder, he climbed up onto the grass.

He then washed his filthy clothes. Something else he hadn't noticed before was that he had a set of clothes different from what he remembered. He must have donned another set of clothes after his meeting with Varic. Instead of a simple black tunic, his garb looked much like the armor of the Khoshekh. It had many designs covering it and was much thicker than the tunic he remembered. His black pants were also made of a thicker material. His boots and belt were also black and had designs on them as well.

He would need new clothes as soon as he could find some. Knowing he couldn't walk around in nothing but his skin, he continued washing his garments and laying them out to dry. Then he lay down next to them to dry himself in the sun's warmth.

In less than an hour, he and his clothes were dry. Putting them back on, he felt almost like he was filthy again. These clothes held on to the things he had done in the past when he couldn't control himself. Despite the way the clothes made him feel—and probably look—he had to press on.

Ryker left the pool behind and continued along the river. He guessed that he probably had another four hours of sunlight left in the day. The Khoshekh wouldn't appear until the small hours of the night, so he thought he had plenty of time. The warmth of the sun, compared to the cold of the Hollow, made Ryker break out in a sweat almost instantly after he left the pool. Even though it was almost too warm, Ryker enjoyed it. He would rather have this than the intense, bitter cold.

His journey along the river took many turns as it snaked its way through the green plains. Every time Ryker rose up on one of the many hills, he scanned the area around him to see if this new hill would reveal anything to him. The only things that were revealed were large rocks sprouting out of the ground and small outcroppings of trees that grew randomly among the tall green grasses. He also noticed a few more pools near the banks of the river as he followed it.

As uneventful as the landscape was, Ryker found it immensely beautiful. The rocks, the trees, and the tall grasses growing on the rolling hills—all were an amazing sight. After seeing nothing but rock and shadow, even the grass he trampled on was marvelous.

The only landscapes he could remember before the Hollow were the shores of Teerah Bay. Many trees grew on the banks, which were lined with millions of small, smooth stones. He had used such stones to skip across the usual calm waters. He would count how many times a stone skipped before sinking into the bay. After he had been abandoned in Tervan, he'd never had the courage to leave the Shuul's borders. He'd often looked out past the Shuul at the landscape, much like the one he was surrounded by now, and wondered what lay beyond. He could remember bits and pieces about the Shuuls and Thraan his father had described to him, about the Spine and the other landmarks on the island. All he wanted to see now was something familiar.

He wished he could travel straight to his parents' old cottage on the shores of Teerah Bay. Maybe there the Khoshekh wouldn't be able to find him. He could work as a fisherman like his father before him. No one would ever know of his past, and he could live out his days there in peace. Ryker truly thought about trading in his quest to warn the Drudin and find the wielder of the light to find his parents' old cottage. He could live like his parents had, and maybe even find himself a wife. But he knew his dark past would eventually catch up to him, so he threw those thoughts of a peaceful life aside.

Climbing yet another hill, he was surprised when he saw something other than more hills. Far off on the winding river, he saw a bridge made of white stone. Expecting to see nothing, this grabbed his attention right away. He hadn't seen it until now because of a large hill blocking his view. Now he had rounded a curve along the river and could see it plainly, but it was still quite far away. The only other thing he could see was what looked like a small wooden building built in the middle of the bridge. He thought he could see the sun glimmering off something on the bridge, but he wasn't sure. Making his way down the hill, he quickened his pace to reach the bridge.

After climbing a few more hills and drawing closer to the bridge, he saw that it was built with great skill and care. He had heard that the Thraans were built of white stone. The King and his army must have crafted this bridge, because it too was made from huge white stones.

It seamlessly spanned the wide river, arching high above the flowing water. Atop it was indeed a small wooden cottage that had been built in the middle. A feeble plume of smoke rose from a brick chimney, revealing someone to be inside.

Standing just outside the door to the cottage was what looked like a man in a suit of armor, much like the Drudin Gaur he had seen in the tavern back in Tervan. That must be what the sun had been glaring off of. Still, being so far off, he couldn't tell for sure.

When he came closer to the bridge, he was surprised at how large it was. From far away, it had looked impressive, but now that he was right up next to it, and the sheer size of the stonework blew him away. The river was more than one hundred yards wide. The bridge arched high above it, spanning the distance without any pillars to help hold it aloft. Great craftsmen must have constructed something this huge. Three carts could pass over it side by side, and there would still be plenty of room between them. On either side of the bridge was a low wall.

Before he stepped onto the bridge, he noticed a toll sign. It read, "Must pay toll to cross, ten pieces of copper, by the order of Drudin Haffin."

Ryker hadn't heard of that Drudin name before. He had only known about Drudin Ashard. This wasn't the river leading to Tervan. He thought for a moment about what to do next. He knew it would be foolish to continue following the river. The sun would soon set, and he would be alone in the dark, awaiting the looming threat of the Khoshekh's appearance to snatch him away. He needed to cross the bridge in hopes that the Gaur would help him. He would almost be better off asking the Khoshekh to leave him alone than for the Drudin Gaur to help him, but he would have to take the chance.

He stepped onto the bridge and climbed its arched stonework. He walked near the right side of the bridge so he could see how high he was above the water. He thought this architecture was amazing. If this was a simple bridge, what would the Thraans look like? Stepping with caution, he caught a glimpse of the thatched roof of the cottage. After taking another step, the bridge gave way to a level spot at its center.

The cottage was built on the left-hand side. Whoever had built it hadn't been the craftsmen who had built the bridge. Unlike the stonework created with great skill and care, the cottage had been simply thrown together. The thatched roof looked like it would let in more rain than it would keep out. The sides were poorly built slats of wood. However, it was a large cottage. It spanned nearly half the width of the bridge.

Ryker saw a Gaur standing just outside the cottage with his head bent down to his chest. He looked as if he was sleeping. He wore a shining breastplate and helm, both very well polished. A long blue feather was sticking awkwardly out of his helm. His limp arms held a spear with which he was propping himself up. He was standing near the doorway to the cottage, and Ryker could hear two voices from within.

The sound of a metal pot being thrown in the cottage woke the Gaur outside. He fumbled with the spear in his hands and had to fix his helmet, which had shifted when he'd been rudely awakened. The helm seemed not to fit on his head.

"Quiet in there!" he yelled to the people inside. "I'm trying to get some shut-eye."

"I'd be quiet if this fool would let me cook the way I have been for the past week!" one voice called back in answer.

"I'm not going to suffer another night of his foul cooking!" another voice said to the first. "I've had enough potatoes to last me a lifetime!"

Somehow the Gaur outside didn't see Ryker. He had once again propped himself up by the spear to go back to sleep. Then suddenly the Gaur must have noticed Ryker, because he shook himself the moment he got comfy and realized that there was someone on the bridge with him.

"That's an odd outfit you have on, kid," the Gaur said, stepping forward. A sword swung from his waist, which Ryker hadn't noticed before. "You look pretty pale," he said mischievously. "Are you all right?"

"I'm fine," Ryker stammered. Then he spoke quickly, hoping his urgency would let the Gaur know the seriousness of the matter. "I need to speak to the Drudin right away!"

"If you want to talk to the Drudin, you have to pay the toll and get an appointment at the tower." The Gaur looked behind Ryker at the now setting sun. "I doubt you'll make it there by sundown, though."

"That's just the thing," Ryker said desperately. "I need to get there before sundown. My life depends on it!" He stepped forward to try to pass the Gaur. The Gaur grabbed his spear with both hands and pointed it at Ryker.

"You won't pass by me without payment, whether in coin or in blood."

Ryker stopped moving forward and put his hands on his hips impatiently, not even recognizing the Gaur as a threat. "I must tell the Drudin something very important. All of Arke is in danger!"

"Well, if all of Arke is in danger, then I need to know about it! So you can tell me, and I'll tell the Drudin whenever I see him next." The Gaur's sarcastic words didn't convince Ryker.

Another pot was thrown inside the cottage, crashing into something with a loud clang that was followed by a curse. "If you touch another one of my pots again, I'll cut you up into tiny pieces and make you into a pie!" one of the voices said in a serious tone.

The other laughed and replied sarcastically, "It'll probably be the best thing you've ever made!" The Gaur in front of him still had his spear pointed right at Ryker's stomach and wasn't paying any attention to the threats coming from inside the cottage.

"The Khoshekh's master, Varic, plans to send Arke into darkness!" Ryker said loudly. "The Drudin must be warned, and Varic must be stopped!" He stepped forward until the Gaur's spear was dangerously close to his chest.

"The Khoshekh?" the Gaur said in disbelief. "You must be one of them: sickly pale skin, black clothes, talking about darkness and the end of the world!" The Gaur spoke like he had just trapped a prized animal. "Hey, boys! I'm going to need a hand out here!" the Gaur yelled, and two more men dressed like him came out of the cottage.

They both donned their helmets and drew their swords as they stepped out. Ryker's instincts almost took over in that moment. He wanted to flee and get away from these armed men. One wrong move and the Gaur holding the spear wouldn't think twice about skewering him.

"Who's this sickly fellow?" one of the newcomers asked. "Who have you got now?"

The pair circled behind Ryker and grabbed hold of his arms just below his shoulders. Ryker struggled for a moment but settled down when one of the men placed a sword on his neck. They held his arms tight, and both of their swords were close at hand.

The Gaur with the spear then lowered it and leaned it against his shoulder. He took off his helmet to wipe his brow and kept it off. "So, what were you saying?" he asked Ryker with a smirk.

"I was saying that the Kingdom of Arke is in danger," Ryker said frantically, pulling away from the Gaur at his sides. "I must warn the Drudin! If you let me cross, I will go straight to him."

"You're dressed like one of them, you look like one of them, and you sound like one of them," the Gaur said, pulling on Ryker's tunic.

"I was taken and tortured by them, but I escaped!" Ryker said. He was panicking now. If the Gaur thought he was a Khoshekh, they might execute him on the spot and throw him in the river.

Ryker struggled between his captors, but when he found he couldn't break free, he spoke up again. "I have seen firsthand what they can do. They are not mere shadows but foes you don't have a chance against. They held me captive along with hundreds of other boys. They trained us, against our will, to one day become like them. I escaped, and I need to warn the Drudin!"

"Sir," said one of the Gaur holding Ryker, "I heard about one of these shadow-keepers appearing in Tervan and taking out two of Ashard's Gaur and almost the Drudin himself before disappearing in a cloud of smoke."

"Oh, shut up. You don't know what you're talking about!" said the Gaur on Ryker's other side who had been arguing with him inside the cottage.

Ryker knew that what the first Gaur said was true. He knew it for a fact, because he had been there. It was funny how he, the one the Khoshekh had been after, wasn't even mentioned in the story.

"Take him back the way he came," said the Gaur with the spear. "If he persists, kill him."

The two Gaur holding Ryker started to turn him around. As soon as they did this, Ryker twisted his body quickly and broke free of their grip. The third man had expected this, and the moment Ryker broke free of the other two, he was ready for him and caught Ryker by the arm.

"What's this?" the Gaur asked, noticing his mark on his hand.

The Gaur held Ryker's hand steady to look at it more closely. When he saw it, his eyes grew large and shifted between the mark, Ryker, and the other two Gaur. The other Gaur now grabbed Ryker once again in a much firmer grasp. The look on the Gaur's face clearly indicated that knew he knew something about the mark that Ryker didn't.

"Where did you get this?" he asked quickly. The Gaur with the spear held a firm grip on his hand. He held it up to show the others.

"Why, what is it?" Ryker asked fearfully. He hoped the Gaur knew what it meant and would tell him.

"Where?" the Gaur asked again, angry and growing impatient. He squeezed Ryker's wrist with his own gauntleted fist.

Ryker wondered if the mark was a bad thing. Maybe it had nothing to do with the light. "When I escaped," he said, "a bright light shone, and the mark was imprinted on my hand. I don't really know how." Ryker spoke the truth, but he was afraid he had already said too much.

"Bind him!" the Gaur suddenly told the others.

One of them sheathed his sword and withdrew a short piece of rope from his belt. "You'll get your wish after all. You're going to meet the Drudin, though not in the manner you wanted."

In a flash, the memories of training came back to Ryker. He moved with great speed and the skill to match. He stomped down with his heel onto the feet of one of the Gaur's who held him. Luckily, the man wasn't wearing metal boots, so the reaction was what Ryker wanted. He then shoved the other Gaur who was fumbling with the tangled rope. He was free of these two. Now he just had to get past the third.

The training from the Khoshekh really kicked in, and his speed was without equal. The third Gaur barely had time to ready his spear before Ryker was on him, yanking the spear out of his grasp and tripping him with the other end of the weapon. The man fell with a loud crash of his armor.

Leaping over him, Ryker dropped the spear and dashed to the other side of the bridge. What he saw waiting for him at the bottom of the bridge was something he didn't expect. Three more Gaur who hadn't heard the commotion yet were looking the other direction.

The Gaur he had just escaped from were trailing behind him, yelling to the other guards, "Stop him!" The other Gaur turned quickly and saw Ryker running their way. Ryker groaned to himself. He didn't know if he could overcome three more of them. Two of them held spears, and another had a large axe. Ryker should have kept the spear he'd dropped only moments before.

Hearing the heavy footfalls of the other Gaur closing in on him, he needed to act fast. The Gaur with the spears stayed near the edge of the bridge, while the one with the axe charged at Ryker. Defenseless, he would have panicked if he hadn't been on a bridge over a river. An escape quickly formed in his mind.

Ryker turned on his heals and ran the other way. The Gaur he had fought near the cottage were almost upon him, and the Gaur with the axe was closing in fast. He hoped the water would be deep enough. It was a long way down, but it was worth the risk.

Running toward the Gaur charging him, he was just about to climb up onto the short wall to leap into the swift current below. Before he got to the wall, he felt the butt end of a spear come crashing down on the back of his head, knocking him forward into the bridge's stone railing. The blow sent stars into his vision and the breath out of his chest. Slowly Ryker's world faded into shadow once again.

17

Bound

Groaning, Ryker woke up to find that he had been bound to a chair. Twisting his body to test the ropes, he pushed and pulled with all his might to break free. The ropes did their job and held him. The movement sent a sharp pain from the back of his head. The throbbing pain made him clench his eyes shut. He could feel dried blood crack on the back of his neck as he tried to shake the pain away.

His eyes fluttered open to find that the sun had set. With the fall of the sun, night reigned, and darkness had resided all around him while he was unconscious. Bright stars were shining in the black void above him. Clouds concealed the moon, although not completely, for its glow could still be seen behind them.

Panicking, he looked all around him. He saw no red eyes, but the feeling that they would appear at any moment haunted him. Scanning around him, he realized that the chair he was tied to was located around the left side of the cottage. Being bound to the short chair cut off most of his line of sight. He was just as tall as the wall on either side of the bridge, so all he could see was the cottage close to his right and the bridge everywhere else. He tried to push himself up to stand, but the way his legs were tied, he could only squat. It was no use. He wouldn't be able to see the Khoshekh coming if they did.

Ryker found it strange that he had been left here outside the cottage without a Gaur watching him. In fact, he couldn't see his captors anywhere. He knew better than to call out to them. If they thought he was still unconscious, maybe they would leave him alone. Maybe he could figure out a way to escape while they thought he was still out cold.

Once again he tested the ropes that held him tight to the chair. They didn't budge. His hands already felt raw from the rough braids of the ropes biting his skin. Still, he struggled through the pain and tried to free himself. He twisted his wrists and contorted them until he couldn't take the pain any longer.

The river below the bridge roared from the swiftly flowing waters. Ryker couldn't hear anything above the noise of the waters, so he continued to search visually in the night. The cottage revealed many slivers of light coming from gaps and holes in the wall. He looked down to see that his chair wasn't mounted to anything, so he began to scoot it toward the cottage.

He was sure no Gaur was watching him, so he figured they were all inside the cottage. The chair made a terrible screeching noise on the stone as he moved, but the loud noise from the river muffled everything. He scooted the chair to one of the larger holes in the wall of the cottage, twisted the chair around, and leaned forward to look inside.

Ryker blinked from the bright light inside the cottage. When his eyes adjusted to the light, he could see into the spacious cottage. The cottage was a very open, with many bunks lining the wall closest to him. On the other end, a fire blazed in the hearth. Near the hearth the Gaur he'd tried to escape from sat around a table. Each had a mug nearby, and they were talking in hushed tones. They still wore their shining armor, which reflected the fire's orange glow. The roar of the river removed any chance of their hearing them. Taking his eyes away from the hole in the wall, he replaced it with his ear. Doing this, he could hear a few of the words shared.

Ryker thought he recognized the first speaker as the Gaur's leader. He sounded like the Gaur who had done all the talking earlier. "Odes and Jerek, both of you will take the boy to the tower at first light." Two other voices groaned in disapproval, and Ryker guessed they would be Odes and Jerek. "On your way back here, gather the usual provisions. This time get better mead. Last time the stuff you brought back tasted like goat urine." Many of the other Gaur added the same comment about getting the good kind of mead.

"Go yourself and pick whatever mead you want," a younger voice shot back. Ryker figured this was either Odes or Jerek.

"You should watch your mouth!" the head Gaur said, threatening him. "It was me who got you this job. Know your place!"

So, Ryker would go to the tower like the Gaur had said earlier. At least that was where Ryker had wanted to go in the first place. There he would meet the Drudin. Hopefully, the Drudin would believe his story and help.

The voices continued talking about the condition of their weapons and armor—and the lack of travelers who brought them tax money, which was what they had been sent here for. Ryker's ears perked up when the one who sounded like the leader spoke up again. "You all know the orders: if we see someone with the mark, whether on flesh or cloth, they're to be taken straightaway to the Drudin. If anyone asks, he showed up in the morning. Otherwise it'll be my head that we didn't take him straightaway."

"It's been a while since I've seen anything on someone's skin," another voice said.

"I've never seen the mark like that before," said another. "It looked like he was born with it!"

The head Gaur spoke once again. "You all know what that mark means. I have been overseeing this bridge for a long time, but I have never seen a mark like this one."

The mark on Ryker's hand must mean something if they were to keep a close watch for anyone having it. Ryker wondered what it could mean. He tried to look down at it, but his bonds didn't allow it. He hoped to find out at the tower, although he knew it probably wouldn't be good news.

One voice said to the others, "All the talk about the shadow-keepers made me question if what the boy said was true. What if there was a threat?" Many of the other Gaur agreed with him as well.

Then their leader spoke up. "Now, don't go getting soft. Guarding this bridge has gotten to all of you! What would we need to be scared of? Shadows can't get through armor!" There was a sound as if he'd struck his armor with his fist. "Besides, the Drudin would've given us word if we were supposed to watch for shadow-keepers. We are, after all, his mighty Gaur!" Many of them cheer and toasted to the strength of the Drudin Gaur.

Ryker pulled himself away from the wall of the cottage. So, they didn't believe a word he'd said, and the Drudin had no idea of the threat Varic posed to the Kingdom of Arke. The protectors of Arke were oblivious to the darkness that was about to consume them. He would have to convince the Drudin otherwise.

Convincing the Drudin while in bondage didn't seem like the best idea, but it might be the only way to interact with him. If he tried to escape again, he would more than likely be killed. Even if he did escape, he would have a price on his head. The moment he showed up in the Shuul, he would be captured. He didn't even know where the Shuul was. His best step would be to go along with the Gaur, bonds and all, to meet the Drudin. They would take him exactly where he wanted to go.

An uneasy feeling came over Ryker. He nervously scanned the bridge around him. All he could see was the gentle arch of the bridge until it fell away. He hoped a few of the Gaur were watching the bridge, but he couldn't count on them. He had almost slipped past one of them in the middle of the day. The Khoshekh could easily get past them in the dark of night without the Gaur even hearing them, let alone seeing them. He knew he would have to keep a lookout himself if he was to stay in the custody of the Gaur. He knew the judgment of the Drudin would be simple compared to the torture of the Khoshekh.

Ryker kept his eyes open for as long as he could. He was worn out from his full day of traveling, but he had to stay awake in case the Khoshekh showed up. The moon still lay hidden behind the clouds; it would be the perfect night for the Khoshekh to appear.

Hours passed, and the roar of the river lulled him to sleep. His nervous mind was no match for his exhausted body. Soon his head was leaning up against the cottage, and his eyes had fluttered shut. He fell fast asleep.

A bucket of water rudely woke Ryker from his sleep. He spit out a mouthful of water, surprised he had let himself sleep. Opening his eyes, he saw two of the Gaur—Odes and Jerek, he figured—standing before him.

One of them held an empty bucket, and the other had a long piece of rope. Their armor shone, even in the first rays of dawn. Each of them had a long feather stuck in his helmet. Instead of the full suit of armor, these two wore only a breastplate and helm of the Gaur's signature armor. The rest of the body was covered by a mail shirt. This would be lighter and easier to walk in.

As it was with the Drudin, the Gaur's appearance meant everything to them. They always wore their shining armor, polished enough to see one's reflection in the steel. Their armor was detailed and well-crafted and had neither dent nor scratch, indicating a priority on appearance rather than functionality.

The one holding the bucket threw it to the ground and drew his sword, gripping it tightly and pointing it directly at Ryker. He said, "Don't try anything stupid or I'll run you through. It won't make a difference to me if we just bring your hand to the Drudin."

The other Gaur untied Ryker from the chair and pulled him up out of it. He then tied a short piece of rope onto the rope that still bound Ryker's hands. He too drew his sword but kept one end of the rope tied to Ryker in his other hand.

"Stay between us, and you'll make it to the Shuul without any holes," said the Gaur with the rope, laughing. He then began to walk to the end of the bridge with Ryker in tow. The second Gaur followed close behind, mumbling something under his breath.

Ryker hadn't noticed before, but neither of these men were in fact men, at least not entirely. Although their helmets covered most of their faces, they didn't look much older than Ryker. He realized that the other Gaur had given the legwork to the young recruits.

When they spoke, they made themselves sound rough and tough, but Ryker now knew better. He watched them more closely. He knew that young men were unpredictable, much like he was. He needed to be careful in order to make it to the Shuul.

Reaching the end of the bridge, they passed by two of the older Gaur. They stood on either side of the bridge with their spears aimed at Ryker. "Have a nice stay at the tower, boy!" said one of the Gaur, mocking him as he passed. "You two keep a close eye on him. He seems slier than a fox."

The Gaur in front of him tugged on the rope to keep him moving, while the Gaur behind laid the flat of his blade on Ryker's shoulder and kept it there while they walked. They sought to intimidate Ryker, but he had endured a life in darkness that the Drudin themselves would fear. He could be out of these ropes with the sword in his grasp before either Gaur knew what had happened. He knew that if he escaped he would only repeat the cycle. It would be better to go with them without any kind of fight. He hoped, if he went along, that he would get an audience with the Drudin.

Leaving the bridge's stone behind, their feet now trod a wide dirt path. It left the bridge and turned sharply left, following close beside the river. The river moved swiftly, its current flowing steadily past them.

Along this side of the river, many more trees grew close to the banks. All around them, more trees seemed to sprout up by the roadside. Although he was well rested, his legs still felt stiff from the day before. The long walk through open and hilly terrain had been very different from his training in the dark.

He was indeed glad he'd gotten some sleep. Even though the Khoshekh could have caught him, they hadn't, and he was still more or less free under the sun. He wondered why they hadn't showed up last night. It would have been the perfect opportunity, as he was unguarded and tied to a chair.

Had the light kept them back? Was it that powerful? He knew deep down that the mark on his hand had nothing to do with the Khoshekh, no matter what the Gaur had said. He could just feel it. The light itself had embedded it into his hand.

The Khoshekh hated the light. They were the complete opposite of everything light stood for. They were cold and dark, instilling despair into the hearts of anyone they came across. He wondered if the Drudin knew more than his Gaur about the mark.

The Gaur led Ryker by the rope as they swiftly followed the road along the river that wound its way through the hillside. Ryker wished he had found a road like this yesterday and not been captured by the Gaur.

Despite their armor, the Gaur moved swiftly up and down the many hills. Having his hands bound in front of him, Ryker found the journey more difficult. The Gaur leading him constantly pulled on the rope, chafing his wrists until, after a time, they were bleeding.

Luckily, the sun was shining, and a gentle breeze blew over the countryside. Although he was bound, he was still in the light, and he was glad for that. It was far more pleasant than being held captive by cold darkness.

As they rose from one of the many hills, Ryker saw far off in the distance a small farmhouse. Sitting close to the river, a large plowed field lay before its door. From this distance, he couldn't see anything in particular.

Getting closer to the farm, he could see a small billow of dust. As they drew closer to the farm, Ryker could see a scrawny old man through the dust cloud. The old man led an even older and scrawnier horse. The duo plowed the dusty fields in preparation for planting. Either the farmer didn't see them, or he didn't pay them any attention, for he didn't look up from his plow.

This sight would become more common the closer they got to the Shuul. In fact, Ryker also saw many fenced-in fields where strong-looking horses grazed. The endless hills beneath them began to level out, becoming a much smoother landscape.

He could see even farther away now, and off in the distance he thought he could see a large blur. He figured that as they drew closer the blur would become the Shuul they were traveling to. He wondered how far away the Shuul might be.

Without thinking much about it, he asked the Gaur. "How far away are we from the Shuul?" Neither of the Gaur responded.

He knew they had heard him, so he didn't bother to ask again. He thought it was strange that the Gaur had not exchanged words, even to each other, since they'd left the bridge. Both of the Gaur had been quiet and walked quickly on the road to the Shuul. The Gaur before kept the rope taunt as he led Ryker. The Gaur behind still had his sword drawn, always keeping it dangerously close as he urged Ryker to keep moving.

When they had left that morning, it had been just after sunrise. Now, from the look of the sun, Ryker figured it had to be close to noon. Without the adrenaline from his anxiety over the threat of the Khoshekh, he began to grow weary. His stiff limbs reminded him of the running he had done in the forest yesterday. The hills and the heat were very different from the bitter cold in the Hollow. The thick clothes he wore didn't help him much out here under the sun. He wished he could just take off the tunic and let his body cool off. Really, he wished he could change clothes as soon as possible. These dark clothes wouldn't help him plead his case before the Drudin.

The road they traveled widened further. Soon other travelers with the same destination accompanied them. Most of them were farmers with carts laden with crops. Some of them led beautiful horses by their bridles. Others walked with empty baskets ready to be filled in the market. All of them gave the trio odd looks. They especially stared at the black-clad young boy in the middle.

Ryker found their looks unnerving. Many of them whispered to one another when they saw him. He found it best to just keep his eyes forward and ignore them the best he could. Luckily, they knew better than to say anything outright to Ryker, for fear of what the Gaur would do. The Gaur barely noticed the people's stares. In fact, they loved the attention they received from the people. Ryker watched as the Gaur leading him put his shoulders back and pulled at the rope every few seconds, showing off his prize.

Occupied by the nearby travelers, Ryker didn't immediately notice the tower that suddenly rose up out of the ground in the distance ahead of them. When he did, it looked like it was reaching up into the clouds, even from this distance.

The King had built the towers long ago, tall and strong. Their structures had withstood countless seasons. This tower could be seen for miles, and it served as the stronghold of the Drudin and his mighty Gaur. It looked absolutely identical to the tower in Tervan. There, it had always seemed to watch over him, no matter where he went.

He would have seen it earlier if not for the Gaur in front of him. His armored frame had obscured the tower standing off in the distance. Now they were going down a small slope in the road, which gave Ryker a clear view to the Shuul's edge not too far away.

Soon the buildings came into view as well. At first they were very blurry, and then their details became clearer. Rising on a hill, Ryker looked down on the Shuul. It was surrounded by three low hills and the river.

Looking at the Shuul, he would have guessed it was Tervan if not for the river flowing in the opposite direction. The structures there were made out of sandstone from the coast, as were the buildings in Tervan. Everything about this place reminded him of the place he had only recently thought of as home.

He wished he could go back to his hideout to find Broff and Shiloh alive and waiting there for him, but he knew he would never see them again. He would be lucky if he ever set foot in the place they had called home.

Far ahead of them, a large cluster of people had gathered, all of them seeking entrance to the Shuul. From this far away, it sounded as if all of the people spoke at once. The chattering noise reminded Ryker of the busy market square. Everything reminded him of that place—the people, the buildings, and especially the tower that constantly loomed over everything.

They had made it to the Shuul. Although Ryker was glad they had made it, he was nervous about meeting the Drudin here. He hoped he was nothing like Ashard, though all of the Drudins might be like that.

Ryker started thinking about what he could say to the Drudin that would make the man believe him. If Ryker told him what he had told the Gaur, he would likely get the same response. But it was the truth, and it needed to be heard. He knew he would suffer either way, so he made up his mind to speak the truth, no matter how unusual it was.

18

Defected

It was well past noon now, and many lazy clouds caught the breeze and made their way slowly across the bright-blue sky. Along the sides of the road were many crop fields. Thousands of perfect rows had been plowed in preparation for the season of planting. Along with many of theses crop farms, there were many fields fenced in by decorated boards.

Looking past the adorned posts and slats were dozens of large, beautiful horses galloping in the green fields. Many boys lined the fences and watched the horses as they ran and played. Men could be seen inside the fences, brushing and grooming the horses to make their hair and coats shine in the bright sun.

They passed by a pair of men, one with a small shovel propped on his shoulder, and the other leaning on the fence that separated them. When the Gaur and Ryker passed by, they both stopped talking and watched the trio walk by. "Hey, what'd this boy do?" one of them asked, pointing at Ryker. Without taking heed of the men, the Gaur continued on. After they had passed, Ryker heard the other man say, "Poor kid. You can look at a Gaur wrong these days, and they'll take you to the tower quicker than you can blink."

Ryker watched the cluster of people who had lined up outside one of the various entrances to the Shuul. Although there weren't any walls surrounding the Shuul, there were arched gateways that the people could enter through. The Gaur utilized each one of them. The buildings were built so close together that these gateways were the only ways into the Shuul. Many of the Gaur stood here, taxing the people who were trying to enter to sell their wares. They even taxed the people who were leaving after buying things in the market.

Instead of going through this entrance, they began to circle the Shuul to the right. As they passed far away from the buildings, Ryker could still see onto the flat roofs. He had always loved running and jumping on the rooftops in Tervan. Those were his own streets, and he knew the quickest ways through the Shuul.

On one rooftop a woman beating an old rug with a stick high caught his eye. She whacked the rug, and dust flew everywhere in a thick cloud. They continued rounding the Shuul until the next arched entrance. Under this archway were three more Gaur. These ones directed a few people who sought entrance to the Shuul around to where a large group of people was seeking the same thing.

"Who have you got in tow?" asked one of the Gaur who stood under the center of the arch. There were three of them guarding the entrance, one near each pillar and the third between them. Each had a sword hanging from his belt and a long spear in his hands.

Without breaking stride, the Gaur continued forward toward them. "Boy with a mark. We're taking him to the tower." Ryker was surprised to hear a response from the Gaur who led him. He hadn't said a word since they'd left the bridge.

"Well, we can take him from here," said the Gaur in the middle. "I'm sure you have better things to do than babysit this boy. After all, there could be more of them out there wanting to cross the bridge."

The Gaur behind Ryker spoke now, pointing his sword at the Gaur under the arch. "You'd love for us to hand our captive over to you! You'd take the credit for finding him in a heartbeat. No, we can take him ourselves to the tower and get our reward. You just stay put and watch the entrance to the Shuul. Just be careful. Many of these farmers can wield a shovel better than you can wield a sword!"

The Gaur standing by either pillar laughed loudly at the mocking remark. Ryker wanted to laugh as well, but he knew he would be beaten for it. Within the slits of his helm, the Gaur's face turned red. "Come say that a little closer, and you'll see firsthand that I can wield a sword better than any Gaur on the island!" he said, dropping his spear and drawing a thick-bladed sword.

Now the Gaur leading Ryker was passing next to the red-faced man under the arch. The three didn't stop but continued into the Shuul. The Gaur following behind Ryker called behind his back to the Gaur at the gate. "I'm too tired from our walk to play swords with you now. On our way back, I'll stop by, and we'll see how quickly you fall." The middle Gaur called out curses upon Ryker and his two guards, but they paid no attention and kept on walking into the Shuul. One of them chuckled to himself at the encounter.

The Gaur leading Ryker knew exactly where he was going. He took many twists and turns, avoiding as many people as possible. Anytime they passed by someone, they got an awful stare. Ryker could tell the people of the Shuul weren't very fond of their protectors.

Ryker kept his eyes focused on the ground as much as possible, while moving through he Shuul. The first few times he'd made eye contact with someone, their facial expressions had showed distaste and disgust. They had no room for pity. From the looks he received, Ryker knew he must look awful. He knew he resembled a Khoshekh and despised himself for it. He hoped his skin tone would go back to its normal tone and that this was only temporary because of his lack of sunlight. He wouldn't mind having one of their black hoods right about now.

In averting his eyes, his ears picked up more than they normally would have, which surprised him. His senses seemed sharper and more tuned than he remembered. The training he had received from the Khoshekh must have had something to do with them. He was well aware of everything going on around him—the sights, the smells, and all the noise.

The darkness he had endured had made his eyes adjust and grow stronger, and he could see small details at a great distance. Although there was much chatter going on in the busy Shuul, Ryker could pick out single conversations, even though he couldn't see who was speaking. His sense of smell was something he wished wasn't stronger. The smells from the Shuul were something he didn't want to think about.

After rounding a corner between two tall buildings, Ryker saw the fifteen-foot wall that surrounded the tower's courtyard. The walls were almost the same height as the buildings they had just passed. The white stone looked exactly like the bridge he had been captured on.

They continued walking beside the wall. Its face was perfectly smooth, without any kind of blemish. The Gaur hurried him toward their destination. They appeared anxious to be rid of him.

Ahead of them, Ryker could see a little of what was happening over the shoulder of the Gaur who led him. It appeared that a man with soiled clothes was speaking to the Gaur with a desperate look on his face. Without hearing them, Ryker could tell that the man needed to see the Drudin.

The Gaur's expression couldn't be seen under his helm. All he did was point in the opposite direction. Walking closer, Ryker could hear the end of the conversation. "You don't understand. I can't leave without speaking to the Drudin. I'll wait all day if I have to!" The man sounded almost frantic.

The Gaur shook his head and simply said, "Drudin Haffin is busy." Ryker hadn't heard this Drudin's name until now. He wondered how far away from Tervan he was, if Ashard wasn't in charge. "Now, leave before I grow impatient!" The Gaur's voice sounded threatening coming through his helm. Knowing that he couldn't change the Gaur's mind, the man hung his head and left the gate.

Reaching the spot where the conversation had just taken place, Ryker realized that it was just before the gate. Its ten-foot-tall wooden doors were flung wide open. The single Gaur watched the entrance to the courtyard of the tower.

Without a single word, only a nod, Ryker's guards passed by their fellow Gaur. He nodded back to them. Hearing something above him, Ryker looked up before they entered the gate. He saw that the rampart above the gate was lined with Gaur in leather armor, armed with bows and arrows, looking down on him. He only got a glimpse of them before they entered under the archway through the wall.

There was a small door to the right, which was closed. Ryker could see through the port that it had stairs on the other side that must lead to the ramparts above. For a moment they walked within the cool shade beneath the wall. Ryker would have loved to remain there for a long while. They didn't, however, but continued through.

Walking past another set of large doors, they entered the courtyard. At first glance, it was very busy with all sorts of activities. The first thing that caught Ryker's eye was the tower that everything seemed to flourish around. Its sheer height was almost impossible. He had never seen the tower back in Tervan this close before. The King had to have built such a masterpiece. It truly did reach up into the clouds.

There were other buildings in the courtyard much less impressive than the tower. They were made of the same sandstone as were the buildings in the Shuul. Most of them were single story with no windows and a single small door in the center. One was a two-story building with a large, flat roof where Ryker could see many of the Gaur polishing their plate armor. They must spend hours up there, he thought to himself.

On the ground floor, which was more or less two hundred yards from wall to wall of the courtyard, Gaur in shining armor could be see throughout. In the far corner on the left side of the tower, Ryker saw a group of about ten or so men. All of them had their right arms raised as one Gaur read them something from a decorated roll of parchment.

Looking to the right side of the tower, a small group of shirtless men trained with swords. Their movements and awkward handling of the blades reminded Ryker of his own training. Even though they were men, they acted exactly as the boys had acted when they'd been handed weapons. The sounds of their swords crashing together could be heard even from this far away.

The shrill sound of a blacksmith's angry hammer echoed around them. Its ringing could be heard far above the striking of swords. Ryker tried to turn to see where the smith was, but the moment he did, the Gaur with the rope yanked him forward. He immediately saw why he had pulled it: Ryker had almost been trampled by a Gaur leading a strong-looking horse. The man was leading the horse in the direction of the ringing hammer.

Ryker found it strange that none of the Gaur gave him a second look. He knew he looked strange—everyone in the Shuul had clarified that—but none of the Gaur seemed to notice him. The Gaur led him over to a well, a low stone wall surrounding a deep hole. A beam was suspended over the hole with a pulley tied to it.

The Gaur behind Ryker dropped the bucket into the well and waited for a splash. He then began to pull on the rope to raise the bucket. Both the Gaur drank directly from the bucket, letting the water spill onto their armor and down to the dusty ground. After they'd had their fill, they continued on without even offering Ryker a drink. He was very thirsty as well, but he knew he would be treated this way as long as he was in their custody.

Crossing the courtyard, they made it to the base of the tower. The gates were made of iron, unlike the gates of the wall, and they were shut. Using the pommel of his sword, the Gaur leading Ryker knocked on the door.

Above them, a Gaur poked his head out of a window. "State your business," he told them.

Ryker thought it was strange that he didn't just let them through. They were all Gaur, after all, he thought. Each one of the men in shining armor served the same Drudin.

"We have a prisoner with the mark," the Gaur next to Ryker called up. "We need to personally bring him before the Drudin." He couldn't help but hear the difference in tone when he referred to Ryker as having the mark.

"I haven't had any word of this matter!" the gatekeeper shouted down to them.

"You're hearing it now!" the Gaur below yelled impatiently back at him.

Ryker could tell that the gatekeeper was obviously giving this Gaur a hard time. "All right, all right, I'll oblige!" he finally said and disappeared into the tower. After a few moments, the iron doors screeched open.

Ryker could hear gears turning as the gate slowly swung open. Once the gates were wide enough, the Gaur entered the tower with Ryker. Once they were through, the gates quickly closed behind them.

Inside the tower was like another world. The thick stone held back all manner of sunlight, and it felt like the dead of night inside, reminding him of the place he had only just escaped. Unlike the sunny warmth outside, the inside of the tower was dank and dark, lit only by torchlight. Ryker was now inside the tower, the stronghold of the Drudin.

It was much larger inside than he had first thought. The circular ground floor was a hundred feet across. Torches hung from the walls, illuminating the place with low orange light. Hanging on the walls amid the torches were many weapons of every sort: axes, bows, maces, spears, and swords. The high ceilings caused a loud echo from the few Gaur who stood within the room, talking quietly among themselves. They didn't pay any attention to the door opening or the trio now entering the room. On Ryker's left-hand side was the beginning of a long stairway that led above. It circled around the perimeter of the wall until it was lost to the next floor above.

At the foot of the stairs sat a boy. He was not much older than Shiloh was. When he saw the Gaur enter with someone, he quickly stood and placed his hands behind his back. One of the Gaur walked up to him. The boy, unafraid, stood and smiled. The Gaur whispered in his ear, and the boy took off up the stairs, running at full speed. The Gaur led Ryker up the stairs after the boy at a much slower pace. As the Gaur climbed, their armor rattled, the sound echoing off the walls.

Rounding the room as they climbed the stairs, Ryker saw many gears of all shapes and sizes built into wall on either side of the gate. Whoever had made this contraption had been very skilled and intelligent. Large stones hung from a pulley system that powered the gears to open the large iron doors. A chain led up to the next floor through a hole in the ceiling. Ryker had never seen anything like it. He wondered who had made the contraption.

The next floor in the tower was lit, not by torches but by sunlight that flooded in through many windows in the stone. Wooden shutters were closed over a few of the windows, but most of them were left open. Standing in front of one of the windows that faced over the gate was the Gaur who called to them before. The chain leading to the gate system hung next to him and traveled through the floor. The man didn't wear a helm, and the only shining armor he had was a breastplate. The rest of his body was covered in rings of mail. He looked out of a larger window and didn't bother to turn as they crossed the room and continued up the stairs to the next floor. Before they climbed up to the next floor, Ryker saw the Gaur by the window look at him out of the corner of his eye.

The next three floors had a wall along the stairs. At each floor there was a wooden door next to the stairs. Torches lit the stairs as they climbed. In this confined space, the echo from the Gaur's armor grew louder and drowned out their heavy breathing. Ryker knew the armor must be heavy from the way they struggled up the long stairs.

The fifth floor was open and had a few Gaur looking through slender slits cut into the tower. They all had longbows and quivers of arrows at their sides. Many buckets full of arrows sat next to the slits as well. A few of the Gaur looked up at Ryker as he and the other Gaur passed by them. A few of them spoke among themselves, while others just turned back around to peer out of the slits.

They continued to climb the stairs, and another wall separated the floor from the stairs. The Gaur leading Ryker stopped him on the stairs just before the door. Two tall, strong-looking Gaur with more elegant and detailed armor stood outside the door. Each of them held a great sword by the hilt, letting the tip of the blade rest on the stone floor. Their thick blades mirrored the torchlight.

The Gaur following Ryker stepped past him and spoke to the Gaur. "We found this boy on the bridge to the north, and he has the mark on his hand, so we've brought him straightaway to the Drudin Haffin."

"We will inform the Drudin," one of them said while the other opened the door to the room and left them. He quickly returned, leaving the door open. "He will see you now," said the Gaur when he returned.

Pulling on the rope still bound to Ryker's wrist, the Gaur yanked him into the room. Ryker was surprised to be looking at a finely decorated room. Richly designed rugs were placed over the stone floor. Sunlight filtering through glass windows filled the room. Between the windows were shelves stacked to the ceiling and filled with all sorts of books and tomes. Many leather-bound chairs were placed next to tables littered with paper. At the far end of the room opposite the door sat the Drudin at a finely carved desk. Behind him, a large stained-glass window let the sun display a rainbow of colors onto him.

Rising from his chair and walking around his desk, he stepped forward to meet his guests. He was a relatively thin man with prominent facial features. His thick eyebrows highlighted his dark eyes. A thin mustache grew just above his lip.

He too wore armor, though his was unlike any Ryker had ever seen. Its steel was polished until it looked like glass. The armor was trimmed in gold. Gold had also been inlaid into the armor all over his breastplate and shoulder pads. At his side hung a thin sword with an elaborately decorated handle.

"Welcome to the tower of Wesfas," the Drudin said in a regal voice. "Whom do I have the honor of welcoming to my tower?"

"I am Odes, and this is Jerek," said the Gaur holding on to the rope.

"I wasn't talking to you, fool. I was talking to our guest!" the Drudin snapped. He changed his tone just as quickly and asked Ryker again, "What is your name, son?"

Ryker was dumbfounded that the Drudin was being so polite. He almost didn't know what to say. "My name is Ryker, sir," he replied in a shaky voice, unsure how to react.

"Well, Ryker, I am the Drudin Haffin. Welcome." He stretched his hand out to Ryker. Seeing for the first time Ryker's bonds, he quickly said, "Let's make you a little more comfortable." In the blink of an eye, the Drudin had drawn his sword, slid it between Ryker's wrists, severed his bonds in an upward slash, and returned the sword to the scabbard at his side. "Leave us!" he said to the Gaur in a rude voice.

The Gaur fell over themselves as they fumbled to leave. One of them snatched up the rope that had just been cut, and they both quickly left through the door, which slammed behind them. Now Ryker was left alone with this unpredictable Drudin.

"Would you like anything to eat or drink?" Haffin asked Ryker politely.

"No, thank you," Ryker said before really thinking about it. He was both hungry and thirsty, but he wouldn't take either from the Drudin. He had heard too many stories about the Drudin to trust them in any way.

"Now, I know you must be thirsty," Haffin said, pushing the matter. He walked over to a table set between two tall chairs. He sat in one of the chairs and poured water from a pitcher into a glass resting on the table. "Please, join me," he said, gesturing with his hand for Ryker to sit with him.

Ryker walked over to the chair and sat, feeling uneasy about all of this. The Drudin handed him the glass he had just filled. Ryker looked at the glass, suspicious.

Haffin pulled the glass back and took a long drink from it. "See, it's not poisoned!" he said impatiently. Pouring another glass, he handed it to Ryker, who drank the entire glass in one long draught. "I knew you would be thirsty," the Drudin said with a laugh.

"Now, why did my Gaur capture you and bring you here?" Haffin asked.

"You wouldn't believe me even if I told you," Ryker said quickly, almost shamefully. "Try me," Haffin replied.

"Well, I have been held prisoner by the Khoshekh along with many other boys. We were made to train in bitter cold and darkness. After I learned their evil plan, I escaped, and I knew I needed to warn someone." Ryker had half expected that the Drudin would stop him before he finished.

"What is their evil plan?" the Drudin asked calmly.

"To cover the Kingdom of Arke in total darkness," Ryker said boldly.

"How do they plan to do that?" Haffin pressed again, staying calm despite what Ryker was telling him.

Ryker had figured the Drudin would become outraged and throw him out, but somehow he was staying calm and seemed interested.

"Their leader, Varic, has an orb that holds some kind of dark power," Ryker exclaimed, standing. "I don't know what kind of power for sure. All I know is that he is very powerful and that the Drudin need to do something to stop him."

"Sit down, sit down!" Haffin said, flapping his hands for Ryker to sit back down. "If this Varic is so powerful, how did you manage to escape from him?" he asked.

Ryker was surprised at how many questions Haffin was asking. It almost seemed like the man believed him. "A bright light blinded me, and the next thing I knew, I was in a forest on the slopes of the Spine."

"The Spine, you say?" Haffin cut in.

"Yes, sir, the Spine. Then I followed alongside the river until I saw the bridge."

"And that was when my Gaur found you," Haffin said as he sat back in his chair, stroking his chin.

"Yes, sir. That was when they caught me and brought me here," Ryker said, looking around the room.

Just when Ryker thought the Drudin believed him and was about to command his Gaur to fight the Khoshekh, Haffin suddenly changed the subject. He asked, "Can I see your hand?" Ryker obliged and stretched out his hand. The Drudin caught it quickly and pulled his hand even closer, almost pulling Ryker out of his chair.

Haffin studied the mark on Ryker's hand for a while. Without saying a word, he turned it over and looked at it from every angle. Haffin's face looked almost disgusted as he inspected Ryker's hand. He then began touching it with his thumbs, feeling each line and studying it further. He began rubbing the mark roughly until Ryker thought he would rub it completely off his hand. His skin felt raw, and Ryker winced from the pain.

Shoving Ryker's hand away from him, Haffin quickly stood and moved across the room toward one of the many bookshelves. His sword swung from his side, and his armor shifted as he moved. Scanning the many tomes, he began to talk to himself. He shifted through many books lying on the shelves as he searched. Ryker stayed in his seat, wondering what the man was looking for.

Quitting that bookshelf, he moved to another. After scanning for another moment, he withdrew a large leather-bound book. A large silver buckle held it closed. He unbuckled it and opened the book, flipping through the pages as he walked over to the table on the other side of the room. He stopped at a certain page and dropped the book onto the table with a loud thud.

Standing back, he looked at the book for a long while. "Come look at this," he called to Ryker.

Ryker hesitated at first, but when the Drudin looked at him urgently, he finally stood and slowly walked over to the table. Ryker stood next to Haffin and looked down at the large book resting on the table. Among the many lines of writing was a large drawing of the exact same image that was embedded into Ryker's skin on the back of his left hand. A chill came over him as his eyes widened. He suddenly felt afraid.

Before Ryker could read what the writing said about the mark, he heard the sword at Haffin's side leave the scabbard. He turned away from the book to see a cruel smile widen on Haffin's face. Ryker froze. Before he could regain himself, Haffin brought the hilt end of the sword down on Ryker's temple, knocking him unconscious.

19

Obscured

Ryker's head rolled on his limp neck and then fell onto his chest with a sudden jerk. Disoriented, he fluttered his eyes open, though he found he was still blind even with them open. He wasn't really blind, but he could tell that something was blocking his sight.

A thick sack placed over his head obscured his vision, though not completely; he could still see bits of sunlight coming through the woven strands of the cloth. It stifled his breathing, and the heat from the sun above made his mouth very dry. His head swam with pain, and he found it hard to concentrate on any one thing in particular. He tried to fight the feeling of disorientation by trying to figure out his current situation.

The first thing he realized was that he was seated on a wooden plank and could feel the grasp of cold iron on both his wrists and ankles. They were heavy, so he figured they were shackles binding both his hands and his feet. He pulled on them for a moment and found that they were chained to the floorboards. There would be no use trying to escape from these.

From the motion of the plank beneath him, he felt that he must be inside a cart traveling on a bumpy road. His mind was still fuddled, and his hearing was nonexistent for some reason or another. His head throbbed with sharp pain, a recurring theme while under the Drudin's care—first the spear blow, and now this. The sack covering his face shifted when he tried to move from beneath it. The movement caused the cloth to pull away from the cut he'd received from the pommel on Haffin's sword. Ryker clenched his teeth under the pain. He did his best to stay as still as he could, despite the movement of the cart he was chained to. The blow had knocked him totally unconscious, and he had no idea where he was or where he was heading.

He tried to remember anything about the page he'd seen before the pommel came crashing down on his head. There had been a sketch of a Khoshekh with dark red eyes and a shadowy face. The mark like the one on Ryker's hand was drawn on the opposite page. Though the Gaur and Drudin often referred to them as the shadow-keepers, above the sketches had been written in bold ink: Khoshekh. He still could hardly believe it. The Khoshekh had somehow branded him with their seal before he'd escaped. The Gaur were right about Ryker. He was one of them.

He would never truly be able to escape the darkness that had threatened to consume him whole. The mark on his hand would always be a reminder of the dark training he sought to forget.

What did the light mean? If anything, he knew for certain that the Khoshekh despised the light and everything about it. So, what did the blinding light mean when he had escaped? The seal had been lit up on the rock, which was what had caught his eye in the first place. He couldn't let himself believe that the Khoshekh were the ones who wielded the light.

However, he knew that Varic was very crafty. He could have fooled Ryker with the light and let him escape. But to what end? What would Varic gain if Ryker escaped? He dreaded thinking about it.

He tried to collect himself. He needed a plan, but he found that trying to form one only made his head hurt worse. It felt like an angry ocean tossed his mind around in its deep, dark waves. Rather than think too hard, he simply let his mind ease. He let it go blank, and he calmed himself until the feeling subsided.

The heat from the sun warmed his tired body, and the jostling of the cart rocked him almost to sleep. He somehow fought the drowsiness and kept from falling asleep. He couldn't rest until he was either free or knew what was going on.

After a while, his mind felt somewhat normal, although the knowledge that the Khoshekh had branded him plagued his thoughts. With his mind now clearer, his hearing returned. Ryker began to try to figure out what was going on.

He could hear hushed voices speaking around him. He figured they were the Drudin Gaur staying close to him in case he decided to try to escape. The noise from the cart reached above the whispers of the Gaur. The cart's wheels groaned and squeaked under the weight of the armored men.

He could also hear the clopping hooves of a horse pulling the front of the cart. It kept the same steady pace as it traveled on a somewhat smooth road. The horse's buckles and belts clinked around as it trotted onward. Every so often he could hear the driver lazily whip the horse to keep it on track.

Ryker tried to see through the woven cloth in front of him, but could see only shadows in front of him. From what he could gather, three Gaur sat in the bed of the cart with him, while a fourth drove. The sun was shining, but he didn't know what time of day it was. The three Gaur seemed to be huddled close together, talking among themselves.

The sack continued to rub directly on the cut from Haffin's sword hilt. It burned with hot pain, but Ryker held back a cry. He didn't want the Gaur thinking a little scratch bothered him, even though it certainly did.

"Well, look who's finally awake!" one of the Gaur said. He must have noticed Ryker moving his head around, trying to get a glimpse of what was happening on the other side of the sack.

Another Gaur yanked the sack off Ryker's face, saying, "Let's see how our prisoner is doing!" The sack tore at the wound on Ryker's head, which made him squeal. He blinked beneath the bright sun and shrank back as the Gaur who had pulled off the sack threw it right back into Ryker's face.

Three of the four Gaur laughed, while the fourth said in a threatening voice, "Leave that on him, you fools!"

"What's the point?" one of them replied. "We're out of the Shuul!" Another agreed with him.

Ryker took the time while they argued to look around the landscape to see anything in particular that would help him if he had the opportunity to escape from these men. He was disheartened to see only rolling green hills in every direction. He was still around the same area as the bridge and the Shuul, so he hadn't traveled very long while he was unconscious. He saw a few trees and rocks like before, but no tower and no farm, and nowhere for him to hide if he needed to. It was a vast green landscape, and he might as well stay chained by the Gaur rather than try to escape and be caught by a much darker force out in the wide-open spaces.

The Gaur who had been arguing with the others grabbed the sack and knelt beside Ryker. The Gaur quickly forced the sack over his head, which caused excruciating pain on his wound. It was worth it, though, because unbeknownst to any of them, a small slit in the sack had ended up right in front of Ryker's eye. He could see out of it vaguely—at least enough to see what was going on around him, which could prove very useful.

"The Drudin would have all of our heads if the boy found out where we're going!" The Gaur who had thrown the sack back on Ryker's head was trying to convince the others to listen to his reason.

"Calm down!" the driver said, laughing as he whipped the horse to speed up. "It's not like he'll live to tell anyone about the forest!"

The forest? What forest? Ryker wondered where they were taking him. Why were they taking him to a forest? He thought the Drudins used the towers as their strongholds in Arke. What did this forest have to do with the Drudin?

"The Drudin gave us strict orders. We're to take him to the forest with the sack over his face so he doesn't see anything and so no one sees him!"

"Were far enough away from the Shuul not to worry about that. Besides, we passed the last farm miles ago. It'll be fine!"

Great, Ryker thought. He was miles away from anyone who might help him—or from a place to hide.

"It will be fine because that sack is staying on him!" the Gaur said sternly, and the others finally gave up and dropped the argument.

They all traveled in silence for a long time. From the slit in the sack, Ryker watched the sun slowly sink into the far horizon. He was hungry from not eating for a day and a half. He felt like something from the sack had stuck in his throat, and his head throbbed with pain. Still the day wore on, and they continued in the rough cart.

As they traveled, the road became bumpier. Slowing the cart, the driver steered the animal along the smoothest course. The other Gaur sat in the cart, silent. Ryker guessed that they had fallen asleep, but from time to time one of them would suddenly look up at him and then look at the rolling hills around them.

At least now Ryker knew where they were taking him, though he was terrified of what would happen when he arrived. What would be waiting for him in this forest?

He knew now that he should never have gone to that bridge. He should never have tried to warn the Drudin about the Khoshekh. He knew better than to think he could trust the Drudin. He should have kept following the river until it met the sea. Maybe he could have found the place where he'd grown up. He could have spent the rest of his days as a fisherman like his father. Now, however, he would likely be a prisoner until the Drudin decided to kill him. But it would be better than living in darkness under the constant fear of the Khoshekh and their hateful red eyes. Anything would be better than that.

After traveling for another few hours, a deep shadow passed over them. Ryker immediately became afraid, thinking that night had fallen on them once more, until he saw through the slit in the sack that they had only entered a dark forest. After passing into the forest, the air became much cooler from the shade of the trees. Soon the path behind them was lost as the trees swallowed them whole.

All around them, Ryker could see tall, strong trees. Though the forest seemed to be thriving, he heard neither bird nor beast. The only noise he heard was the hoofbeats of the horse pulling them and the steady clinking of the tackle connected to the cart.

The sunlight filtering through the trees reminded him of something. He wasn't certain of what, though. He gazed up, passed the pillars of back, at the leafy ceiling of the treetops. The sun made it through the cracks and gaps of the living roof and shot down beams of white light through the branches.

This place felt so familiar, yet he knew he had never been here before. In a flash, he remembered his dream of the old man. The trees, the sun, the weightless movement through the forest—the only thing missing were the sounds of the birds.

The wind blew through the treetops, tossing branches as the leaves caught the air like tiny sails. Some of them broke off and flew away on the breeze. Above the cracking bows of the forest broke the foreboding silence within the forest. The tall, dark trees were daunting as they loomed over the travelers.

Ryker now wondered if the decaying Thraan was actually within the forest. What of the old man? The dream had felt so real, so vivid. It had roused him from the darkness that plagued his mind. It had somehow overcome the power Varic had wielded from the Xahlbris. If this truly was the forest in his dream, then maybe the forest Thraan was here too.

If the Thraan was here, then the old man should be here as well. It was a far-off hope, but it was all he had. He needed to know the truth about the mark on his hand. Was it a seal of light or darkness?

The road they traveled on through the forest was rough and tossed Ryker around. If not for the chains holding him in place, the bumps in the road would have thrown him out on more than one occasion. The cart rocked back and forth as the driver swerved from side to side, leading the horse on what smooth parts in the path he could find. Ryker could see through the slit in the sack that the road was littered with exposed roots and deep ruts from many carts passing through here.

The cart now sped along the forest road on a much smoother stretch. Then one of the wheels dipped down into a deep rut, and the cart came to an abrupt stop. It sent the Gaur in the back of the cart falling all over each other. Ryker would have fallen over too if not for the chain that held him.

"What was that?" one of the Gaur asked as he pushed himself up off the others.

Another Gaur who had already freed himself from the pile of men and metal jumped out of the cart to investigate, while the driver whipped the horse continuously to get it to move. He whipped the horse again and again, but despite the horse's efforts to pull it free, the cart was immobile.

Throwing his whip, the driver exclaimed, "We're stuck! All right, everybody out." Each Gaur jumped out of the cart, leaving Ryker to sit alone.

The Gaur stood near three of the four wheels, stretching their stiff muscles. Ryker tried to look over the edge of the cart to see how they were stuck, but he could only see the ground through the hole in the sack.

"On my count, push," said one of the men as he placed his hands onto the worn and dirty wheels of the cart.

The other Gaur got into position, and when one of them yelled, "Push!," they all heaved on the wheels to get them to turn.

Each man groaned and blew out straining breaths of air. The driver cracked his whip, and the horse whinnied and neighed from the weight, its muscles rippling across its dark body. The cart sounded like it was about to fall apart from the stress. Still it didn't budge.

The Gaur all stopped to take a break, and the driver jumped down to calm the horse.

"Pull the boy out, and we'll try again!" one of the men said with labored breath through his helm.

Now was his chance, Ryker thought. If they freed him from his chains, he could run and lose them in the dense forest. Adrenaline started pumping as he readied himself for his escape. He had to wait for the perfect opportunity.

Ryker was watching the rear end of the cart for a Gaur to climb up and loose him from the chains, so when the driver came from behind him, he was shocked. The Gaur was at his feet, loosening the bolt to his chains. He calmed himself down, and when the bolt was pulled out of the cart, he almost felt freed already. The Gaur led him to the back of the cart and handed him to two other Gaur who roughly pulled him down onto the forest road. One of them pushed him to his seat and turned back to the cart to try once more to get it moving.

The chains were still on Ryker's hands and feet. He moved them, seeing how far they would allow him to stretch. After looking at them, he knew he couldn't run as fast as he normally could but he still might outrun the Gaur in their full armor.

He waited for them to get into position on the wheels of the cart. That was when he would make his move. The driver whipped the horse and shouted. All of the Gaur pushed on the wheels to help them turn. As they strained, Ryker rose to his feet and tore through the trees, still bound by the chains and making all kinds of noise.

Being bound hindered his running much more than he'd thought it would. His strides were cut in half by the chain that connected his feet. The chain that bound together the chains from his hands and feet swung awkwardly in front of him. He pulled the slack from it with his hands, which helped him run much more easily.

Luckily, the Gaur had been preoccupied, and he was a good twenty yards or more into the thick forest before they noticed that he was gone. When he heard them shout, he tried to double his speed, but the chains forbade him from running any faster than he already was. If he had run any faster, he would have tripped and fallen flat on his face.

He could hear the Gaur's shouts and curses coming closer behind him. They were gaining on him. They moved much more swiftly in their armor than Ryker would have thought they could. He needed to find a place to hide as soon as possible. If not, they would catch him.

Just ahead of him, he saw a tree that had fallen over, leaving a dug-out stump the same height as him. Running to it, he squeezed himself into it and did his best to calm down his breathing. He flattened himself inside the log so no one could see him from the outside. The decaying tree was brittle, and anywhere he touched crumbled and fell to his feet. He could feel tiny insects all around him, but he couldn't move. He had to stay perfectly still, or the Gaur would see him.

The moment he got himself settled inside the log and perfectly quiet, two Gaur ran by, passing right in front of the stump. They didn't even look where he was hiding, and their eyes could hardly be seen in the slits of their helms. A third Gaur came into view, running a little slower than the others, and his head weaved back and forth through the trees. Ryker's breathing stopped when the man approached the stump. He was close enough that Ryker could have reached out and touched his armor. Once the Gaur passed from Ryker's view, he let out a sigh of relief. He had escaped.

Suddenly the chain between Ryker's hands shifted upon itself and made a deafening clinking noise within the stump. Just when he'd thought he was free of them, an armored arm shot into the stump, pulled Ryker by the chains, and threw him to the forest floor. He lay sprawled in front of the stump where he had just been hiding.

"Clever boy!" the Gaur said, breathing heavily through his helm. "I've got him!" he called loudly to the others. He walked over and struck Ryker in the face twice with a steel fist, producing stars in his vision, and once in the stomach with his heel. Ryker groaned in pain as the Gaur hauled him up. "That'll teach you to comply!" the Gaur said cruelly with more labored breath.

The fist blows had sent Ryker's head into a swirling mess. What hurt worse was the fact that he had failed to escape. He knew his fate would only worsen if he tried again. The Gaur was right; he would comply now. The only thing left for him to do was to take whatever the Drudin or their Gaur threw at him. He had suffered plenty. This would be easy for him. His life had never been kind to him. Why would it start now?

The Gaur yanked Ryker up off the ground and shoved him toward the road. He was covered in leaves and dirt, which fell all around him as he rose. Ryker's lip and nose were bleeding under the sack, and his eyes watered from the pain of the Gaur's blows. Keeping a strong hand on Ryker's shoulder, the Gaur followed close behind him as they made their way back through the forest toward the cart.

When they reached the cart, the Gaur threw Ryker down and put his heavy boot on Ryker's chest, preventing him from another attempt to run.

"So you managed to catch our runaway," said the cart driver as he slid out from under the cart.

Ignoring the driver, the Gaur who had caught Ryker said to him, "Bring me some water! I'm parched from chasing this rabbit through the forest!" The driver brought him some water and took over watching Ryker. He picked him up and tied him to a loose rope tied to a ring on the cart.

Soon afterward, the other Gaur returned, crashing out of the trees with labored breaths. They too took a drink of water from the skin the first Gaur had asked for. After all of them had rested, the driver spoke up. "While you three were out chasing the boy, I found out why the wheel wouldn't budge. One of the wheels is stuck between two roots! We'll never get it out by pushing! In fact, I think we made it worse." The others complained about the state of the cart. One of them stood and kicked the wheel.

"Which one of you has an axe?" one of the Gaur asked the others.

"I've got this!" One of the Gaur pulled out a small throwing axe from his belt. "I was hoping to test it out on the boy in the woods," he said slyly as he gazed at Ryker through his helm. Ryker was glad he had found the log when he had. He may have had a lot more to worry about than a few blows to the face if he hadn't.

Ryker observed, mostly through listening, though he could see bits and pieces through the small hole in the sack. Meanwhile, the Gaur began to work on getting the cart out of the roots. The sound of an axe cutting on the roots beneath the cart broke the silence of the forest. One Gaur got to work on cutting the roots, while the others stood by, telling him he was doing it all wrong.

After a lot of arguing, many curses, and taking shifts at cutting, they freed the cart's wheel. The Gaur untied Ryker from the rope and chained him once again to the bolt in the cart. Then they piled into the cart around him. The driver whipped the tired horse, and they were on their way once more.

Ryker was glad to be back on the road. He hoped they would reach their destination before nightfall. He still was unsure if the Khoshekh would come for him or not. These Gaur would be no match for a dozen Khoshekh in this forest after nightfall. A hollowed tree wouldn't hide him from their dark sight either.

The driver was more cautious now and drove much more slowly, despite the complaints of the other Gaur. "Do you want to cut me out of another hole, or should I go slower?" he asked them, which shut up their complaining.

Ryker watched the driver as he swerved between roots and ruts in the forest path. It would have been faster just to walk through here, he thought. Once they came to a smoother part in the road, the driver whipped the horse hard to break him into a quick trot. They made up time now that the road was smoother.

The sooner Ryker could have this awful sack off of him, the better, he thought. Though the heat wasn't unbearable, the sack still stifled his breathing and smelled terrible. The bright sun had slowly sneaked behind them, leaving the forest with little light. The thick canopy above had let through only a very small amount of light during the brightest part of the day, and now that the sun was setting, it seemed like nightfall within the forest.

The driver cracked his whip, which made the fearful horse pull the cart noisily. The cracking of the whip was all that could be heard over the sound of the noisy cart. Making their way swiftly through the forest, they sped along the road, driving headlong over any rut or root that was in their way.

The driver sought to make up for lost time, so he didn't bother steering around any of these, which made the ride in the back of the cart almost unbearable. Ryker looked around in the jostling cart and found that he could scarcely see the Gaur seated around him. Although he couldn't see their features, he could tell that they were searching the forest beside them. Ryker wondered if they were drawing near to their destination.

The silent forest dramatically changed in an instant with the noise of clamoring of steel. The sound was still somewhat faint and far off, but there was no mistaking it. Through the trees the sound echoed off the bark of the forest. Ryker could hear the distinct sound of steel striking steel.

Drawing nearer to the clamor, he heard what could only be described as the hoarse cries of men in combat. Fear overwhelmed him. The Gaur were taking him into the middle of a battle. The fact that he couldn't see anything only increased his anxiety. Despite the noise of battle, they continued down the forest road. Through the hole, Ryker could see that the Gaur were unaffected by the sounds of war. He could even sense their calmness toward it, and he did his best to calm his own fear. They obviously knew something he didn't.

Though the sunlight had faded and was barely making it through the canopy of leaves, Ryker saw that they had made it to an encampment of Gaur. It filled the forest around him, tucked away under the thick cover of foliage.

The driver slowed as they entered the camp, until the horse was walking at a quick pace.

The noise he had heard earlier was the sound of Gaur training with swords. Flashes of steel could be seen before they struck and crashed against each other's weapons. The shouts he had heard were other Gaur practicing formations with shields raised. Ryker traveled through the camp, gazing at all of its busy activity.

Now there was no hope of escaping through the woods. It was hard to tell their number, but Ryker guessed there were hundreds, if not thousands, of them training. A large Shuul made from a thousand tents had been raised in the middle of the forest. None of them paid any attention to the cart, let alone the prisoner with the sack on his head within it.

Ryker wondered why the Drudin held such a sizable force hidden here in the forest. Their occupation, given to them by The King, was to keep peace in the Shuuls and Thraans of Arke. They were also meant to keep the bridges and roads safe for travel. This multitude of Gaur was far more than enough for those small jobs. What could the Drudin be planning? He wondered if they had been called to assist The King in faraway lands. If not—and if the Drudin planned on staying—maybe Arke stood a chance against the Khoshekh and the darkness with which they threatened to cover the island.

Though the hole in the sack provided a chance to see some of the camp, Ryker heard more than he actually saw. It was busy with activity beside the training. Gaur were polishing and shining their armor while talking about the many problems Arke faced. He could hear dozens of blacksmith's hammers pounding away on raw metal. The noise caught his attention, and he looked to see through the shadowy forest to see a smith's shop. A burley man hammered away at a piece of red-hot ore on his anvil. The sound of the hammer striking the metal slowly faded as they continued along the road.

Soon, most of the noise from the camp also faded as they passed through it. When Ryker heard the driver say, "Finally!" he knew they must have made it to their destination.

He turned to look through the sack and saw a looming wall in the darkening forest. Its height was twice that of the wall surrounding the tower they had just come from. The white stones had turned a greenish color and were covered in moss in some areas. A few places along the wall had collapsed and been repaired with much darker stone. The stones that had fallen were left to litter the forest floor. This place looked exactly like the dream he'd had. Where in all of Arke could he be?

20

Judged

Reaching the gate, they waited for it to open. Ryker noticed that the light of day had finally been spent, leaving the forest in deepening shadow. Though the sun had set, it was still some time before nightfall officially consumed the sky. They were in the twilight hours, when dusk had not quite settled and nightfall had not yet arrived completely. The world around them was almost absent of all color. The images were only dark and darker, having little contrast between them. The sky was bleak with colors of dark blues and shades of gray. Shadows overcame the once bright sky through the trees overhead. The sound of the old gate creaking open pulled Ryker away from gazing through the trees above him as he tried to get a glimpse of the first stars.

The cart pulled through the gate, which immediately closed behind them with a disheartening thud. He had arrived at the Drudin Thraan. There was nothing he could do now to escape. The area inside the wall was much like the courtyard of the tower, with many buildings surrounding the outer rim of the wall. Some of the buildings had crumbled, leaving behind piles of rubble. Tall trees grew above the walls and stretched their longs limbs over the ramparts and into the courtyard from the forest outside. Many trees grew within, although they were much smaller in size compared to those that grew along the roadside they'd traveled that day. The grounds of the courtyard were wide, with grass covering the floor. Above him the Thraan left a large opening in the canopy of trees. The branches and leaves had covered him all day long, and it was nice to finally see the sky again, even though it neared nightfall.

In the center of the courtyard rose the citadel. Compared to the tower he had seen the day before, this was incredible. Its tall stone rose high above the courtyard that surrounded it. The citadel was not only very tall, but it was also wide, taking up almost the entire courtyard within the walls.

The citadel had a large main tower from which many other taller towers and spires rose. Each tower was a different thickness and a different height. One in particular stretched up and loomed over the trees of the forest. Even though it was nearing the dark of night, Ryker could still tell that it was very elaborately decorated with all sorts of masonwork. Almost every window in the many spires of stone held stained glass within them.

With the sack still over his head, Ryker couldn't see very well. He wished he could have gazed at this place unhindered and in the full light of day. This was indeed the Thraan built for the Drudin, for they loved boasting of their beauty and wealth. Why they had built it in secret, hidden within this forest, puzzled Ryker.

The Gaur roughly tossed him out of the cart and onto the grounds of the Thraan. The driver had stopped the cart close to the citadel's main gate. As soon as the Gaur and Ryker were out of the cart, he heard the driver crack his whip and continue on through the courtyard, leaving them.

The Gaur roughly shoved Ryker forward. Moving him so quickly hindered him from seeing through the sack. He stopped suddenly when he felt two sets of hands on him. He heard a terrible screeching noise, which sent an icy chill down his spine. He moved his head beneath the sack, trying to force the slit in the fabric in front of his eye.

Once he did, he saw a large metal portcullis rise. He could hear gears pulling on chains from behind the walls as the contraption pulled the large gate upward. Its metal teeth yawned to let them enter, releasing its hold on the ground it had recently devoured.

A Gaur shoved Ryker through, and he moved swiftly underneath the threatening teeth, not wanting to stay under them for long. Now they were inside an inner courtyard, which was much smaller. Many torches lit the courtyard, revealing fountains and all manner of landscaping. The fountains basked in the orange glow of the torchlight, making the grim atmosphere of the Drudin's citadel less dreadful.

Ryker knew when they had entered the citadel, because the air had become much cooler than the warmth of the forest. The Gaur knew all the twists and turns of the corridors, which resulted in Ryker's having a hard time keeping up with them. What made matters worse was that in all the shoving and turning, the hole in the sack had moved, obstructing his vision yet again.

Now he had to rely mostly on his hearing to find out anything he could about this place. He listened to every door opening and every footfall as they moved through the maze of corridors and hallways. The Gaur shoved him through a large main door, and after that a series of smaller doors and a few stairwells.

They stopped him abruptly in what seemed like the main room. From the echo created by the room, he knew that it had to be very large. One of the Gaur held onto the collar of his shirt, while the others, from what he heard, climbed up a flight of wooden stairs nearby.

From the sound of the Gaur's clanking armor, it was a long flight of stairs. The Gaur's armor-clad footfalls stepped onto what sounded like stone and then finally fell silent. The Gaur had reached the top. One man's voice echoed as he spoke in a forced, ceremonial tone. "Hail Vas Drudin Rhenus! Hail Drudins Haffin and Ashard," he cried, and it sounded like he hit his armor with his fist. "We have brought the boy from the bridge who bears the mark on his hand."

A reply came from a voice known to Ryker. It was Drudin Haffin, the very man he had sought out for help. The help that Ryker had envisioned couldn't have been further away, seeing how he was being treated now. He didn't want Arke to suffer from the Khoshekh, and he knew that the Drudin were the only ones who could help. And now he knew that they would offer nothing of the kind. In fact, they would deliver the complete opposite.

"Bring him forward!" Haffin commanded the Gaur. His voice echoed down to where Ryker and the other Gaur were standing.

Ryker heard the Drudin's voice echo above him. Haffin ordered his Gaur to bring Ryker forward, though the Gaur holding Ryker at the base of the stairs remained still. Although the Gaur spoke vilely and treated him like a dog, they somehow held to some method of order, always seeming to pride themselves on their military might. Ryker had seen the might of the Gaur in action that night in the bar. It had left him unimpressed.

Ryker felt two sets of hands grab him away from those who had been leading him through the citadel. These new guards led him forward toward the stairs, helping him somewhat up the steps. At first it was hard for Ryker to move up the unseen steps, and the Gaur practically carried him up the long staircase.

Reaching the top, he felt a sudden rush of fear and anxiety. Without his vision to aid him, he instantly became aware of how large the room was that he had just entered. He felt as if he was back in the Hollow with darkness all around him and unseen enemies watching him from every shadowy corner.

"Take that disgusting sack off our guest at once!" Haffin commanded, sounding absolutely repulsed by the way his Gaur treated the boy.

He was yet again trying to gain Ryker's trust by showing him kindness, but no matter what he said or did, he wouldn't have it this time. Ryker knew now to never trust these Drudin, even when they spoke kind words. They were no longer the protectors of Arke that they had once been. Ryker saw that they were just as much a threat to Arke as the darkness the Khoshekh sought to unleash.

Ryker's heart pounded at the thought of being revealed to the Vas Drudin. He felt as if the sack concealed his identity, and he feared what might happen when the Vas Drudin saw him. He had never even heard of, let alone seen, the Vas Drudin. Ashard, however, he knew, and he was afraid that the Drudin might remember him.

Ryker felt a hand on his head as a Gaur quickly pulled the sack from his face. He immediately squinted as his eyes adjusted to the light of the room. He shrank away from the steely gaze of the Drudin. He then peeked through his eyelids to see the bright light brought forth by many torches that hung along the wall. A dozen or more chandeliers hung above them, filled with candles burning brightly. The room was filled with an orange glow from the light of the candles and torches.

For a moment, Ryker stood in awe of the huge room. It was very wide and twice as long. He was taken aback by the height of it as well. He gazed up at the multiple chandeliers hanging from solid oak beams. The beams held up the tall ceiling, and arches spanned from one wall to the other for even more support. The ceiling was so tall that the orange light barely reached past the arches and beams. Hanging along the walls between the arches draped long, dark curtains that reached from the ceiling all the way to the floor.

Ryker switched his eyes from everything above to what lay in front of him. A long blue rug stretched out across the entire length of the room, and he stood in front of one end of it. On either side of the rug, close to where it ended, there rested seven beautifully carved stone thrones. There were four on the left side of the rug and three on the right. The Drudins Ashard and Haffin sat on two of these thrones on the left-hand side of the rug.

At one point in time, there had been a fourth throne on the right-hand side as well. A worn place on the floor was all that remained, revealing that it had been removed ages ago. It only made sense to have eight thrones, because behind each throne, set between two pillars, stood a life-size, lifelike statue of each of the Drudins.

Behind Ashard stood his statue. It was a depiction of him on the field of victory, holding his great sword in triumph. His mighty armor and horned helm could easily be seen in the masonwork.

Haffin's statue looked much more composed. In one hand he held a scroll, and in the other he held his thin sword, the blade resting on his shoulder.

Though Ryker had never seen the other Drudin, he knew now what they looked like from their statues. Each of them differed slightly from the others, although all of them wore beautifully decorated armor and held an array of weapons. Each one looked terrifying. He hoped he would never have to meet them.

The remains of a destroyed statue stood behind the absent eighth throne. The torso and legs of the man stood intact, but the rest had been cut off and lay in a pile its feet. Resting at the foot of this statue among the rubble was another statue of what looked like a large beast. It was just as large as the other statues of the Drudin. It lay curled up at the foot of the statue. It looked like what Ryker's father had described to him as a lion. A man who could have tamed a lion was someone even the Drudin would fear. He wondered why this statue had been destroyed and why the throne had been removed. Who was this missing Drudin?

At the far end of the hall, Ryker saw another set of statues. These were much larger than the ones standing behind the thrones. A huge tarp covered most of the statues' features, though it didn't conceal the shapes of the bodies. Ryker could tell that they were a pair of men standing right next to one another. The statues both had their hands outstretched, reaching out from beneath the tarp. All he could see of the statues' stonework were their forearms and outstretched palms.

Sitting at the foot of the statues was a large man in bright-white armor. His armor was made much like that of the others, but there was no mistaking the fact that it was a bright-white color. Ryker had never seen steel like that before. Resting in the man's lap was a long sword. Its elaborate scabbard held many jewels and gems. The man's hands lay on the sword as if he was always ready to strike someone down.

He leaned back in his tall throne, looking very relaxed and unaffected by Ryker's entrance into the room. His helm had a tall fin on the top of it that ended at his nose. Two small slits were cut for his eyes, and many holes lay in front of his mouth. The tall helm concealed the features of his face. Like the other Drudin, he too sat on a throne, though his was twice as large and far more elegant. It was strange, Ryker thought, for the leader of the Drudin not to have a statue of his own.

"Leave us!" Haffin broke the foreboding silence with a command to his Gaur.

The Gaur shoved Ryker forward and went back down the stairs. Their shifting armor echoed throughout the quiet hall. When they had left the stairs, the hall became unbearably silent. Ryker thought the gazes of the three Drudin would burn a hole straight through him. Their locked gazes seemed to last for hours until they were finally broken.

Haffin again broke the silence. "Come forward, Ryker! You won't be harmed." His kind words stung Ryker like a wasp. He knew better than to believe that he wouldn't be harmed.

Ryker stood in place for moment. He was terrified, waiting to be judged by the Drudin. When he stepped forward to face them, his fate would be sealed. There was nowhere for him to run, nowhere to hide. His life now lay in the hands of the same men he had hoped would help free him from the darkness. But now they would place on him a darkness that resided in the full light of day.

Reluctantly he obeyed and stepped onto the long rug. Still bound by the chains, he shifted his feet to step toward the Drudin. If not for the rug, it would have been a clamorous journey. The chains at his hands and feet clinked and clanked as he walked along the long rug.

He shifted his eyes between the three Drudin. Both Ashard and Haffin had their helms resting in their laps, so he could see the expressions of contempt displayed on their faces. The Vas Drudin Rhenus, however, kept his helm on, and through the slits, Ryker could see neither the whites nor pupils of his eyes. It seemed that a shadow lay beneath the gleaming white helm.

Ryker stopped when he stood directly in front of Vas Drudin, with the others just at his side. His heart hadn't stopped pounding in his chest since the sack had been removed. His sense of fear and anxiety had doubled by the time he stood at the judge's feet.

The outcome of this meeting would determine his fate for the rest of his life. He should never have set foot on that bridge. He should have escaped the Khoshekh and found a place to hide for the rest of his life.

Haffin, still the only one who had spoken, spoke again using careful words. "Welcome to our Thraan. I personally hope the ride here was comfortable."

Haffin was about to continue when Ashard spat out, "Enough with the flattery, Haffin. This boy is our prisoner, and we shall treat him like the traitor that he is. I didn't come all this way to listen to you blabber away with your fancy words!" His was the gruff, loud voice that Ryker remembered all too well.

"It would do you good to learn some manners!" Haffin shot back.

"Enough!" Vas Drudin Rhenus yelled. His deep voice, muffled slightly by his helm, bellowed throughout the hall. The other Drudin immediately stopped their bickering and sat back in their thrones. The hall was silent while Rhenus's booming voice continued to echo throughout.

When the hall was completely silent, Rhenus continued. "Haffin, I will see this mark you spoke of with my own eyes." The Vas Drudin rose up from his throne.

Turning back to his throne, he set his sword on the ground, leaning it against the armrest of the throne. He then took long, slow steps toward Ryker. His white armor shone brightly now, as it was directly beneath the chandeliers. Elaborate patterns were inlaid all over the white steel, which was something Ryker hadn't noticed before.

The Vas Drudin's armor made little noise as he moved, though his footfalls were heavy, and with every deafening thud, Ryker's resolve seemed to flutter away. With every step closer that the Vas Drudin came, Ryker's heart beat faster. Rhenus's long blue cloak swept behind him, following him as he walked toward the trembling boy. Ryker's eyes stayed focused on the slits in Rhenus's helm, where his eyes seemed to be absent.

Now the leader of the Drudin stood at arm's reach in front of Ryker. He was so close, in fact, that Ryker could hear his slow and steady breathing from under the large helm that concealed his face. Rhenus stood there for a few moments, neither moving nor speaking. Ryker could feel his intense stare burning into him. His heart felt like it was about to burst, and the thumping in his chest now felt like a pounding in his head. He couldn't tell if the hall echoed with his heartbeat or if it was only in his head.

The movement wasn't sudden, although it still stopped Ryker's racing heart within his chest. Rhenus reached out and grabbed Ryker's chained hand with his gauntleted one. With an immense amount of strength, Rhenus pulled Ryker's arm up to his eye level. Ryker almost thought he would have picked him up completely off the ground, his grasp was so strong. The chains holding Ryker's wrists together dangled above him, filling the quiet hall with their metal clinking. Ryker kept his face turned away, shamed by what was burned into his flesh. He felt the Vas Drudin turn his wrist over and spin his hand almost upside down. Ryker thought the man was going to break his hand off, his movements were so rapid and painful.

Throwing the boy's hand away from him, Rhenus turned and returned to his throne, this time more quickly. Ryker tried to rub his wrist beneath the shackle, having been bruised by the Vas Drudin's rough inspection. Ryker lifted his head and watched the Vas Drudin walk away from him, his long blue cloak flowing close behind him and leaving a trail of cloth is his wake.

The other Drudin moved their gaze along with Ryker's toward their leader and waited for his command. He was solely responsible for Ryker's fate. Ryker was terrified at what he would say, but Rhenus's words didn't come until he had sat down again on his throne and placed the sword in his lap.

"It is as you said, Haffin," Rhenus said simply. The tone of his voice hadn't changed at all. He still seemed calm and reserved.

Ashard, however, spoke to Ryker in a rage of questions. "How did you get that mark on your hand? Where did it come from? Where did you get those clothes? Tell me now!"

"Calm down, Ashard!" Haffin said. "All will become clear later. The boy told me everything. Right now we need to decide what to do with him." Haffin finished his speech and extended his hand toward Ryker.

"Isn't it obvious?" Ashard shouted. His rage toward Ryker could only mean that he remembered the boy from the bar. "He will go to the mines in Vesthraan!"

The mines? Ryker hoped they weren't anything like the Khoshekh mines his friend had had to endure while Ryker had trained. That hole was dark and filled with despair. He didn't know which had been worse in the Hollow, training to become a Khoshekh or slaving away at mining for some dark purpose.

Ryker's life lay in the hands of the Drudin. Once again he had no control over his future. But all his fear in not knowing what was going to happen to him was coming to a close. Soon he would know what his fate was.

"That is not your decision to make, Ashard!" Rhenus boomed as he raised his voice. "I alone will decide the boy's fate. He will go to the mines only if I say so!" Ashard lay back in his own throne, shrinking away from the Vas Drudin. "Haffin, you questioned him in the tower," Rhenus continued. "What did he tell you?"

"The mark alone tells you his allegiance, my Vas Drudin." Pausing, Haffin rose from his throne to continue while standing. "He told me of a threat to Arke that will cover the kingdom in utter darkness. He confessed that the shadow-keepers would lead the assault. He said they had trained him against his will and that he had somehow managed to escape and get to the bridge where my men apprehended him." Haffin spoke the truth, but the way he said it was menacing. It made Ryker sound as if he was one of those vile creatures he had been enslaved by.

After Haffin had finished, the Vas Drudin seemed to ponder his words for a long while. The room stayed silent while Rhenus sat back in his throne and stared straight ahead of him. Ryker thought his heart would suddenly burst out of his chest from the anxiety of the situation. He stood there, perplexed, waiting for his fate to be sealed.

Finally Rhenus spoke. "Boy, you hold a claim that I see as treason to the Kingdom of Arke, treason against The King himself, The Great King who gave the mighty Drudin power and authority in his absence." Rhenus's voice rose as he stood before his throne, pointing the hilt of his sword toward Ryker. "You say you escaped the shadow-keepers, but I see you dressed as one of them. Your skin is ghostly pale, and you are as thin as the shadows they dwell in. You bear their exact mark branded on your hand. I see the only threat to Arke standing before me!"

Rhenus spoke the truth, and Ryker realized that he had been lying to himself all this time. His face fell in disbelief. Everything Rhenus had said was true. After all the training and being surrounded by the darkness for so long, he thought he had escaped it all when he'd left the Hollow. But he hadn't escaped it. He had become a part of it.

"You will be sent to the dungeons to have that mark removed by any means necessary. Then you will be taken to Vesthraan. There you will serve until your dying breath." Vas Drudin Rhenus had sealed Ryker's fate. "Take him!" Rhenus concluded as two Gaur, whom Ryker hadn't even heard approach him, grabbed him and hauled him away.

"No," Ryker whispered in disbelief and horror. Had he truly become what he despised? His mind was flooded with questioning thoughts, too many to count.

One word was all that came across his lips: no. He whispered it again to himself. Soon he realized what his future would hold. Comprehending his dire situation, he began to say the one word his mind could form, and he spoke it louder and louder. The word grew until it was a hoarse scream as they dragged him away. His eyes were filled with tears, and he didn't even pay attention to where the Gaur were taking him.

Somehow he didn't even care. He wanted to be anywhere, as long as he left the presence of the Drudin. The very men who claimed to serve the absent king had condemned an innocent boy to slavery. The only thing Ryker was truly guilty of was being enslaved and tortured, and for that reason he would be thrust into slavery once more.

He had been stolen off the streets and forced into training. These Drudin who lived by the law and resided with order hadn't given him a fair trial. Where was the justice in forcing a boy who had been abandoned by his family, stolen off the streets, and forced to train in darkness, to spend the rest of his life in bondage?

Not realizing how long he had been moving through the inner chambers, he suddenly found that the Gaur had stopped before a large wooden door reinforced with iron slats. Torches burned on either side of it, lighting the threshold before the large door.

Somehow it looked familiar to him. He blinked away the tears that puddled in his eyes and rubbed them off with his shoulder. It was the exact door from the dream he'd had in the Hollow. The forest, the decaying Thraan, and now this door—how had he not seen it before?

Could the old man with the young eyes be waiting for him in the cells below? A spark of hope flickered in the depths of despair that filled his heart. Though the dream had brought more questions than answers, it had also brought hope.

One of the Gaur withdrew a ring of keys and unlocked the large door. The lock clicked and echoed in the narrow hall. On the other side of the door was a steep flight of steps leading downward. The torches hanging near the wall only shed light on the first few steps, and the rest of the stairwell was lost in dark shadow. The other Gaur shoved him through the door, grabbing a torch as he passed. He continued to shove Ryker down the steep, slippery steps.

The air immediately became cooler as they descended, and the stench of death and decay filled Ryker's nostrils, making him want to gag. The lower the stairs went, the cooler the air became. The darkness confined him, reminding him of the Hollow. His mind urged him to retreat up the dark stairs, but he knew he would be thrown down if he tried to flee.

The torch the Gaur held behind him helped his awkward feet descend the stairs, even though they were still chained together. Leaving the stairs, they entered a long, murky hall. Green moss grew on the old walls. Puddles of what he hoped was water lay all over the floor and along the walls. The ceiling was low, and many of its bricks lay scattered on the floor so that they had to step over or around them. Only a few torches lit the hall.

The Gaur that had the torch led Ryker, while the second stayed behind the boy and shoved him forward. Both of them stayed silent, letting Ryker's own thoughts plague his mind. Their words couldn't harm him any more than his own thoughts already did.

They passed by many iron-barred doors that were firmly locked along the wall to his left. Ryker couldn't tell if any other prisoners lay inside the doors. The silence of the dungeon was haunting. The only noise he could hear were the heavy footfalls of the Gaur and the quiet roar of the torch as it burned the oil-soaked cloth.

They continued down the long, dark hall of the dungeon. The farther they went down the long hall, the worse the walls' condition became. Some of the walls looked like they had been dug out of the ground without even being reinforced with anything.

Finally stopping at a cell door, the Gaur with the keys pulled them from his belt again. Producing one from the ring, he used it to unlock the metal door. He swung it outward, stepping out of the way as the hinges screeched in agony, filling the hall with a terrible noise that made Ryker cringe. Even the cells screamed in terror, Ryker thought.

Thick darkness abode within the cell. Even Ryker's eyes, which had become accustomed to this, found it hard to see into the cell. The light of the torch lay in a pool of orange at the threshold of the cell. The darkness within forbade even the flame's light to enter.

The second Gaur walked Ryker into the cell and stood by while the other Gaur produced another key that freed Ryker of his chains. The Gaur made quick work of unchaining Ryker, and he could tell that the Gaur wished to be out of this dark place as soon as possible.

The Gaur threw the chains in a corner near the door, and they left Ryker in the cell alone, surrounded by deepening shadow. They slammed the door and locked it. Though Ryker had been freed of the chains that bound him, they had been replaced with a much larger and darker prison.

"I hope you're not afraid of the dark, though it would seem you belong here in the darkness." One of the Gaur reminded Ryker of the fear the darkness had always seemed to instill in him, but he felt that the Gaur were more fearful of this dark place than he was.

The Gaur went back up the hall the way they had come, taking the only light with them. No torches hung on the wall near his cell, leaving him in darkness that compared to the Hollow.

Tears again filled Ryker's eyes as he began to weep in bitter sorrow. He felt the walls in the darkness to find a corner of his cell to hide away in. He shrank to the ground and curled up on the floor. He wept bitterly.

He had thought he'd escaped the darkness, but the darkness always seemed to find him. It waited for him in cracks and corners, waited patiently for him to be alone. Then it shrouded him in shadow and whispered vile things into his ears. He would never be able to escape from darkness for good—whether it was unearthly darkness that the Khoshekh brought or this dark cell that the Drudin had plunged him into. He knew he would never be freed of darkness.

Every last thread of hope began to leave him. The old man from his dream wasn't waiting for him here in this darkness. Only despair awaited him. He was a prisoner of the Drudin, condemned for treason against The King and the entire Kingdom of Arke.

The training from the Khoshekh came to him in unexpected memories. Horrific nightmares plagued him, memories he wished would stay unknown to him. He held a past inside him that he had been blinded to. Now that he was free of the darkness that the Khoshekh had instilled in him, he was being reminded of his blind obedience. Scenes played over and over in his mind of the things he had done within the Hollow when he had given in to the darkness and let it consume him.

It took hours of weeping before Ryker finally fell asleep in the dark cell. Whether his eyes were open or closed, he felt a presence within the cell, as if the darkness was a being in the cell with him, pressing in on him and seeking once again to strangle him.

Whether the presence left or his weariness overcame it, he fell asleep. Slipping into a restless slumber, he escaped from the dungeon cell for a brief moment. His mind graced him with a glimpse of the dawn he had watched when he'd broken away from the forest.

21

Condemned

Ryker woke to a fitting noise for a dungeon. A faint and muffled cry came echoing up through the hall. His eyes shot open to his dark cell as his ears were filled with the horrifying moan.

To whom the voice belonged, he was unsure. He didn't know how long he'd slept. Despite the circumstances, he felt somewhat refreshed. As the drowsiness of sleep left his mind, the sound became even louder. Cries of pain filled the dungeon, shaking the very walls around him.

He pushed himself up off the cold floor of his cell and moved toward the door. The next cry he heard sent shivers down his spine. It was a howl of absolute agony. The sound seemed to come from farther down the hall, as though someone was being tortured deep within the dungeon.

Moving his head to one side of the cell door, Ryker tried to see down the hall where a few sparse torches burned low, fending back the shadows within the dark dungeon. Far off he could see a faint sliver of light along the length of the floor. It seemed like light coming from beneath a doorway, and his eyes became fixed on the stretch of brightness. But when another cry came, he shrank away from the cell door.

He squatted down and took a seat with his back against the wall near the entrance to his cell. As he sat there, he felt beneath him the cold chains that had bound him earlier. He picked them up and hurled them against the far wall. With a crash of iron on stone, they hit the wall and fell to the floor. He leaned his head back against the wall and pitied whoever had to endure such pain. Such wailing could only be the result of great suffering. He wondered if the cries had just started or if they had been going on without his hearing them.

His time would come as well, he thought. He knew that the Drudin Gaur would remove the mark on his hand, no matter what the cost to Ryker. The more he thought about it, the more he began to accept the idea of the mark being removed. If the Khoshekh had somehow branded him with the white flash before he had escaped, he would almost be glad to rid himself of it. If the Gaur could remove the mark from his flesh, maybe he could begin to forget about the dark past he had been forced to endure.

He wondered what his life would have been like if the Khoshekh hadn't had shown up on the rooftops of Tervan all those nights ago. He knew his life would have been vastly different from the one he led now. How could a world be so cruel to such an innocent boy as himself? He wished he knew the answer, but he didn't. All he could do was take the pain and hope that one day it would all end.

More cries of desperation came blaring down the dimly lit hall. Although Ryker felt terrible for whoever had to withstand such pain, he felt better knowing that he wasn't alone. Someone down here shared with him in suffering at the hand of the Drudin and their Gaur. In a strange way, it brought him a little peace to know that he wasn't the only one. Another cry came tearing through the dungeon halls.

Suddenly the cries of despair elevated to screams of horror. The sudden increase in volume made Ryker's skin crawl with terror. A door suddenly swung open at the far end of the hall and then closed immediately with a loud crash.

The cries down the hall ended, and soon Ryker could hear the heavy footfalls of someone coming up the hall. Ryker shrank back in his cell. He tried to hide among the shadows that shared the cell with him. He tried to get a glimpse of whomever was passing by, and as the footfalls became louder, he grew more curious at who the person was.

Though it was still pitch-black in the cell and in the hall on the other side of his door, Ryker could almost see the white armor of the Vas Drudin Rhenus as he passed by. His armor seemed to glow in the shadowy dungeon. His feet moved swiftly as he passed, and soon his echoing footfalls fell away as he climbed the steps to exit the dungeon.

Why was the Vas Drudin, the very man The King had left to govern the kingdom in his absence, deep within the dungeon overseeing a torture? It didn't make sense, Ryker thought. Who could that screaming man be—not only that he had to withstand such grueling torture but that he had also drawn the personal attention of the leader of the Drudin? What could he have done to deserve such pain and suffering?

After the Vas Drudin had left, time wore on, and the cries of pain slowly faded. Ryker could no longer hear the ear shattering cries for help. Now he couldn't hear anything past the door at the end of the dungeon. The shadows within the dungeon seemed to grow until the silence that the shadows brought forth flourished.

The darkness that dwelled in the cell with Ryker became a deafening silence almost worse than the cries of pain he had listened to for hours. He almost laughed to himself as he compared this dungeon to the darkness within the Hollow. Nothing could compare to that dreadful place. The very air one breathed was filled with fear and despair.

Just then, the door at the end of the dungeon swung open with a thud. Ryker could hear two sets of feet making their way down the hall toward him. As they drew closer, he could hear what sounded like something being towed across the floor. Ryker's heart began to beat rapidly as the Gaur's footsteps drew closer. He became lost in wonder. He inched his way closer to the cell door until his face was touching the metal bars that enclosed him. Ryker wanted to look upon the face of the man the Drudin had brutally tortured. He had to see the person with whom he shared this dungeon.

An orange glow pushed away the shadows that surrounded the threshold of Ryker's cell. The torchlight bounced off the walls as the Gaur drew closer. The sound of their ironclad feet echoed throughout the dungeon. Ryker could see their armor shine in the torchlight as they drew nearer.

Two Gaur carried a battered and bruised man between them, his limp body sliding over puddles and across rocks that littered the dungeon floor. Ryker saw something shimmer on the man's head. A jagged metal crown has been thrust onto his head, and blood ran down into his hair and down the sides of his face. The Gaur continued down the hall and soon passed by Ryker's cell. He could faintly see the side profile of the man's face, which was battered and bruised. Through the stains on the man's face, Ryker saw that it was an old man with long, graying hair and a beard—speckled with his own dried blood.

Ryker's eyes grew wide, and he fell back into his cell, realizing that his earlier dream had come true. Even in the darkness, Ryker knew that this was the old man from his dream, the man who had spoken one word to wake Ryker from the dark slumber that had been covering him and shadowing his thoughts. Quickly Ryker got back up and looked outside his cell to stare at the old man in disbelief. He was gazing at this man for the second time, though now it was with his own physical eyes. How could he have seen a man within a dream whom he had never seen before—and then see him again in reality? Who was this man?

After they had passed by his cell, Ryker watched as they stopped at the cell next to his. Letting the limp man fall to the dungeon floor, one of the Gaur held the torch aloft, while the other unlocked the cell. From the glow of the torch, Ryker saw that the old man's back was covered in blood and that his clothes had been torn to shreds. Dozens of wounds covered his skin from what looked like the cruel marks of a whip. The old man lay there, lifeless. Ryker couldn't even tell if he was breathing or not.

The cell door swung open, and the Gaur scooped up the old man and threw him carelessly into the cell. Ryker heard him hit the floor inside the cell with a sickening thud. He fell away from the entrance to his cell and slowly made his way toward the back. His mind swam with thoughts and questions about the dream he'd had. After seeing this old man in real life, he didn't know what to think. He heard the Gaur slam the old man's cell door and lock it. His eyes became fixed on the door to his own cell.

The orange glow from the torch outside crept through the iron bars into his cell. He watched in horror as the Gaur began to unlock the barred door. Ryker tried to crawl backward against the wall to get farther away from the Gaur. He knew what they were going to do to him, and he was terrified of the cruel ways they would use to try to remove the mark on his hand. He now had little time to think about the dream and the old man.

The cell door opened with a screech, and the cell was filled with the glow of the torch. The light hurt Ryker's eyes, as they were already accustomed to the dimly lit dungeon. The Gaur rushed inside and grabbed both of Ryker's arms. Despite Ryker's struggle, the Gaur seized him and held him fast. Ryker's strength was drained by his lack of food. The Gaur holding the torch searched his exposed skin and held Ryker's hand aloft when he found the mark.

"It's just like they said," exclaimed the Gaur. "It's here on the back of his hand. It looks like it was branded on him."

"Then we'll just have to burn it off!" said the other Gaur. Pulling a mace from a ring at his belt, he struck Ryker in the gut, who winced in pain as he doubled over. The Gaur pulled him back up and spit in his face. "We heard you're a runner. That's to teach you: if you run from me, you'll get hit! Don't be foolish in thinking you can do anything to escape this dungeon either. There is only one door, and thirty feet of earth separates you from the forest above. It would take you a year to dig your way out." The Gaur laughed.

Ryker knew it would be foolish to try to escape, at least right away, but if the opportunity presented itself, he would try. He would never stop trying to get away from these men, the very men who were supposed to protect Arke and its inhabitants. Instead of doing their job, they were busy torturing innocent boys and old men.

"I know you heard all that wailing from the old man, so I hope you've prepared yourself," one of the Gaur mocked. "We have plenty of special things in mind for you!"

Ryker could immediately tell that these Gaur thrived on the pain of others. It would take all of his strength not to break under their cruel torture. Growing bold, Ryker blurted into the Gaur's face, "I have endured darkness like you can't imagine! Not even your precious armor would shine in that place!"

The outburst took the Gaur aback for a moment. Ryker could tell that they had never had anyone talk back to them before. Pleased with himself, he let the Gaur shove him roughly through the cell door and down the hall. He knew he would suffer worse if he continued to quarrel with the men who had been sent to torture him.

The torchlight helped guide him down the hall over puddles and rocks that seemed to worsen as he journeyed deeper into the dungeon. He could feel the Gaur behind him, burning a hole in the back of his head with their intense stares. He even heard one of them mumble something under his breath.

Up ahead he saw the open door that led to the torture chamber. His heartbeat quickened as he dreaded what would happen once he stepped inside. Unconsciously his steps became slower, and he felt a rough push from the Gaur who followed close behind him. The Gaur became impatient, and both men seized Ryker and forced him through the door. One of them slammed it behind them, locking the bolt.

Ryker's eyes filled with tears of fright as he looked around the room. All the darkness that the Khoshekh had instilled in him couldn't prepare him for this. The room was stiflingly hot, as a fire burned low from within a large hearth that covered almost one entire wall. Torches hung all over the wall, shedding light over many terrible things within the room.

The smell of the room was something Ryker had never tolerated. It smelled like blood, sweat, and suffering. A table littered with many tools lay in front of the hearth. All along the walls and hanging from the ceiling were many chains, some hooked to shackles. Residing in two corners of the room were a table standing upright and another lying flat. Both of them had straps built into them to hold down their victims.

The Gaur threw Ryker into a chair in the center of the grotesque room. One of them threw the torch he held into the fire. Its embers sprang up from the torch. The Gaur rummaged through a barrel near the hearth and added a few logs onto the embers. The shifting of the embers caused tiny sparks to shoot through the air above them. The heat from the embers immediately licked the dry wood, and the flames grew. The other Gaur got to work strapping Ryker into the chair, using many leathers belts and straps to buckle him down.

The heat of the room rose as the flames ascended higher within the hearth. The smoke flew up through the smallest of chimneys. He knew there would be no way he could fit through it, even if he got the opportunity. Ryker immediately began to sweat, and his mouth quickly became parched. He watched as one Gaur went to a rack near the wall that held many long metal prodding tools with wooden handles. The other man held Ryker's arms folded and glared at him.

"Where to begin?" the Gaur asked himself as he looked through the rack.

The Gaur who stood in front of Ryker left him and walked over to his fellow. Pushing him aside, he pulled out a prodder with a leafed tip at the end of it. Without a word, he poked it into the red-hot embers beneath the fire.

"Well, that's not what I would have started with, but you pick whatever you want," said the other Gaur as he walked back to Ryker.

"As much as I'd love to stay here all night, I'm ready for a drink. I'd like to be done with this boy as soon as possible!" said the man with the prod. When he pulled the leaf tip out of the fire, it was already as red as the embers surrounding it. The Gaur spit on the end, and the hot metal sizzled. Turning from the fire, he walked toward Ryker, aiming the prodder at the boy. "Hold him!" he told the other man, a cruel smile spread across his face.

Ryker began to squirm in his chair at the sight of the red-hot metal coming closer to him. He wished he could tear free from the chair that bound him. The straps and strips of leather held him firm. The Gaur put another thicker piece of leather around his wrist and began to pull it away from his body to keep it outstretched.

The other Gaur drew closer until the metal was near enough that Ryker could feel the heat. He began to shake all over in terror. Without hesitation, the Gaur pressed the red-hot leaf onto Ryker's hand. He screamed in absolute pain as his skin hissed beneath the hot metal. Wisps of smoke rose from his hand. Ryker's head swam. He thought he was going to pass out from the pain.

Ryker's agonizing screams stopped when his vision began to blur from the pain. To his relief, the Gaur pulled the burning metal away from his hand. Ryker fought through the pain to look down at his hand, only to see that the mark was still intact. No hint of the leaf had been transferred onto his hand. No trace of the hot metal could be seen on his hand. The mark remained in the exact spot where it had been before. But now it looked like it was bright red, as if the heat of the metal had stirred something within it.

Ryker was just as surprised as the Gaur when the mark remained on his hand. "How is that possible?" asked the astonished Gaur holding Ryker's hand. His voice sounded muffled by the throbbing inside Ryker's mind.

"I just didn't get the metal hot enough," said the other.

The Gaur went back to the fire and angrily thrust the tip into the hot embers. Laying the handle on the stone hearth, he walked over to the side and pulled down on a handle that pierced the stone. Ryker felt a rush of hot air as the Gaur worked the bellows that were behind the wall.

The pain on Ryker's hand did not go away when the metal was removed. It still felt like his skin was burning, even though the leaf-shaped metal had left no mark. He wondered how the seal had remained on his hand despite the cruel effort of the Gaur. Breathing heavily, Ryker watched the metal heat up among the embers. He didn't know if he could take another surge of pain, and the next could be worse if the Gaur intended to make the metal hotter than before. Passing out wouldn't be the worst thing to do in this situation. Maybe if he did, they would bring him back into his cell.

Quitting the handle on the bellows, the Gaur returned to his prodder and pulled it out of the now roaring fire. The metal leaf at the end of the prodder was now white-hot. The Gaur had succeeded in making the metal much hotter than before.

"It'll work this time!" he said in a cruel tone, almost smirking as he walked over to the terrified boy.

Ryker turned away as the metal was once again brought down on his hand. Searing pain erupted through his hand and passed through his entire body. His eyes clenched shut, and he bared his teeth, trying to fight through the pain. He wanted to scream out, but no sound came out of his open mouth. He was in so much pain that he couldn't even make a sound. He could hear the skin on his hand hiss again. Soon his whole body shook, and the Gaur who was trying to hold him down could do nothing as Ryker's arm began to flail.

22

Punishment

The bit of metal on his skin slid off as his arm flailed, singeing the leather around his wrist. The tension from the Gaur pulling on the leather sent him falling backward onto the floor, holding the singed leather in his hand. The other Gaur pulled up on the prodder too late and tried to help his fellow up off the floor.

The Gaur on the floor slapped his hand out of the way. "You almost burned me with that thing!" he yelled. He grabbed the prodder and threw it across the room.

"You should have held him down better!" the other shouted back at him.

Ryker's head hung low in exhaustion. Though he had only lasted minutes compared to the old man, the burning on his hand had taken its toll on him. He couldn't even find the strength to lift up his head to see if the mark was still on his hand. With the throbbing in his hand, Ryker would have found it hard to believe that the seal could still be there.

"It's still there!" one of the Gaur said in disbelief.

Ryker heard him, but he couldn't bring himself to move. He heard one of the men shifting through the instruments that lay scattered on the table in front of the hearth. Ryker jolted up in the chair when the other Gaur doused him with a bucket of freezing cold water. The water surprised him, but it also revived him. Thankfully, some had even landed in his parched mouth. He savored every last drop. Despite the pain that still erupted through his hand, he sat and watched as the Gaur spoke quietly to each other. Their backs were turned to Ryker, so he couldn't tell what they were talking about.

The Gaur spun around from the table. When Ryker saw what he held, despair crept into his heart. One of them held a small knife in one hand and a stone in the other. He set the blade to the stone and sharpened the knife. A wicked smile spread over his face as he scraped the steel on the stone.

"If we can't burn it off you, then we'll have to carve it off!" the Gaur said as he set down the stone. "You hold him this time!" he commanded the other man as he stepped closer. The other Gaur walked behind the chair and put his side to Ryker's shoulder. He grabbed ahold of Ryker's forearm and held it firmly for the other Gaur, who now stood in front of him.

Ryker's heart pounded within his ears, and huge drops of sweat dripped down his face. A lump grew in his throat at the thought of the knife on his skin. He felt the cold steel press against his skin but was surprised when he felt no pain. The burning must have destroyed the feeling in the topside of his hand, he thought. He could still feel the blade and the pressure from the Gaur pushing on his hand, but nothing more. He felt neither pain nor blood from the knife. The Gaur holding his arm cut off his view to the side, so he couldn't see exactly what was going on.

"Hold him still!" said the Gaur with the knife as he pressed the blade down even harder.

"He's not even moving!" the other replied.

"Well, it's not working!" Pulling away from Ryker's hand, the Gaur walked back to the table. Grabbing the stone, he ferociously began sharpening the blade upon it.

"Give it here. You're not doing it right!" The other man grabbed both the stone and knife from him and felt the edge with his thumb. A small drop of blood formed on his skin. "It's plenty sharp! You just weren't pressing down hard enough!" He threw the stone away and came back to Ryker. "He's not just a boy. He's an enemy to Arke! Just look at him, dressed all in black with eyes full of hate. He would cut both of our throats if he wasn't bound!" He pointed the knife into Ryker's face as he finished speaking. Ryker kept his mouth shut, although he wouldn't have argued with the Gaur's words.

The Gaur bent down and held the blade almost flat on Ryker's hand. He pressed much harder than the other man had. Still no pain or blood came forth. Ryker could see that the Gaur was becoming angry. Wrinkles formed on his brow, and his face turned red. He pressed harder until his entire weight was on Ryker's hand. Turning the blade upright, he sliced Ryker's hand as he stood up. On either side of the mark where the blade had hit his bare skin, a thin line of blood formed.

The Gaur threw the knife, yelling in frustration. The blade hit a chain that hung from the ceiling, rattling it, and then slid across the ground. Ryker almost cracked a smile at the failed attempts of the Gaur and the frustration he knew they felt. The Gaur must have seen the joy spring up in Ryker's eyes. The Gaur pulled back his arm and struck Ryker in the lip.

"What do we do next?" the other man asked.

Laughing at the pain he had caused the boy and seeing the blood dripping down his chin, he walked back toward the table. He looked over it, not seeing anything he wanted to use. Then the Gaur walked over to a small shelf in the far corner near the hearth. There Ryker thought he could see vials of many shapes and sizes. The Gaur grabbed one of these and walked back toward Ryker.

"We can't use that!" said the Gaur near Ryker.

"And why not?" the other asked, pulling the cork from the vial with his teeth. He spit the cork out onto the floor and walked toward Ryker.

"You know we're not supposed to use that without the consent of the Drudin, especially not in their absence!" The dissenting Gaur snatched the cork from the floor and tried to take the vial away from the other man, who pulled the vial away from him and continued to move toward Ryker.

Ryker wondered what could be in the vial, or how the Gaur intended to use it.

"The Drudin told us to remove the seal on the boy's hand by any means necessary, and this is one of those means!" Without another word, he poured the vial's contents directly onto Ryker's hand. Once it hit his skin, it foamed up on his hand in a dark, bluish color. The pain it caused was triple that of the hot metal. It froze and burned his skin at the same time.

Ryker clenched his teethed and thrashed violently within the confines of the chair. The pain intensified as time wore on, and Ryker knew he had reached his breaking point. He couldn't control himself any more.

He cried out, "Stop, please stop! I can't take any more!" He wept bitterly—to the amusement of the Gaur.

"So the little shadow-keeper can't take any more. I thought you had endured worse than we could offer."

"I didn't know," Ryker said through labored breaths. "I didn't know it would hurt so bad!" He exhaled and hung his head.

"Not as tough as you thought you were, boy!" the Gaur laughed. "Clean the foam away so we can see that mark underneath."

One of the Gaur poured some water onto Ryker's hand. The cool water felt remarkable as it washed away whatever foam the vial's contents had formed. He raised his head and looked at his hand. His heart sank when he saw that the seal remained.

"What?" the Gaur roared. He lashed out and grabbed Ryker's hand and began to rub at the mark on it. Ryker was almost numb to the pain it caused.

"Where did this come from?" one of the Gaur thought aloud. "It's unlike anything we've ever come across before!"

"Shut up!" the other yelled. "If the Drudin heard you talk like that, you would be in the same seat as the boy!"

"What do we do now?" Both of the Gaur stood over Ryker and looked down at him. His head still hung low, and he peered up at them through his half closed eyes. He knew what would come next. The thought had loomed in his mind when the Vas Drudin had spoken it.

"The only thing that's left to do. Find me the axe!" the Gaur said as he began to stack square logs onto each other near the armrest of the chair.

The other Gaur searched throughout the room for the axe. When the man near Ryker had stacked three of the square logs, he unbuckled Ryker's hand from the armrest of the chair and tied a stout bit of leather to his wrist. He pulled on it until Ryker's wrist was in the center of the log. Sure that the logs were in the right place, he began to help the other Gaur look for the axe.

"You still haven't found it?" he asked as he went through the prodders hanging on the wall.

"I've looked high and low. It must be missing from this room. I suppose we'll have to use a knife." Walking over to the table, he picked up another knife. This one was a little bigger than the one they had used before.

"Do you know how long it would take to do that with a knife? With an axe it would only take one quick chop!"

"Well, unless you can find an axe, this is what we'll have to use!" said the Gaur holding the knife.

"We can find an axe in the courtyard above."

"We can't leave the boy here alone!"

"He's already borderline unconscious, and he's tied to that chair." He pointed to the door. "Besides that the door will be locked."

"All right. I'll go find an axe, but you stay here and watch him. The Gaur who brought him through the forest said he fought them all the way from the bridge and nearly escaped twice." Putting the knife down, he made his way to the door.

"Trust me. He'll be fine. And I need a drink! We'll both go." Without waiting for a reply, he began to tie Ryker's wrist to the chair again.

"All right, come on. We just need to be quick!" Walking over to the large door, he unlocked it and swung it open.

"Agreed," said the other, finishing with Ryker's bonds and moving toward the exit. The door shut behind them, and Ryker heard the lock click.

Ryker sat up in the chair and searched his bonds to find the weakest point to start working on. He wasn't going to waste any time. Although pain was still coursing through his whole body, he knew this would be his only chance before he lost his hand. He would have to escape before the Gaur returned.

The Gaur hadn't tightened the buckle on his left wrist. He had hurried in strapping Ryker in, leaving room for Ryker to wiggle his wrist underneath. The leather strap rubbed his skin raw as he twisted and pulled, trying to get his hand through the loose strap. He could barely hear the departing footfalls of the Gaur as they walked down the hall. He was sure to have enough time to get out of this chair. After that, though, he wasn't sure.

Though the strap was loose, it wasn't loose enough for his hand to slide through it. He couldn't bend over, because the strap draped across his chest held him upright. The only movement he could make was with his fingertips. So he tried another approach to escape the bonds. He slid his arm in the other direction as far as he could and tried to bend his wrist toward the buckle to undo it. He could barely touch it with his fingers; it would have to be enough. He tried to push the strap back through the buckle with the tips of his fingers. It was slow going, but it might work.

After pushing the strap through the buckle for what seemed like hours he had finally inched it all the way through. Now he would just have to get out the metal prod that went through the strap and slide out the other side of the strap. He'd thought sliding the strap through had been difficult, but removing the metal prod proved nearly impossible using only the tips of his fingers. Luckily, all the pulling on the strap while the Gaur had tried to remove the mark had worn out the hole in the strap.

If he twisted his wrist just right, he could almost reach the clasp with his finger. After a dozen failed attempts to remove the metal prod, he let himself rest. His wrist was already sore from the pain.

Suddenly he heard the sound of footfalls returning down the dungeon hall. The Gaur had already returned! He tried frantically to remove the clasp. If he at least freed himself, he would have a fighting chance against his captors. With every step he heard, the Gaur drew closer. His heart raced as his finger fumbled with the strap still binding his wrist. This would be the last time he would ever use this wrist, he thought.

He did it. The prod released from the strap, and he slipped his wrist out of it. He quickly swung his arm toward his other hand to free it as well. From the sound of the footsteps, the Gaur would open the door at any moment. He had both hands free now and he worked them both to free the rest of his body from the straps that held him to the chair.

The lock clicked, and the door swung open. Ryker didn't even bother to look up as he heard the Gaur rush in. All he had left were the straps at his feet, and he fumbled with them. He had almost freed himself.

Running toward him, one of the Gaur slammed Ryker in the face with a backhanded swing of his mace. The blow nearly knocked Ryker unconscious. It did manage to knock him back into the chair as he saw stars float all around him. The other Gaur made quick work in strapping Ryker's wrists again. After the Gaur put his mace away, he helped the other strap Ryker in.

"What did I tell you?" the Gaur said as he pulled on the last of Ryker's straps. "I knew he would try to escape!"

"He didn't succeed. And he wouldn't have gotten past the door, even if he did get out of the chair."

"You don't know that. I've heard that the shadow-keepers can appear and disappear like the very shadows they resemble."

"If he could do that, don't you think he would have by now? Now, what should we do with him?"

Ryker ignored the Gaur and fought to regain his swirling mind. He was relieved to see through his blurred vision that the Gaur did not have an axe. He wondered what they would do with him now?

"We'll just find one in the morning before they send him to the mines," said the Gaur with the mace.

"What if the Drudin find out?" asked the other.

"They wont!"

"He can stay in his cell through the night. He can give the old man some company." The Gaur laughed. He pulled out his mace again and picked up Ryker's face with the end of it. Blood began to trickle down Ryker's chin. "You know what will happen if you try anything on the way to your cell."

They unstrapped Ryker and picked him up out of the chair. The Gaur held on to his arms and walked toward the door. Without letting go of Ryker's arm, one of the Gaur opened the door and grabbed a torch that hung on the wall. A cool draft flew in through the door. The coolness of the hall froze Ryker as they left the warm room, which was still lit by the many torches and fire. Ryker's head still throbbed from the blow, and he relied on the Gaur to steady him as they walked down the dark hall.

More than once, Ryker tripped over a rock on the ground. When he did this, the Gaur holding him simply picked him up and over it and continued on. He could feel their frustration peak. He could easily tell that they were ready to be rid of him.

They made it back to his cell and threw him in without a word. The Gaur slammed the door and made sure it was locked before they left, taking with them the only light left in the dungeon. Ryker fell headfirst onto the cell floor. After a moment he rolled over onto his back and lay there for a while.

Sorrow quickly found him lying there on the cold floor of his dark cell. He didn't know what was worse: being branded by the Khoshekh, or having his hand removed from his arm because of it.

He crawled to the rear wall to rest his back against it. On his way, he stumbled upon the chains that had bound him in the cart. He set them in his lap and sat back against the wall. He dreaded the future that was laid out before him. He leaned his head back and thumped it twice against the stones. Tears began to well up in his eyes. Alone in his cell, he began to weep.

He had been left alone, still branded by the darkness. He would have endured all that pain gladly to have the seal removed from his flesh. The fact that he'd had to go through so much pain only for it to remain embedded in his skin made him distraught. The Khoshekh had made him theirs for eternity by branding him with their mark, which was never to be removed.

Without another thought, he quickly tore the hem of his tunic and wrapped it around his wrist, concealing the dreadful mark. Though he couldn't see it in the dark cell, he knew the cloth covered it. Even if he were to lose his hand tomorrow, at least he wouldn't have to bear the sight of the mark one more time.

Why was this happening to him? What had he done to deserve such pain and sorrow? He wished he had ended it all in the black sea underground. He should have let Broff endure that little bit of pain so that he himself could escape the lifelong suffering that awaited him now. He knew he couldn't escape from this Thraan. Soon he would be left with only one hand. What would he do when he reached the mine with one hand? He knew his fate would be a lifetime of torture that he wouldn't be able to do anything about.

Gripping the chains that lay in his lap, he looked down on them through the darkness. A sinister thought began to form in his mind. He weighed both ends of the chain in his hands. He remembered seeing a long chain hanging from one wall, and he rose and slowly walked toward the place where he thought it would be. He reached up and found that he could touch the chain. Throwing the shackle and chain up onto the chain that hung from the wall, he tangled them together. Pulling down on them, he tested them to make sure they were firmly connected. He stood with his back against the wall on the tips of his toes and wrapped the other shackle and chain around his neck.

He hadn't escaped such bitter darkness just to be enslaved beneath the light. He would be free in life, or he would escape with his death. He was fed up with being enslaved and bound, thrust into the will of whoever had bound him. He had never controlled his own fate—until now. He would control the outcome of this night. He would leave this cold, dark world that had no pity on him. He would leave everything that sought to make his life miserable.

Raising his feet off the ground, all of his weight began to pull at the chain wrapped around his neck. Immediately, the chain cut off the airflow to his throat. A sharp and terrible pain cut into his neck. It would be worth it to rid himself of this cruel world.

He opened his eyes and saw nothing through his tears. There was no light in the cell, and he couldn't see anything in the darkness. It was a reflection of his life. In a matter of moments, his mind began to swirl, spiraling downward into the black abyss that always stood by, waiting to consume him, once and for all.

23

Reunited

Ryker could feel his mind slowly escape into eternal darkness. With every passing second that he didn't receive air, his mind began to fade, sinking into the shadows around him, melting into them until he became one with them.

Just before his light went out completely and he forever left this world, the chain around his neck loosened, letting him fall to the ground. The shackle that had been wrapped around the chain on the wall had come undone. The chains had untangled from each other, and Ryker found himself on the cell floor. He coughed and gagged as his body forced him to inhale precious air that had been cut off by the tight chain.

With every breath of air, his mind steadily became clearer. What had he done? What was he thinking? He began to weep silently. A chill ran over his body. He didn't know if it was from the cold cell or the fact that he had tried to kill himself. He whimpered in the cell alone. He had truly tried to leave this world. His fate had looked dark, without the hope of light to be seen anywhere. He knew now that it had been a foolish and selfish thought. What more could death hold for him than life could?

Ryker clawed at the chain that was still wrapped loosely around his neck. Unwrapping it, he hurled it across the room and rubbed the bruises it had left behind. He drew up his knees to his chest and hugged them close to his body. Letting his head fall into his lap, he wept loudly now. Tears began to roll like torrents down his cold cheeks. He was at the end of himself. He felt that he was no longer Ryker but some kind of shell of his former self. He was a tool for the Khoshekh to use, a prisoner of the Drudin who could do whatever they wanted with him.

With every passing moment that he wept, he could feel the darkness in the cell growing around him. It drained him as if he were in the Hollow. It drained him of something he didn't even know he had. His mind was clearer now, and he could almost feel it. The darkness took away something precious, the way the cold took warmth away from the bones. It stole the light from inside him.

He could hear whispers that grew in the shadows. He began to hear dark voices echoing in the halls. He didn't know if they were in his head or in the cell with him. They were dreadful voices, and their words were vile and full of hate. Though they weren't clear, he knew in his heart what they said. The words they spoke broke him down even further. The words felt like crashing waves upon hard stone, and he slowly began to crumble against the onslaught.

The sound of a click echoing throughout his cell silenced the voices. This noise he knew. It wasn't in his head. It was real. The lock in his cell door had suddenly snapped, echoing through the cell and the hall outside. Had the Gaur returned to finish the job? Ryker's eyes searched in terror for his captors to appear out of the shadows and grab him. He shuffled backward on the floor, sprawling to reach the back of the cell. When he did, he pushed himself up off the floor and rose, pressing his body as far as he could into the corner farthest from the door. He hoped he could hide from the Gaur for as long as possible.

When Ryker saw no light, he knew the Gaur weren't down here. He stayed in the corner for quite some time, expecting the Gaur to come around the unseen corner of his cell and snatch him. When they didn't, he slowly crept forward. Listening closely for any sound in the silent dungeon, he made his way to the door. Hearing something, he paused and listened, but there was nothing more. He continued slowly, moving toward the cell door. His footsteps seemed to echo loudly in the cell. His stiff limbs fell heavily to the floor as he crept. The silence that hung in the dungeon made every tiny noise seem deafening.

When he reached the other side of the cell, he felt the smooth wall beside the door. Letting his hand glide on the stone, he felt for its opening. He could feel the cold iron bar that was embedded into the stone that the door locked into. Feeling further, he could feel the open space between the walls. The door was indeed open.

He pushed his head out into the hall and looked in either direction. The dungeon was completely black. No torches burned, and Ryker couldn't see a thing. Though his cell door had been opened, hope still hadn't found a place in Ryker's heart. He knew better than to let hope make its way into his heart when there was no room for it, especially when there was no reason for it. It was only a matter of time before he was caught.

One question formed in his mind as he stood peering out of his cell into the hall that was cast in complete shadow: how had his cell opened? He stood on the threshold and felt the bars on the door that had been locked earlier.

He knew it wasn't the Drudin Gaur. They would have been carrying a torch and would have immediately grabbed him to finish their work of removing the mark on his hand. Who else would have the key to open his cell? Then a thought sprang up in his mind and sent terror into his body. What if the Khoshekh had finally caught up to him?

He slammed the cell door closed, though it swung back open because it wasn't locked, and rushed back to the corner of the cell. They had finally caught up to him and found him in this dark place, which was much like the Hollow where they resided. Dread gripped him as he frantically searched the black void of his cell, expecting to see it filled with their red eyes. He began to sweat, despite the cold air, as he stood in the corner, fearful of what was about to happen.

As time wore on and the Khoshekh didn't appear, he grew even more worried, thinking they would appear as soon as he let himself calm down. He couldn't let himself believe that he was safe. He needed to stay alert.

Maybe he could escape before they reached him, he thought. His cell was open, so he had a chance. It might be slim, but it was all he had. He quickly made his way through the darkness and out into the hall. Peering through the deep shadow, he felt his way along the hall toward what he thought would be the stairs that led to the Drudin citadel above.

This might be exactly what they wanted him to do. They would let him think he had a chance of escape, only to capture him in the end. Whatever the case, if he could get out of this dark dungeon even for a moment, it would be worth it.

As Ryker passed by the cell next to his, his eyes caught a glimmer of something shining from inside. After seeing only the darkest of shadows for so long, his desperate eyes could pick up the faintest of lights in the darkest of places. He could see a tiny glow of what he thought to be a light coming from the cell. Though it shone in the frailest of ways, it pushed back the shadows within. The light splashed onto the wall opposite the cell. Moving slowly, he followed the wall until his hand met the metal of the cell next to his, its door stood open as well. He gently turned his head and peeked into the cell.

Inside, a single candle sat on a thin rock shelf in the back of the cell. The small candle held a weak flame that flickered on its wick. The candle was only about the size of his finger. Though the candle was small, its flame almost lit the cell with a soft glow.

Below the candle and beneath the light, a man lay in a heap on the ground. His body was bloodied and bruised. The rags that covered him were ripped and torn, revealing his skin underneath. This was the same man who had been dragged down the hall past Ryker's cell the night before. Ryker had heard his screams and cries as the Gaur had brutally tortured him. Now, seeing him face-to-face, Ryker knew there was no mistaking it: this was the old man from his dream. He wore the tattered rags and the thin, gray hair and beard. He was the very same man who had spoken to Ryker in the dream that had woken him from his life of darkness.

His terror of the Khoshekh was diminished with the small bit of light. The fear of the Gaur showing up dwindled away as well. Neither of them found a place in his heart or mind now. Ryker only wanted to help this old man who had saved him.

Ryker stood at the entrance to the cell and stared upon the old man's face. He was so still that Ryker thought for a moment that he was already dead. He stared blankly at him, hoping he would stir at any moment.

When he didn't, Ryker's heart sank. He was too late. When he had made up his mind that that man was in fact gone from this world, he whispered silently to himself, "I am sorry." His heart ached for a man he had never even known.

Ryker was about to turn and leave, when he noticed wisps of hair stirring near the old man's lips as shallow breaths passed over them. Though the hair only moved in the smallest of ways, Ryker knew that he was not gone, at least not yet. Realizing that the man still had life in him, Ryker rushed into the cell and fell at the old man's side.

Ryker gently took off the jagged iron crown that had been thrust onto the old man's head. It looked terribly painful, but the man didn't stir while Ryker removed it. The multiple metal points had cut deep into his head, and blood trickled down his face. The crown was covered in blood and was much heavier than Ryker had expected. After he had taken it off, he laid it beside him, wishing he could cast the wretched thing away.

Ryker pushed the old man's messy hair away from his face, saying, "I wish I had some water to give to you, sir."

"Thank … you." The old man coughed to clear his throat before he continued. "I'm afraid … that nothing … will be able … to save me now. I am on the edge … of this life, standing on the shore … awaiting … the tide."

His speech was labored and sounded like it hurt him. Every so often, the old man would suck in a deep breath of air before continuing. Ryker could tell by the way he spoke that he was indeed near the end of his time.

"Were you the one who opened my cell?" Ryker asked. He had so many questions building up inside of him, but he knew he couldn't burden this poor old man. He tried to stay calm and ask simple questions.

"Yes," the old man said, almost laughing, which caused him to cough even more. After a few moments of coughing and trying to catch his breath, he muttered, "These old bones … still have power … though, not as much …

as they once did." The old man shifted his body while saying, "Help me sit up, son."

Ryker set his arms under the tattered man and helped him sit up a little bit straighter with his back resting against the wall. In helping him, Ryker could tell that one of the man's arms was broken, and it seemed like his legs were as well.

Again a question rose in Ryker's mind, and he asked it without holding back. "Were you the same old man from my dream?" Ryker felt like he had known the man all his life. He felt so relaxed with him. The man somehow seemed familiar to him.

When Ryker asked this, the old man's eyes finally flicked open, and Ryker saw that they weren't the bright-blue ones in his dream. They were different. They were gray. It seemed they had been clouded over after long years in utter darkness. "It was I who woke you … from that dark slumber, yes." The old man's voice was no longer so feeble and weak when he spoke these words. Ryker could hear a difference in his voice, as if strength had been reawakened.

"Who are you?" Ryker asked in wonder. He had not even thought of who this old man with such impossible power could possibly be.

"I am … my father's … son," he said slowly. Ryker's eyes grew wide when he heard him speak those words. Suddenly he knew that he was face-to-face with The King's son. The man's breathing became more labored as he spoke. His strength was noticeably waning again.

Raising his limp hand, he pointed weakly at Ryker's hand, which was still wrapped up with the hem of his tunic. "You bear … my father's seal," he said as his hand fell.

So many thoughts flooded Ryker's mind as he realized who this man was. He looked down, and in the candlelight he could see the tip of the same mark escaping from the edge of the cloth covering his hand. This was The King's seal? Just as Ryker opened his mouth to blurt out a thousand questions, the old man spoke up again. His voice began sounding weaker. With every word the man spoke, Ryker could hear him lose strength.

"Listen to me … Ryker. I know … I know you have many questions, but our time … together … is short." The strength in his voice began to fade rapidly as he spoke, and it was no more than a whisper now. "You must … trust me … in this. You will escape … this place."

Now the old man spoke with feeble breaths that were barely audible. "Ryker, come closer. My eyes … they have grown dim. I wish … to look closer … upon your face."

Ryker leaned closer to him until he was almost hovering over the man's broken and bloodied body. Ryker could see how much strain just speaking had put on the old man. "I shall ... give you ... whatever power is left ... within me. Find me again, Ryker! Find ... me."

The old man stretched out his hand with his last breath. The movement wasn't from someone with fading life in them. He grabbed ahold of Ryker by his arm with much more strength than Ryker would have expected. The moment The King's son touched Ryker, the mark on his hand began to glow beneath the cloth strip. He spoke words that Ryker had never heard before. When he heard them, his heart began to race, and his body felt rejuvenated. Instantly, warmth unlike anything he had felt before began to saturate his arm until it filled his entire body.

Peace rushed through Ryker. Every worry he had ever felt seemed to fade away into the back of his mind. The dark memory of the Hollow seemed faint and far away. The mark on his hand now began to grow warm, though not with heat like the Gaur had used to burn him. Rather, it was a welcome heat, a warmth that Ryker had never felt before. In a whirlwind of light, Ryker felt power course through him like nothing he had ever known.

He could feel everything within him grow strengthened. The cell around him began to swirl with the wind of a hurricane. The darkness around him fled. The candle's feeble light was replaced by a light that no shadow could ever hope to hide from. The mark on his hand lit up with a white-hot light that seemed to burn away the cloth covering it. For a moment, Ryker thought he had gone blind. With one last, mighty breath, the old man gripped Ryker's hand tight—and then was gone. His hand fell from Ryker's arm, and his body went limp.

The light from the seal was gone. The candle still burned, despite the sudden whirlwind. The King's son lay still before Ryker. He had given Ryker his remaining power, and with that deed, he was gone. It was a gift Ryker wasn't worthy of.

The man's limp, cold body was still propped up against the wall. His head hung limp on his chest. Ryker knew he couldn't simply leave the old man like this. He hadn't even known the man, but he had saved Ryker from the depths of the Hollow and from his doom at the hands of the Drudin.

Tears welled in his eyes as he looked upon the man who had just given his own life in hopes that Ryker could be freed. How could someone who hadn't even known him do something like that? Moments ago Ryker had been so selfish as to try to leave this cruel world. But now he had found kindness in the most unlikely of places.

This old man was The King's only son. Ryker was amazed. He had thought The King's son had left the island along with his father. Why would the Drudin capture the person they claimed as their leader? How long had he been suffering down here? Ryker knew it had to be ages. How could someone possibly survive so long under such torture?

Knowing that time was precious and that he couldn't grieve for the man in his cell, Ryker plucked the candle from the small bowl it sat in and searched the room for something with which to cover him. He wasn't surprised when he found absolutely nothing in the room with him. Placing the candle back on the shelf, he gently slid the man off of the wall and laid him on his back with his arms folded over his chest.

Not wanting to leave The King's son alone in his dark cell, Ryker left the candle. At least he could do that much. He would rather stumble around in the dark hall than leave The King's son surrounded by shadow. Turning to leave, Ryker stopped himself at the cell door and turned to look back upon the face of The King's son one more time.

"Thank you." Ryker spoke softly. He wished he could give the son of The King a proper burial, but he knew he had to escape this place before the sun rose on the forest outside or the Gaur returned.

Ryker searched in the darkness near the wall opposite the cells and found a torch to help him see. He returned to the cell to light it from the candle. He looked down at The King's son lying there on the ground. He looked peaceful, as if the thick shadows of this dungeon couldn't touch him. Ryker hoped, if nothing else, that he could find some way to repay him for offering his last strength.

Touching the end of the torch to the candle, Ryker lit it and returned to the hall outside the cells. The torch shone bright in the dark hall. Moving silently and very slowly, he began to walk down the dungeon hall toward the stair. With every step he took, he waved the torch back and forth, searching the hall.

He passed cell after iron-barred cell. The shadows held within them felt like they might lash out at him. The closed doors made it feel like each cell held something terrible locked away. He was glad to have a torch to help guide his way. Ryker made it a point to stay as far away from the cell doors as possible. He walked near the blank wall where the other torches hung.

He continued along the hall of the dungeon. Every small noise made him stop quickly and listen to whatever it was. As he walked, he felt like something was always behind him. He would turn quickly to look, but when he saw nothing, he would turn back around and continue.

A rat scurried out of his way as he approached it. Ryker jumped back even before he realized what it was. Squeaking, it ran off into an empty cell. Ryker was more afraid of it than the rat was of him. Ryker, who had been trained in the Hollow, constantly surrounded by dark figures, was scared of a rat.

Passing by more and more rats, he easily got used to their noises and didn't even stop when he passed by them.

Something crashed behind him. Spinning around abruptly, he lifted the torch to cast its light before him. The light shone on a pile of rubble where he had just been standing. A rock must have shifting from the ceiling and fallen to the floor. He was glad it hadn't fallen right on top of him.

The torch he held lit the way through the shadows that clung to the walls and the ceiling. He was glad to have a light to help guide him over the puddles and fallen stones that littered the floor. Otherwise, he would have stumbled over them.

Soon he saw up ahead a faint light breaking through the shadows near the ceiling. He could barely see the end of the hall and the beginning of the stairs. As he drew closer, his torch added to the dim light above. The light of the torch revealed where the stairs met the worn dungeon floor.

Ryker laid his torch down at the foot of the stairs and began to climb, knowing he wouldn't need the light at the top. It would only be a beacon to the Gaur and reveal his whereabouts. Between Ryker's torch below and the light above, there was enough light to help him climb on all fours up the long flight of steps.

Nearing the top, he slowed and crept up the stairs. He was very careful to make absolutely no noise. He listened closely to anything that moved above him. It was nearly impossible to hear if anyone was on the other side of the thick wooden door above.

Reaching the top, he saw that all the light was coming from the cracks above and below the large door and even through the large keyhole. He stood there, gazing at it. He became momentarily lost in the beauty of such small beams of light pushing away such large amounts of darkness. Realizing that he needed to hurry, he stepped up to the door and looked through the keyhole.

The first thing he saw was that the hall was filled with many torches and candles. Along the floor were many carpets, which would help him when tried sneaking past all the Gaur, he thought. Seeing no one around, he put his ear to the keyhole and listened for a long while. When he didn't hear anything, he knew he had a chance.

His heart pounded as he clenched the two metal rings to pull on the large door. He squared himself up with the large wooden boards and gave the door one mighty pull. The door didn't budge. When that didn't work, he let go of the rings and placed his hands on the wood and pushed. He pushed with all his might, but the door didn't open. It was locked.

He tried once more to push the door but to no avail. Hoping to jiggle the lock free, he tried to shake the door slightly, which caused it the make an awful noise. He stood back from it, paralyzed after making so much noise.

He thought for sure that a Gaur would come rushing into the room beyond the door at any moment. He stood still and listened for a few moments before daring to look through the keyhole once more.

He slowly bent down to the beam of light flooding in through the hole. He had to blink a few times before he could see anything. He was relieved when he saw no one. Ryker breathed for the first time since he had made the noise and sat beside the door, leaning against it.

Turning as he sat, he felt the keyhole and tried to get his fingers to shift the locking mechanism inside. His two smallest fingers on either hand could fit inside. He could feel where the key would move the bolt, but his fingers weren't strong enough to move the bolt to relieve the lock. Already frustrated, he continued to try to unbolt the lock with his fingers. His hands began to shake under the pressure he was putting on them to budge the bolt. Pulling them away, he sank to his seat and dropped them into his lap. They were covered with small cuts from the keyhole.

Having nothing to use as a tool to open the lock, he knew it would be foolish to continue trying to open it with his fingers. He rose and left the locked door behind. He walked back down the steep steps, the light of the torch below casting long shadows over them. Maybe he could find something to use inside the torture room, he thought. He hoped it had been left unlocked. Making it to the bottom of the stairs, he picked up the torch and walked back down the hall.

A hissing laugh erupted within the hall of the dungeon. Ryker froze as it echoed throughout the dark halls, piercing his ears with panic. He had no idea where it was coming from. The echoing halls made it sound like it was all around him.

He knew that laugh. It was the evil, hissing laughter he had listened to constantly in far darker places. A Khoshekh was inside the Drudin's dungeon with him.

His worst fear had come true. They had finally caught up to him. Knowing he had nowhere to run, he quickly made up his mind that he would fight them, no matter how many, no matter if it cost him his life. He wouldn't go back to the Hollow without a fight.

Holding the torch aloft, he tensed his body and spoke boldly. "Who's there? Show yourself!"

He felt a new strength against the darkness. He wished he had had it when he'd first been forced to reside within it for so long. The King's son surely must have given him something, because he indeed felt stronger and bolder against the darkness around him. He scanned intently through the thick shadows that swarmed past the light of the torch, waiting for a set of eyes to appear. He had almost gone all the way back to where he had started. With every step he took, his fear grew.

Suddenly, blazing red eyes appeared where he least expected them. Ryker leaped back to the wall and stabbed at the eyes with the flame. Beside him, on the other side of one of the barred doors, a Khoshekh stepped forward out of the dark cell. Its laughter grew louder, and the hissing noise pierced the shadows within the entire dungeon.

Its laughter stopped long enough for its hissing voice to say, "The son of our great enemy has died this night. I can feel it." He broke into a laugh for a moment and then continued. "I was privileged to listen to him suffer. They will be celebrating within the Hollow tonight." The hissing voice would have made Ryker tremble if not for the light The King's son had given him. When the Khoshekh was finished speaking, it continued to laugh.

Ryker stepped forward and thrust the torch into the cell with the Khoshekh. It slunk back from the light that splashed over the entire cell. The Khoshekh hissed madly at Ryker and tried to hide its face with its hands. Ryker pulled the torch back and took two steps away from the cell, hoping to lure the Khoshekh back to him.

When the Khoshekh stepped closer to the door, Ryker looked deep into the red eyes shrouded in darkness and said, "I have suffered years under the torturous training from your master, but I prevailed! I escaped the darkness of the Hollow, and I will escape this place! All I have ever known is bondage, and that ends tonight!"

Then Ryker tore off the cloth and held up the mark on his hand. It still glowed slightly from the contact of The King's son. "I know now that this isn't the brand of the Khoshekh. It is the seal of The King! He wields a light that will burn away all the shadow and darkness with which Varic and you Khoshekh seek to cover Arke!" Ryker could feel his strength peak, and he puffed out his chest and clenched his fist. He believed every word he had said, though it seemed as if they had come from somewhere else.

The Khoshekh burst into a wickedly hysterical laugh. Ryker watched as it fell with its red eyes to the floor and rolled around, its evil laughter growing louder and more hideous. It hissed and screamed as Ryker slammed the door and left it there in the cell. As he walked away, he could hear the Khoshekh stumble and rise.

The Khoshekh shouted through the bars of its door, "My brothers will find you! They will find you and bring you back to our master!" Its laughter screeched after Ryker as he continued to walk away.

Ryker stopped at the cell where he had left the old man. The Khoshekh's laughter still reverberated on the walls of the dungeon. Stepping through the door, Ryker was amazed at what he saw—or didn't see. He stood in shock when he saw that the cell was empty. The candle had already burned low, and it gave off a faint, yellowish light. He rushed to the corner where The King's son had lain, but all that remained was a large bloodstain and a torn piece of clothing. Tears began to fill his eyes. Ryker would have wept in the cell for hours, but he heard a loud noise up the hall that made him press on.

He heard, or thought he heard, the noise of the bolt on the lock shifting at the top of the stairs and the large door opening. It was a very distinct sound. He was almost certain that was what it was. He quickly stepped out of the cell and flew down the long hall toward the chamber at the other end of the dungeon. The torch in his hand burned brighter as he ran. The flame roared against the air blowing past it. He only hoped he could find something that would enable him to escape. He knew The King's son wouldn't have wasted his remaining strength on Ryker only for him to be caught and killed.

Though he'd heard the large door open, he didn't hear any noise other than his feet crashing on the stone floor. Even the Khoshekh's laughter had stopped, or maybe he was just too far away to hear it. He was expecting the Gaur to come after him at any moment with their sharp blades and foul tempers. He was glad as time wore on that they didn't, and he remained alone in the dungeon.

The darkness flew away from the light of the torch as he ran. Passing cell after empty cell, he was eager to break free from this place. Making it to the end of the hall, he almost crashed into the large door that sprang suddenly out of the shadows at the light of the torch. He stopped himself just in time and was glad to find the room unlocked.

He quickly closed the door behind him and locked the bolt, even though he knew that the Gaur would have a key if they found him. Running around the room, Ryker lit every torch and stirred the fire in the hearth. He threw multiple logs into it, and soon the fire blazed. Now light and warmth flooded the room. It was a good feeling to have light all around him instead of the dungeon's more natural darkness.

Heading back to the door, he shoved and piled anything he could move in front of the door—boxes, barrels, anything he could easily shove across the floor to barricade himself in. If the Gaur made it here, they would have trouble opening the door, even if they had a key.

Turning back to the room, he began searching everywhere for a secret passage or any other way out. He ran his hand over every wall, looking up and down each one until he'd scanned every brick. When he found nothing, he began looking through all the tools and contraptions that filled the room. When he came up with nothing after that, he walked over to the hearth.

The fire burned hot, but Ryker dared to step near it and inspect the small chimney the smoke escaped through. He leaned almost directly over the flames, which made him sweat instantly. He had noticed the chimney when he had come here the night before. Now, after seeing it up close, he realized that the Drudin had built it small enough so that no one would ever be able to fit through it. The chimney was no bigger than the size of Ryker's head, and besides that, a metal grate had been built about a foot up into the opening, blocking any passage.

He moved over to the center of the room and looked around. "What am I missing?" he asked himself. He knew he had to be missing something.

He thought long and hard about his options. He knew that one way or another he could get out of this place. He had to. He could gather a few things here that might help him fight off the Drudin upstairs. Maybe he could find something to pick the lock in the door at the top of the stairs. Then an idea sprang up in his mind: what if there was a passage inside one of the empty cells within the dungeon?

He then began frantically throwing aside all of the things he had just piled in front of the door, tossing them away so he could search the rest of the dungeon. He knew that looking through every cell would take all night, and he could only hope that he had enough time to find an escape before morning, before the Gaur returned and he lost his hand.

Soon he threw the last barrel out of the way and unlocked the door. He pulled it open, pushing the remaining things aside. With the door now open, he peered out of it to make sure the coast was clear. He was glad he did, because far off down the hall he could see an orange tint to the black dungeon. Someone with a torch was at the other end of the hall.

Ryker threw himself back into the room and shut the door, quickly but quietly. Was it already morning? There was no time for him to search the other cells. There had to be something he had missed in this room. He knew now that he didn't have enough time to pile everything back in front of the door. He had to find a way out or be captured.

"Ach!" he cried out suddenly.

The seal on his hand stung with a sharp pain. It stole his racing mind away from all of the thoughts that flew through it. He looked down at his hand to see that the seal was glowing with a soft white light. He raised it up to his face to inspect the light and watched it brighten, though only slightly. Stretching it out in front of him, it grew brighter again. Taking a step toward the door it dimmed. Was the seal on his hand guiding him? Turning, he took two steps toward the back wall, and it brightened again. How was this possible?

The next thing he knew, he found himself standing at arm's reach in front of the back wall. He placed both hands on it and began searching every crack and every brick. His left hand somehow stuck to a spot on the wall, and despite his frantic pulling, it wouldn't move. Unexpectedly, the seal on his hand began to pulsate with light. Suddenly, all of the torches went out, along with the fire, and the air around Ryker began to swirl with a mighty wind. The seal began to flash with a white light until it almost blinded him. Then he could feel a fire burn through him, which started in his chest and flowed through his arm until it escaped out of his hand.

"Se Kruh Ke!" The words sprang out of Ryker's mouth, unknown words from an unknown source.

As the words left his lips, a force stronger than the burning sensation erupted through the center of Ryker, ran through every muscle in his arm, and went out through his hand. With a sound like a clap of thunder, the force sent stones and earth flying as it blasted a hole through the corner of the wall and ceiling. Chunks of debris flew everywhere. The explosion lasted only a moment, but the shower of dirt and dust hung in the air for a while. Ryker was knocked backward by the blast, which sent him to the floor.

24

Immersed

The wall and ceiling where Ryker had been standing had been blown away. His ears rang from the blast, and his body felt tremendously weak. He felt like he couldn't move. It was as if the blast had used some kind of unknown energy, leaving him drained.

Ryker coughed. His throat was dry from all the dust in the air. He wiped the debris off his face and labored to sit up. Pushing away a few stones that had fallen on him, he scooted back to the table behind him. He leaned his back against one of the legs and rested there. He felt weak just from sliding on the ground and sitting up.

Looking through blurry eyes, he took in his new surroundings. Where the wall had stood, there was now an even slope up to the forest above. Through the hole he'd made, he could see the tops of the trees as a bright moon shone through their canopy. Whatever power The King's son had given him was certainly a gift. He had somehow made his own path out of the dungeon.

Ryker sat on the floor for a while. His head pounded and his ears rang. He was completely dumbfounded at what had just happen. The wall had just exploded because of him, because of the seal on his hand, because of the strange words he had spoken.

He sat there while the dust and dirt continued to rain down on him. He couldn't bring himself to move. Whatever power he'd used, whether it was The King's son's or his own, it seemed to have drained all his energy. He knew he needed to move, but he just couldn't bring himself to do it. He needed to start running. Every Gaur in the Thraan would have heard that explosion. Soon he would have the mighty Gaur of the Drudin searching for the source of the noise.

Picking himself up, he slowly climbed up and out of the hole. His weary limbs ached as he used them to climb over the stones and rocks that had once held him confined.

When he neared the top of the slope, he had to jump up and get a grip on a tree root to pull himself out. He rolled onto the grass and lay on his back, admiring the trees flowing in the nighttime breeze. He sat up and felt the wind blowing fresh air all around him. He breathed in deeply. He was free from the dungeon.

Looking all around him, he couldn't see the walls of the Thraan. He knew he was close, but luckily he wasn't close enough to be seen. He needed to get into the forest and find a place to hide before anyone saw him or the Drudin found out about the hole he had made in their dungeon. He knew he hadn't escaped just yet.

Many trees grew around him, standing many feet apart from each other in a glade. In one direction he could easily tell that the trees thickened and grew closer together. The moon above shone brightly all around him and almost as if it was the light of day, though this light was bluish in color. Short grass grew beneath his feet. The trees around him reminded him of his journey here and the cart ride through them.

A shrill noise sprang up from behind him through the trees, stopping his heart. A horn blasted in the night, signaling the Gaur that he had escaped. They must have heard the explosion, he thought. Who in the Thraan wouldn't have? In the direction of the sound of the horn, he could see specks of orange high above the ground. Now he knew where the Thraan was. He needed to get as far away from there as possible—before the Gaur showed up.

Ryker rose off the ground, his legs still feeling very weak, dusted himself off, and began to jog deeper into the forest. The moon was shining bright overhead, which made his trek through the trees easier. He swerved through the trees as they swayed in the breeze. The wind blew through the forest, stirring up fallen leaves.

His heartbeat quickened, and though his limbs felt like mush, he pushed himself into a run. His legs felt stiff under him, but still he ran on. Soon he could feel his strength returning to his body, and he picked up his speed. He knew he was only going to survive this night if he made it out of the forest and hid somewhere on its border. The beat of his heart was the drum that kept him moving.

Suddenly another horn blew through the air. It stopped Ryker dead in his tracks. The wind in the forest picked up and carried with it the sound of dogs baying at his scent. Now he had no hopes of hiding. The Gaur had dogs to help them find their missing prisoner. Two more horns sounded. The whole Thraan sounded like it had been emptied to find him.

Knowing he had no other option, he ran. Over fallen trees, under low-hanging branches, and through the moonlit forest, he ran. He didn't know exactly which direction to run, so he simply listened the best he could over his swiftly moving feet for sounds of his pursuers. Flying between the trees, Ryker ran for his life.

Rounding the corner around a cluster of trees, he saw ahead of him through the forest a pair of Gaur. How they were in front of him this far from the Thraan was a mystery. He knew he didn't have time to hide and wait for them to pass, so he quickened his speed, hoping he could pass by them through the trees.

They must have been on patrol in the forest, because they were heading back toward the Thraan. One of them held a lantern and a sword, and the other had a long spear. Seeing Ryker running away from the Thraan, they knew he was the reason the horn had sounded.

"Stop right there!" one of them shouted. When Ryker didn't comply, he yelled again. "I said, stop!" The Gaur speaking held a lantern in front of him, which cast its light around the trees where he stood.

Ryker continued running and attempted to pass them with a wide birth. The other Gaur saw what he was doing and made for him with his spear held forward. Ryker knew he had the advantage in the dark forest, so he would fight this one and run from the other. He needed to keep moving.

The Gaur charging at Ryker suddenly tripped over a root in the dark forest and fell. He slid on the ground, and his speed threw dirt into the air. Ryker seized the opportunity and ran toward the fallen Gaur. The weight of all the man's armor held him down and gave Ryker time to close the gap between them. Without breaking his speed, he ran over to the Gaur sprawled on the ground.

Ryker stepped on the man's back and leaped past the other Gaur, pushing the first man farther into the dirt. The second Gaur slashed his sword blindly through the air, hoping to hit Ryker as he passed. The swipe nearly missed Ryker as he sped by, but he wasn't quite fast enough, and the tip of the blade had found its mark in his leg. However, the Gaur who had cut him didn't seek to finish the job and helped the other Gaur rise instead. This gave Ryker enough time to clench his teeth and keep running, fighting through the pain erupting in his leg with every step.

Pushing away the pain, he rushed on, his mind focused on reaching the edge of the forest. The cut in his leg slowed him down, but he wouldn't let it stop him from getting away. Every other step became more and more painful. Soon his running became a hobbled jog. He never let himself stop moving, though. He knew if he stopped it would be hard to start again. Ryker fought through the pain.

He knew the Gaur would soon return to the others and tell them the direction he had run, so when he knew he was far enough away for the Gaur not to see him, he switched directions. He turned slightly to his left, hoping to see the edge of the forest soon.

The bays and cries of dogs suddenly pierced the forest air. Ryker stopped in his tracks and turned. He searched through the moonlit trees behind him, half expecting to see multiple dogs leaping out from behind the trees he'd sped by. But they didn't, and he knew that standing here looking at the trees and waiting for them would only lessen his chance of escape. He turned around and headed toward what he hoped was the edge of the forest.

Above him, past the tops of the trees, a cloud concealed the bright moon, leaving the forest in deep shadow. Luckily, Ryker could still, more or less, see the shapes of the trees he wove between.

From the corner of his eye, he thought he saw something. He turned his head slightly to see what it was, but nothing was there. Turning forward again, he pressed on. Then it happened again on his left side. He turned to look, but there was nothing.

This time, he knew he had seen something. It was almost right in front of him and a little to the right. It was a set of red eyes. The eyes glowed in the dark forest, and though he saw no other shape, he knew the hood of a Khoshekh was wrapped around them, his black armor hidden below. The figure vanished as soon as he saw what it was. Now there were Khoshekh in the woods.

His hopes of escaping plummeted at the sight of the Khoshekh. It would have been hard enough with the Drudin Gaur to worry about. But he couldn't stop now. He would much rather that the Drudin catch up to him than that the Khoshekh take him back to their darkness. He would gladly give his hand rather than be sent back to the Hollow.

The cloud above shifted, and the moon once again shone down into the forest through the trees, sending down blue beams of light through the branches and leaves. Once it did, Ryker could see that the trees ahead of him were beginning to shrink and grow farther apart. He hoped this was the edge of the forest, but he had no idea what lay beyond. He would soon be out in the open with no place to hide. He could only hope that there would be a house or cave or any place for him to hide.

Through the thinning trees, Ryker could see horses rounding the trees to his left and right. They looked like they were circling the forest and were about to meet each other. The riders carried torches. There must have been more than a dozen of them, and they were no more than a hundred yards away from him. If they saw him, he would easily be run down. He didn't hear or see any of the dogs he had heard before, so he had a good chance of hiding from the riders.

Ryker turned slightly to his left so he would end up behind the riders once they passed by. His leg was beginning to grow numb, and it became harder to run on it. He watched as the riders met each other and formed up together. To his horror, they entered the forest, moving slowly on their mounts through the trees with their torches raised. Some of them even headed straight toward Ryker.

Suddenly the dogs' loud barking and wailing sounded like they were right on top of him. Ryker had almost forgotten about the dogs. He turned his head to see that they were still nowhere in sight. His sight was cut short by the trees, so he knew they were more than likely just out of his sight. His escape was looking feeble. Even if he made it to the edge of the forest, what then?

Despite the glow of the moon, he was surprised and terrified to see dozens of red eyes all around him in the forest. Some of them were standing among the trees. Many of them were hanging above him in the branches of the tall trees. Their laughter pierced the night sky and sent chills down Ryker's back. The laughter of the Khoshekh mixed with the baying of the hounds. Ryker could also see that the Gaur were almost upon him. He wondered who would get to him first, the Gaur or the Khoshekh?

"This will not be my end!" he said to himself.

Ryker's entire body still felt weak from the explosion in the dungeon, but he pressed on. He had been running for nearly two hours or more through the dark forest, but he pressed on. The cut on the back of his leg sent agony up his body with every step he took, but he pressed on. Whatever gift of power the king's son had given him helped him to press on.

He ran with all of his might. The dogs barked, the Khoshekh laughed, and the Drudin Gaur drew closer with every step. Ryker didn't know how must more he could run. His lungs felt as if they were going to cave in. His mind pounded with the beat of his heart. His mouth felt dry and held a terrible taste within it. Despite everything being against him, he pressed on and ran through the trees.

Ryker's feet unexpectedly fell out from under him. He hadn't tripped on a root or stumbled over a rock. The ground beneath his feet had simply disappeared. The moment he'd broken from the line of trees, a huge gust of wind had blown over him, seeming to pick him up and throw him over a ledge. A scream barely passed over his lips as he fell through the air. He tried to get a glimpse of the ground below him, but his body spun so wildly that he couldn't see anything. His vision was blurred, and his heart felt like it was about to leap out of his mouth.

Suddenly his body hit water. The impact of the water almost knocked him unconscious. Luckily, the shock of the ice-cold water roused him. The moment he hit the water, he sank deep beneath the waves. His heavy clothes from the Khoshekh weighed him down. He swam upward to the surface to reach the air above.

The waves above him crashed against each other, creating a current that sent him deeper under them. Every time he swam to reach the surface, the waves crashed and sent him sprawling below. The waves above him died down for a moment, just long enough for him to swim to the surface and desperately suck air into his lungs.

Treading water, he looked up to see what he had fallen froma sheer cliff, right at the edge of the forest. High above him, he could see many tiny figures cast in orange light. He had done it. He had escaped.

Shivering, he searched the shoreline, but he saw only jagged rocks below the cliff. He hoped he could make it to shore somewhere. He began to swim toward the foot of the cliff, hoping to find a flat rock to rest on.

As he drew closer to the cliffs, the waves surrounding him began to overpower him and toss him around in the water. Suddenly a wave crashed over him and sent him underwater. Another wave crashed, and then another, and soon he found himself deep below the waves. He swam madly to break the surface of the water. Waves crashed atop him, over and over. Just when he neared the surface and could feel the air with his hands, another wave pushed him back down.

He could feel the tide pulling him toward the cliff. His mouth was full of water as he fought the waves. He was no match for the strength of the sea. A huge wave came crashing down on him, and in a swirl of bubbles, he spun over and over himself. He tore blindly through the icy water, trying to correct his position.

Then his head struck a rock, his body went limp, and his mind went blank.

Author's Note

The kingdom we live in now has forgotten and forsaken our great and mighty God and His Son Jesus. Our world began in much the same way that Arke did, but acts of human selfishness took us further away from the light of the King. I believe that God helped me to create the Kingdom of Arke to tell the story of His infinite love toward His creation.

We cannot fathom how desperately God loves us. He loves all of us so much that He sent His Son, Jesus, to dwell among us and teach us how to serve Him and shed light on the world. Jesus took on the darkness of sin itself for all of us, and He destroyed it at the cross with His crucifixion. With the darkness destroyed, Jesus rose from the grave and poured out His spirit of light for each and every one of us.

I hope that this story will reveal to others the light that I have found. I want everyone to see the terrible contrast between light and dark within this world. I believe there is a darkness that is consuming all of us, one that we don't even see, that we are not even aware of.

I believe we are allowing sin's shadow to suffocate us and blind us from the beautiful light of God's love.

There is hope. The light shall come forth and consume all shadow of sorrow and fear. It will rise like the dawn, evaporating the cold and bitterness of night, bringing a glorious new day.

With all my heart, I hope the words you have read have helped you to see the light—to see it for the first time or to see it anew. I hope these words speak into your heart, speaking life over death and joy over sorrow. I pray that you will draw closer to the light.

Let us become citizens of the light, keepers of its infinite glow. Let us rid this world of all shadow. Let us shine forth until all might see His light through us.

About the Author

Michael Bergman is an aspiring young author from western Kentucky. He works full time as a marine technician and an electrician. Michael's family operates an orphanage located in Hinche, Haiti, which currently provides for thirty-five children. While growing up, Michael was an avid reader who hoped to someday become an author. He was especially inspired by the works of C. S. Lewis and J. R. R. Tolkien. Michael resides in Eddyville, Kentucky, with his beautiful wife, Marissa.